I'LL KISS ALL YOUR WOUNDS

JESSICA N. WATKINS

JESSICA WATKINS PRESENTS

SYNOPSIS

A once blissful day in an Uber with a beautiful driver turned into utter chaos for Lyfe Miller.

Ocean was the driver's name, and it fit her perfectly. Just looking at her, he knew that her beauty was endlessly deep and behind the allure in her eyes was violent turbulence. She was beyond her curves, chocolate skin, and artistic features. Despite her youth, life had dealt her a bad hand. She had the eyes of a fighter—determined and unafraid. Her pain was evident in the creases of her brow and the natural pout of her full lips. Her amazing eyes revealed a broken soul, fighting to put itself back together.

Their chemistry was instant and an explosive inferno. Their kiss was flooded with authentic animalistic passion. It tasted like they were meant to be. He could taste the sweetness of her soul and the bitterness of her past.

But some wounds never truly heal and bleed again at the most inopportune moments. Will the wounds of Ocean and Lyfe's pasts cause their explosive chemistry to fizzle before their opportunity to live happily ever after?

* *This standalone was previously released <u>exclusively on the author's website</u> as Rideshare Love, but will now be released on Amazon. Though the characters and storyline remain the same, it has been revised and improved with additional scenes.*

 Created with Vellum

ABOUT THE AUTHOR

National Best Selling Author, Jessica N. Watkins, was born on April 1st in Chicago, Illinois. She obtained a Bachelor of Arts with Focus in Psychology from DePaul University and a MasterS of Applied Professional Studies with a focus in Business Administration from the like institution. Working in Hospital Administration for the majority of her career, Watkins has also been an author of fiction literature since the young age of nine. Eventually, she used writing as an outlet during her freshmen year of high school as a single parent: "In the third grade, I entered a short story contest with a fiction tale of an apple tree that refused to grow despite the efforts of the darling main character. My writing evolved from apple trees to my seventh and eighth-grade classmates paying me to read novels I wrote about kids our age living the lives our parents wouldn't dare let us".

In September 2013, Jessica's novel, Secrets of a Side Bitch reached #1 on multiple charts, which catapulted her successful career in the

Urban Fiction book industry and labeled her a national best-selling author. Since, Watkins' novels have matured into steamy, humorous, and realistic tales of African American Romance and Urban Fiction.

Jessica N. Watkins is available for talks, workshops, or book signings. Email her at authorjwatkins@gmail.com.

CHAPTER 1
OCEAN GRAHAM

"I still can't believe you're an Uber driver."

My eyes slightly rolled at Ivory's playful insult. "Why not?"

I grabbed the bag of Doritos from my passenger's seat. I then returned to the comfortable recline of my driver's seat.

"First of all, because you have a job."

I did, in fact, have a job that paid me a comfortable salary. I was a rental broker. My job was to serve as a liaison for landlords or property management companies, and potential renters. I worked for an agency based in Hyde Park that was completely dedicated to serving the rental market, which meant I was well-informed on what properties were available in any given locality. Most of my agency's properties were in influential neighborhoods in Chicago, like Hyde Park, Bronzeville, the South Loop, and many others. The money I made from the commissions was quite lucrative, especially for a twenty-seven-year-old high school dropout.

"So what if I have a job? I can have *two*," I argued with Ivory. "I told you I have too much idle time on my hands. I needed something to do to occupy my time, and this is perfect."

Before becoming a rideshare driver, I found myself spending so much time alone that my demons were attacking me. Recent failures had caused a major depression. The same monstrous thoughts that swallowed me whole as a child and led me down a deadly path were starting to haunt me once again. Too much time alone was in no way beneficial to my physical, mental, or emotional health. I needed something to do outside of work that was healthy and constructive. So, I decided to become an Uber driver.

"I can figure out a bunch of things for you to do with your time."

Chewing on Dorito after Dorito, I replied, "I'm sure you can, and those things will only deplete my bag rather than add to it. I've only been doing this for two months now, and I've already made a lot of extra money. My savings account is getting *fat*, boo boo. Plus, it gives me a reason to get out of the house, and I can make some money while doing it. I'd rather be doing this instead of spending money in a mall, restaurant, or bar."

"Why not just get a part-time job at a bar or something? That way, we can at least meet boys in the process."

"Tuh!" I grunted as I admired the block in Hyde Park out of the window of my parked BMW.

I loved this neighborhood. Its diverse population of people, beautiful landscaping, and adoring architectural design were always great to gaze at, especially on a hot summer June day.

"I'm not going *back* to any type of school to learn another trade, and I'm married," I reminded her, though there was no way she had forgotten.

"Barely," Ivory groaned.

I chuckled. "Touché."

I couldn't argue with her. My husband was always busy on the road. He was a truck driver and was frequently taking loads in his big rig as far as California. He would be gone for days and even weeks at a time. I never complained because he was the only individual solely responsible for turning my life around. In addition to that, he paid all the bills in our twenty-five-hundred-square-foot home in Bronzeville. Considering the way I was raised, and my sketchy past, I figured it a blessing that I was even married, let alone living so comfortably. So, his absence never bothered me. He was very loving toward me. He was just there emotionally more than physically. Admittedly, I missed the physical, though. I missed it so much that I often fantasized about having the courage to give another man a chance at banging my back out, especially since it was often weeks in between the time that me and my husband, Irv, short for Irvin, had sex.

Ivory sucked her teeth. "You agree, but you ain't gon' cheat, though. Scary ass."

I sat back, popping another Dorito into my mouth. "Judge yo' mama."

"She's a scary heffa in a lonely marriage too," Ivory replied.

I laughed, insulting her. "You're such a bitch."

Ivory was always encouraging me to cheat on Irv. She thought it was offensive that he was away all the time. She felt that she and I were too young to have such inactive sex lives. But since she was single, she could be as sexually active as she wanted with no restrictions. I couldn't, which was also another reason I was a rideshare driver. It kept my mind on working instead of my sexual urges and desires.

"Anyway, you can at least be doing something that doesn't require strangers to be in your personal space. It's too much craziness going on in the world right now for you to willingly put yourself in harm's way."

I shrugged off her warnings. "Girl, I'll be fine. I keep my gun on me. You know how I roll."

"I *gueeess,*" she sang sarcastically. "Are you sure you just aren't running yourself like this because you want to avoid thinking about—"

"Unt uh!" I snapped. "Don't go there, Ivory. I'm actually having a good day today."

I hated the ritualistic pity that Ivory gave me. Ever since we'd met sophomore year, right before I dropped out of high school, our friendship was based on her giving me empathy and charity.

Right on time, my Uber app chimed, signaling that there was a requested ride in the area. I sat up and hurriedly accepted the ride on my business phone.

"I gotta go," I told Ivory. "I have a passenger to pick up."

"Okay," she mumbled. "Be careful."

"I will."

"Call me later. I'm bored. Let's go get something to eat and have some drinks."

I grabbed the bag of Doritos, closed them, and then put them inside my purse. "Sounds good to me. Talk to you later, chick."

I hung up and started the car. I then reached into the console for my car freshener and sprayed the linen scent to get rid of the pungent smell the Doritos had left lingering in the air.

As I pulled off and headed to the passenger's destination, I looked at the person's picture and felt some relief. Though I never left the house without my gun, I was still very antsy about picking up certain passengers. Since I was young and, in my opinion, an attractive woman, I was hesitant about picking up certain kinds of people. However, the picture and name were obviously an older woman, so I felt no concern as I headed to the destination.

♫ *I want to sit on it*
So tell me why you deserve it
Come on and prove, why I should move
Spit on it ♫

I started snapping my fingers and bobbing my head to "On It" by Jazmine Sullivan. The sensual and lustful lyrics turned on my abandoned center. It had been about three weeks since Irv and I had had sex. Even then, it was short and sweet because I had kindly taken it from him before he hit the road. Since then, he had been home more, only having gone on short two-to-three-day runs, but he and I had been so busy with work that we hadn't had time for sex.

After five years of being in a relationship and a year of marriage, I realized that sex and marriage were far from what I had perceived them to be before I said, "I do". I had had this false narrative of butterflies dancing in my stomach for the next sixty years while me and my husband made mad, passionate love every other day. I'd imagined hurrying to fix dinner and put our children to bed so I could climb on top of my longing husband.

That was not the case in our marriage.

Me and Irv's sex life was obviously far from mad or passionate. Because of his schedule, we didn't have sex often. When we did, it was good, but I was missing the passion I'd felt when we first met.

There were no children. I had yet to get pregnant. When we'd first married, I was more focused on getting my life together. Back then, it was particularly important to me that, since Irv had found it in his heart to marry such a basket case, I put myself back together again. I focused on getting my GED and my real estate license. Once I found a job and actually had a *legal* income for the first time in my life, I was too excited to slow down that check by becoming a mother. Though Irv was thirteen years my senior and childless as well, he hadn't been pressed for a pregnancy either.

Two years ago, I felt more in control of my life than I ever had before. I was finally ready to have children, at least one. However, my husband spent so much time outside of our home that it had been difficult to get pregnant. A year ago, I finally did, and I was so happy that I was about to have a child of my own. However, three months ago, my baby boy was stillborn. Unfortunately, nearly half of all still-births do not have a known cause. So, I wasn't given a reason why. But I still felt responsible. His death was on my conscience. The guilt was unbearable. I knew the things I had put my body through in the past had caused my baby to be stillborn. It was either that or all the bad I had done coming back in a heartbreaking form of karma. I saw no healthy way to deal with such pain and guilt. Old habits wanted to nurse the suffering in the only way that I knew how. Instead, I avoided dealing with the feelings and kept busy.

Once I pulled up to the destination, I double parked and turned on my hazards. As I waited, I turned from Jazmine Sullivan's lustful crooning to a more professional genre.

I took rideshare driving very seriously. It was good money, it was helping me stay on the straight and narrow, and I often met some remarkably interesting people. It had only been since I had met Irv that I had even put myself out there fully into the world. I was still looking at everything and everyone with fresh eyes because it was all so new to me.

"Urgh." I fought hard to hide my groan as I pulled my eyes away from the address that my passenger was coming out of. Instead of the older, Black woman that had been pictured in the passenger's profile, there were two young guys bopping toward the car, pulling up their pants, which were hanging around their knees.

I was a product of the streets and had even lived in them for years. There was nothing about the hood that scared me. Considering my past, there was no way I could judge anyone. Yet, some of the younger generation had become so ignorant of their ways of mayhem and violence that they were frightening.

As soon as they opened the passenger's doors, the bitter smell of weed floated into the car.

"Great," I mumbled before asking them, "Rebecca?"

"Yeah, that's my mama," the one sitting behind me replied as he plopped into the back seat.

I put my car in drive, and once they closed the doors, I pulled off without another word. At this point, I knew who to have a conversation with and when. Nothing about these passengers told me I would have a productive conversation with them. As I peered into the rearview mirror, I quickly took in their scruffy and disheveled appearances. They were the textbook definition of fitting the description. I knew it was wrong of me to put them in that category as a fellow Black person, but, gawd damn, they could have at least–

"You can't smoke that in here!" I spit as I saw the one behind the passenger's seat attempting to light a blunt.

"I can roll the window down," he had the nerve to suggest casually.

"Window down or not, you can*not* smoke in my car," I insisted, with shock still lingering in my tone.

"My fault, shawty. *Shiiid*, you looked like you would be cool with it."

The one behind me chuckled. "Hell yeah, I thought she would want to hit it."

"How do I look like I would want to hit a blunt?" I challenged them.

"You just look like you're down," he answered.

That's what I get for dressing so casually today.

7

"My name Wap. What's yo' name?" he then pressed.

I fought the urge to roll my eyes since I was sure they were looking at my face through the rearview mirror.

"Ocean," I spit quickly.

"How old are you?" Wap continued to quiz me.

"Too old for you," I attempted to answer without my irritation showing.

"How you know that?"

"I can just tell."

Suddenly, he sat up, startling and alarming me as he entered my personal space.

"Can you sit back, please?" This time, I was way more direct.

As Wap reluctantly sat back, I slipped my left hand between my seat and the driver's door, where my gun was tucked. My past had left me scared of very little. I'd had to use my gun more times than I wanted to admit and in circumstances that still embarrassed me. Therefore, I was more than ready to up this thang on him if he didn't get out of my personal space.

"You finer than a motherfucka," he then grunted lustfully.

Shit. I glanced at the app, relieved that we were ten minutes away from their destination. I pressed the gas, increasing my speed so I could get there faster.

"Yeah, she is," the other passenger added.

I was used to being hit on by passengers. I had thankfully matured into a beautiful young woman. My chocolate skin was smooth and glowing. There were no blemishes that I needed to cover with makeup, but when I did wear it, it enhanced my perfection. My slanted eyes always bore into any soul they landed on, snatching and demanding their attention. And despite how I had abused my body in the past, now that I was healthy again, I had grown into quite a curvaceous woman. My mother had always been frail in size because of her deathly habits, but I had often heard that she was stacked like a stallion before she had allowed addictions to ruin her. Now, I knew that it was indeed the truth because I was what my grandmother used to refer to as a "brick house" before she passed away two years ago.

"How you figa you too old for me?" Wap pressed.

After clearing my throat, I replied, "I just know."

"Age ain't nothing but a number. I got cougars sweating me."

Eww.

"You should give it a chance before you knock it."

Oh my God.

I chewed the inside of my jaw to calm my nerves. "No, thank you. I'm married."

I wasn't so naïve that I didn't think men would try to make advances at me, especially as a rideshare driver. However, most of them had enough class to let it go once I respectfully declined, especially when they learned I was married. But not this clown.

"I don't care about your husband, shawty," Wap ignorantly proclaimed.

"But *I* do," I quipped.

Then he had the audacity to sit up, interjecting himself in my space again.

Since I was speeding down a one-way at seventy miles an hour, I didn't want to turn my head to give him the death threat that was lingering in my eyes. I gripped my gun in case I needed to use it as I told him, "You need to sit back *now.*"

"Forget all that. I'm trying to get a piece of this." Then he actually began to run his hand over my hip that protruded out of my seat belt.

I slammed on my brakes, causing Wap's body to jolt into the

front seat even more. His friend's face and body crashed into the back of the passenger's seat.

I whipped my gun out of its hiding place. Startled, Wap thrust himself upright with bulging eyes.

Aiming the gun into the back seat, he jumped back, barely missing the gun's barrel colliding with his wide nose. Their eyes ballooned wider. I didn't think of the possibility of them having guns as well because I was caught in the moment. Having been in situations like this so many times in my younger years, I always overreacted first to any sign of danger.

"Get the fuck out of my car," I seethed.

"Okay, okay!" Wap urged in submission as his body pressed against the backseat, away from the gun. "*Damn*, I was just flirting with you. You can keep driving."

My eyes narrowed as I pointed the pistol at his face. "Do I look like I'm about to drive you any further?"

"We're only a mile away. You gon' put us out?" Wap argued.

Clearly, he was used to having guns aimed at him.

I gritted, taking the gun off the safety quickly. "Get *out!!*"

"C'mon, man," the other passenger hurriedly urged Wap as he opened the door and jumped out.

Wap frantically clambered with the lock and then hopped out as well.

I sped off as soon as he slammed the back driver's door. My heart was pounding from a surge of adrenaline. I was attempting to calm down while appreciating the high that the adrenaline was giving me. It was a feeling I had chased for years that had nearly led me to lose my life countless times.

CHAPTER 2

OCEAN GRAHAM

"That's why I don't want you doing that shit," Irv growled as I flew toward our home.

I had figured that the last ride was a sign to call it a night. I was too flustered to go to dinner with Ivory. She had known me for so long that she would see the frustration in my face, pull it out of me, and then scold me for the rest of the night with sprinkles of many *I told you so's.*

I didn't mind telling Irv what had happened, though. There wasn't anything I did not tell my husband because he knew so many deep, dark, and embarrassing secrets about me before he'd even married me.

"I know you need it, though," Irv said, a bit of remorse dangling in his tone. "And I know you know how to take care of yourself."

I forced a smile to appear through my frustrated glower. "You know it," I boasted.

"Did you report those motherfuckas?"

"Yes, sir."

"Good girl."

His dominance caused a blush to coat my brown cheeks.

I pulled onto the block that our brick home sat on. When his black Ram came into view as it sat in the driveway, I gasped. "You're home?!"

Irv chuckled just as I floored the gas. I flew to the middle of the block and sped into our driveway.

Giggling excitedly, I asked, "Why didn't you tell me? I've been fussing on this phone for thirty minutes."

"I wanted to surprise you."

"Mission accomplished." I was still blushing as I ended our call. I threw my car into park, turned off the engine, and hastily collected my purse and phone. Then I rushed into the house, feeling my center pulsating and tingling with excitement.

After bursting through the door, I followed Irv's familiar masculine scent toward the den.

"Hey, you." I was purring with a shy grin still plastered across my expression as I entered the den.

Irv's bedroom eyes danced atop his mischievous grin as he looked up at me from his reclining position in his favorite recliner. Just as I approached him, he dropped the remote onto the coffee table next to him. I plopped down on his lap, and his mass easily handled my two-hundred-plus-pound frame.

I wrapped my arms around his neck and gazed into his eyes, taking him in. I always missed his presence whenever he was away. Since meeting him, I had gotten dependent on it. When he was home, it was so painfully evident that I needed him there more. Beyond his swag, sexiness, and alluring face, I yearned for the protection and security he had given me since the day we'd met.

"Stop acting like you missed me," Irv teased amidst a boyish grin that he was failing to hide.

I lay a soft kiss on the plump lips that protruded out of his full beard. "You know I miss you."

I melted into his lap. Just as he began to lay soft kisses on my neck, I cringed, feeling the perspiration that had pooled on my skin all day meet his lips.

"Let me go take a shower, baby," I said softly as I slid off his lap.

"Okay." He grinned into my eyes, and I was glowing as if we had just met.

I hurried out of the den and up the stairs to the master bedroom. No sooner than I entered the room, I began to strip off the top and jeans I had been wearing all day as I showed condos to prospective residents before I drove Uber. I also stripped the frustrations and weariness off of my shoulders so I could focus on my husband. I showered off the stress that stayed with me on a day-to-day basis, the sadness, the horror of the memories of my past, and the frustration that Wap's ignorance had left behind.

By the time my quick shower was over, my center was leaking sweet juices that were yearning for Irv to drink them.

I didn't dress. I simply dried off and wrapped myself in a towel that was small against my curves. It left nothing to the imagination and barely closed. I then slipped my feet into my furry slippers and hurried out of the room and down the stairs. I could hear the ESPN correspondents still talking excitedly about the upcoming NFL season.

Yet, when I entered the den, Irv's head was back, his eyes were closed, his mouth was agape, and a soft rumble was flowing from his lips.

"Shit," I mumbled quietly with a pout. The uttermost feeling of defeat crept into my feminine essence.

Still, I padded toward him, my toes sinking into the soft carpet, and sat on his lap. I hoped that would wake him, but to my dismay, his snoring continued.

I softly lay a kiss on his neck before calling his name, "Irv? Baby?" Rumbling replied to me.

"Irv?" I nearly begged this time, slightly shaking him.

He only stirred in his sleep but didn't wake up. He was in a deep, comatose sleep.

Sighing with disappointment, I left his lap. Looking around, I found the throw that usually draped our couch. I then grabbed it and covered Irv with it. I didn't bother encouraging him out of his sleep and into our bed, even though I had been so lonely that having him hold me all night as we slept would have been just as satisfactory as sex. He worked so hard that I often put his need for true, restful sleep in his own home above my needs.

Yet, I was growing beyond tired of being a humble and lonely housewife. I hadn't had a mother to teach me what being a wife truly meant or how a good husband was supposed to treat his wife. However, I did have sense enough to know that this wasn't what marriage should feel like.

THE NEXT MORNING, I had awakened in bed alone. I sat up, listening for the sounds of Irv. The house was disturbingly quiet. I assumed he was still fast asleep in his recliner. Before leaving the bed, I searched the covers and pillows for my phone. Finding it under a random pillow, I unlocked it to check messages for work. However, a text message notification from Irv snatched my attention first.

Irv: I had to grab this load early this morning, baby. It's some good money. I'm driving to Arizona, so I will be gone for a few days. Call me when you wake up.

Sucking my teeth, I left his message on read without replying. I checked my work emails, feeling the fire of disgust churning in my belly. I had always been an understanding wife, considering the ashes that Irv had pulled me out of. However, his absence was starting to get ridiculous. He was now leaving town like a thief in the night without even waking me to kiss me or say goodbye, let alone make love to me. We were starting to feel more like roommates than husband and wife.

After checking my work emails, I was riddled with further disappointment because I didn't have any appointments for viewing that day. There weren't even any inquiries for me to answer. Unfortunately, my bosses were so lenient that they didn't require me to come to the office unless it was an extreme necessity, so that left me with even more free time than I could handle.

The usual chills came over me that arrived when I was forced to sit with my own thoughts. Refusing to go down that depressing rabbit hole on this beautiful Friday morning, I jumped out of bed and decided to make some money.

This was why being a rideshare driver had somewhat saved my life. I needed to keep my mind occupied to keep from going to the dark places that my memories and past often took me to.

After showering and getting dressed, I hurried out of that silent dwelling that was slowly starting to feel like a prison to me. I didn't even stop to eat breakfast. The need to escape was more prevalent than my hunger, so I hurried out of the house.

It was a beautiful day. The sun was shining. One could even hear the birds chirping over the sounds of the city. I just wished that I naturally felt as beautiful on the inside as the city looked that day.

Once in the car, I turned on the radio and then my Uber driver's app. Immediately, I got a passenger, so I threw my car into drive and backed out of the driveway.

"Lyfe?" I questioned aloud, reading the unusual first name of my passenger. "That's an interesting name."

This passenger had, in fact, ordered three consecutive trips, so I was eager to make this money and pass my idle time with something to keep my mind off things.

Twenty minutes later, I arrived at Lyfe's pick-up destination. I pulled into the driveway of the home and started to shift through my iTunes playlist for riding music since all three trips were calculated to take an hour and a half.

Deep into choosing the right vibe for the ride, suddenly, the back door opened. Startled, I looked back to see the same face peering into the back seat that had appeared on my Uber app. My breath hitched as my eyes fell upon his masculine, alluring, dark toffee features. The picture on his profile had given him no justice... *zero*. Lyfe was a captivating man with a caramel complexion and charming deep-set eyes that were lined with heavy lashes that I envied. Since it was nearly eighty degrees that day, he was wearing a short-sleeved, black tee. I was appreciative of the opportunity to admire the colorful art that bounced off of his skin.

"Lyfe?" I asked him.

"Yeah, that's me." When he spoke, a voice deeper than any abyss tumbled out of his throat.

I was engulfed by the depth of his voice. It was almost brooding. I would've feared it had I not looked back as he tossed a Louis Vuitton bookbag into the back seat before climbing in.

It had been so long since I had been this attracted to and

intrigued by a man who was not some unattainable athlete celebrity that I lusted over on television or social media. I could n take in any more of him physically without it becoming odd that I was staring at him. So, I hurriedly turned around, started the trip, and backed out of the driveway.

"You have an interesting name," I told him.

I wanted to spark up a conversation. Surprisingly, I found interest in this perfect stranger with only a few words being shared between us.

He chuckled deeply. "I know."

Shit. He sounded like the best intro to a slow and sexy R&B song. I kept asking him questions just to keep him talking. "Do you mind if I ask where it originated from?"

"My mother told me the one thing she wanted to do was bring life into this world. She tried for so long and didn't conceive until her mid-thirties. So, that's where the name came from. She changed the spelling so it would read more like a name."

Listening to that history made my lips curve upward. I suddenly was more comfortable as we rode through the city. "That's dope. She sounds like a very creative woman."

"She was."

"*Was?*" I questioned, raising an eyebrow. "Oh... My condolences."

"Thank you. There is no pain like losing a parent."

"I lost my mom as well a long time ago."

Unfortunately, however, I didn't know the pain of losing a *loving* mother, though.

That left me in profound thought of my own mother or the lack thereof and the life that I had so desperately wanted to bring into the world that had been snatched away with no explanation other than the fact that I had finally reaped the many bad seeds I had sown.

"Did you hear me?" Lyfe's deep rumble penetrated my thoughts, snatching my attention away from the sudden sadness and heartbreak.

I shook it off. "No. I'm sorry I didn't."

"Where did you go that fast?"

Looking into the rearview mirror quickly, I was blown away that he had noticed my change in mood, despite the professional smile plastered on my face, and had cared to ask. Yet, his enchanting eyes were so breathtaking that I forced my focus back on the road.

"I didn't go anywhere," I lied.

Yet, he pressed, "Yeah, you did."

A swarm of chills ran down my spine. I discreetly took a deep, soothing, long breath, trying to push away the demons that my thoughts often made surface. "What did you say to me?"

"I said you have an interesting name as well."

I chuckled, saying, "I do."

I couldn't keep my eyes off of him. They kept drifting to the rearview mirror. Sometimes, our eyes would meet, and I would feel a jolt of electricity that scared and intrigued me. Then, other times, he would be busy on his phone, and my eyes would grow immensely jealous of the device.

"Where did your mom get that from?"

I shrugged. "I have no deep story behind that. My mama was just ghetto as hell." I giggled at my own insult.

He chuckled. "Oh, word? Nothing wrong with that. Most of us are from the hood if we were raised in the Chi. What part of the city are you from?"

"Southside. You?"

While having such a casual conversation, I felt the total opposite. I found myself checking myself mentally for being so attracted to a complete stranger. Yet, I couldn't help it. From his face to his seductive grin to his swag and down to his cool conversation, I was so drawn to him, and my abandoned core pulsated, wondering about his potential in the bedroom.

"Same. What high school did you go to?" he asked but quickly suggested, "Nah, let me guess." He then sat up.

Unlike the night before, I didn't mind at all that this passenger was in my space. I didn't feel any fear. In fact, I felt comfort and security.

Taking me in, he nodded with confidence. "You definitely look like you went to Kenwood or Whitney Young."

I laughed, asking, "How so?"

"That's where all the pretty hood girls went to high school," he replied, returning to the back seat.

I nearly choked on my laughter. "*Hood?*"

"You're not hood?" he challenged, laughing along with me.

Still giggling, I replied, making a right turn. "I am."

Initially, my appearance gave an illusion to others of delicacy, sophistication, and upper class, but my past was painted with such despair that my experiences lived on my skin and told of my street experiences.

"So, which one was it?" Lyfe pressed.

"Actually, I went to Dunbar."

His thunderous voice flooded the car's interior yet again. "Oh, *yeah*, you hood than a *motherfucka*. I'm in good hands then."

Raising my eyebrow, I looked into the rearview mirror.

Our eyes met.

I then felt things I'd wanted to feel with Irv for months: electricity, passion, and chemistry.

Clearing the unexpected tension from my throat, I then tore my eyes away from his daring gaze.

With shaky breaths, I asked, "What does that mean?"

I quickly looked at him, seeing him shrug with a boyish grin that made his swag a bit less threatening. "Nothing."

That one simple word, mixed with his animalistic tone, sounded adventurous.

CHAPTER 3
OCEAN GRAHAM

I was too intimidated by the tension choking me to press him further about what that meant. I was immensely riddled with guilt, so I couldn't say much of anything else anyway. I turned the music up slightly and started to marinate in the guilt that was bubbling in my stomach. I had seen other attractive men before, but I had never lusted for another man the way I had immediately begun to lust for this stranger.

Once at his first destination, he told me, "Be right back," and hopped out of the back seat. After he got out of the car, I finally felt like I could breathe.

I fought the urge to admire him as he walked away, his book bag in hand, but I couldn't help myself. My eyes were drawn to him as if his body was the most powerful magnet. I hadn't been able to fully take him in when he was in the back seat, but now I could take in his towering height and massive build. His bow-legged walk was confident and intimidating. I bit my lip, imagining the way he most likely pleasurably punished his sexual victims.

I shamefully tore my eyes off him. I then picked up my cell phone.

I needed to call my husband. I had to get rid of this resentment I was feeling toward Irv. Being upset at the way he had left that morning was leading me down a thot-ful path that I hadn't been on in years.

I was no longer the hoe I used to be. But I was well aware of my mind and vagina's potential to make bad decisions. My entire past was full of regrettable, terrible choices I had anxiety about falling back into the practice of. I had been faithful to my husband since the day he had claimed me. And there was no way that some stranger could make me break bad with Irv's love and loyalty. But the fact I was even thinking about this man in this way had me riddled with guilt and fear.

As I waited for Irv to answer the phone, I watched Lyfe approach the house and ring the bell. Irv's cell continued to ring as I witnessed the front door open. A guy appeared, and Lyfe stepped inside the doorway. However, I could still see his soaring outline standing on the other side of the screen door, propping it halfway open with his backside.

"You've reached Irv. I'm unavailable to–" Sucking my teeth, I ended the call in the middle of Irv's voicemail greeting. This was usual. If Irv was busy with a load or in a dead spot on the highway, he couldn't answer the phone. So, not only was he often gone on the road, but I couldn't always talk to him when he was.

Lyfe was only in the doorway for two minutes before turning and trotting down the steps. He adjusted his bookbag on his back and hurried toward the car.

I remained quiet as I drove the fifteen minutes to the next destination. I was occupied with thoughts of my abandoned body and love life, with rumbles of Lyfe's vocal perfection interjecting in the background as he spoke to someone on the phone.

"Be right back," he repeated once at the next destination.

I admired him once more, envying whatever woman had the pleasure of experiencing him.

"I need some dick," I muttered.

This was becoming ridiculous. I was now lusting after a random passenger. As a married woman, I should not have felt so abandoned and in need of attention.

Yet, my misfortunes faded away as my interest was piqued. Lyfe had again only been in the doorway of the residence for a split second before he rushed back to the car.

"Unt uh," I grunted curiously.

Something was up. I felt the urge to pry, but I kept reminding myself that it wasn't my business. I was getting paid to mind my own business, in fact.

But as I headed to the next destination, he asked me, "Aye, can I pay you to drive me around all day?'

My eyes blinked owlishly as I quickly peered into the rearview mirror. "All day?"

Stop looking at him, I thought to myself as I tore my eyes away. *Focus on the road.*

"I got a lot of deliveries to make, and you're good company."

"Deliveries? What kind of deliveries?"

My eyes wouldn't listen. They kept traveling to that mirror.

His jaws tightened, fighting a shy smirk. "C'mon now. You know."

"No, I don't. What is it that you're doing?" I pried.

"Dropping off some stuff."

"Some stuff like what?"

23

Still peeking in the rearview mirror, I saw his boyish blushing as he peered up at me with guilty eyes.

I fought the urge to bite my bottom lip as I fell in love with the adorable expression that painted his face.

"What?" I pushed, fighting my own blushing. "Just tell me. I'm not a snitch."

His chuckle interrupted me. "Oh, I can tell."

Almost feeling offended, my eyes slightly bucked. "You can tell? What does that mean?"

"It's not hard to see the trauma in your eyes. You've been through some shit that has humbled you and made you real comfortable in the streets."

Unfortunately, I had just approached a red light. Therefore, there was nothing else for me to concentrate on except him. Despite my every attempt not to, I stared at him through the rearview mirror. His piercing eyes seemingly were peering right through me, into my soul, reading all of my dirty laundry like a scandalous gossip blog.

Looking me directly in the eyes, he told me, "I'm dropping off weight to my customers."

My heart dropped to my stomach. The thought of drugs being in my car sent tingles down my spine.

"I like to use Ubers to do it because I'm less likely to get pulled over," Lyfe went on. "I'd rather pay you to do it because the next kind of driver I get is a gamble. I've had drivers refuse to take me to my next destination before because my looks and actions are suspicious. I can't take the risk of driving myself around because my family at home needs me. I'll pay you a couple of yards to take me to the next few spots. It'll be a few hours tops. That's more than you'll make driving today, right?"

A couple of hundred dollars for a few hours sounded really good for my bank account. However, I couldn't be around him and what he was doing. I was still weak, still vulnerable. It had been years, but no time was long enough to build the type of courage necessary to fight that demon.

Yet, for some reason, I wanted to be around Lyfe, be near him, despite knowing better. That was the lonely, retired bad girl in me who wasn't quite dead yet and yearned to come back out and play every now and then.

Besides, driving Lyfe around was a better option than driving all day with boring passengers that weren't even as entertaining or fun to look at before going to my even more uneventful home.

"Okay," I agreed.

"You sure?"

I nodded, saying, "Yeah."

"Cool." His kissable, moist lips slowly turned up into an adorable curve that I couldn't take my eyes off of.

Looking at him, I felt dirty. Only because his features and swag were so sexy that the lust he pulled from me left me feeling shameful and sinful.

Then some impatient, rude driver behind me started to blow their horn aggressively and repeatedly. I tore my eyes away from the rearview mirror, realizing the light had turned green.

LYFE MILLER

I chuckled as Ocean was forced to pull her beautiful spheres away from me. It was obvious that she was making herself behave. That was cute and made me want to break her down even more.

Ocean was gorgeous. I had noticed that the moment I'd hopped inside the Uber. But I ran into beautiful women every day, so that was nothing new. However, I found Ocean intriguing and different from the many alluring women that populated this city.

Her name fit her. Just looking at her, I could feel that she was deep, and behind the beauty in her eyes was violent turbulence. She was beyond the curves, chocolate skin, and attractive features. I could see that, despite her youth, life had dealt her a bad hand. She had the eyes of a fighter—determined and unafraid. Her emotions weren't easily hidden on her innocent face. Her pain was evident in the creases of her brow and the natural pout of her full lips. Her amazing eyes revealed a broken soul fighting to put itself back together.

Everyone that had survived the streets had that same look in their eyes. Anyone who had battled the trenches and had come out alive, fighting to live the straight and narrow, to mature, and to be responsible, possessed a fire in their eyes that told of their experiences, of their edge, and of their ability to be trained to go at the drop of a dime.

I saw that same fire in Ocean's cat-like eyes. Something about her inability to hide that edge intrigued me. That gave her essence so much passion. Passion mixed with that much depth was sure to lead to some toxicity that my dick couldn't help but yearn for. That gave her beauty so much definition.

"How old are you?" I asked, feeling the deep need to get to know her.

"Twenty-seven. You?"

"Thirty. Do you have any kids?"

She paused, swallowing hard. "Nope. You?" The hesitation that occurred before her answer told me that there was more to it.

"Nah. I got responsibilities, though." Before she could pry into that any further, I asked, "Why don't you have any kids?"

Since I was sitting behind the passenger's seat, I could look into the driver's seat and see a cloak of sadness drape her eyes.

"It just wasn't in the cards for me."

I wanted to push, but by the look in her eyes, I knew this wasn't the right time.

She then cleared her throat. "Why don't you have any?"

"I could never take on the extra responsibilities."

She inquired, as most did when that was my answer to that question. "What does that mean?"

Before I could answer, I realized we were about to ride past the next destination. "That's the house right there."

"Oh," she replied, coming to an abrupt stop.

"Pull into that driveway behind that Range Rover."

"That's a sexy truck," she complimented as she gazed at it.

"Yeah, that motherfucka clean."

As she put her ride in park, I grabbed my backpack, hopped out, and rounded the trunk of the car. I was relieved that she had agreed to be my driver for the day. I knew that doing this with Uber was being too precautious, but after fighting my last case and winning by the skin of my teeth, I wasn't in the position to be anything more than extra cautious.

Before heading toward the porch, I stopped at her window. Noticing me standing there, she rolled it down, the cool wind from her air conditioner flowing out.

"You need something?" I asked. "Water? Anything?"

"Just a bathroom. I'll stop before we head to the next spot, though."

"You can come in."

She looked suspiciously at the house.

"Trust me. This is my family's spot. You're good. C'mon."

When she continued to hesitate, I opened her door. I then offered her my hand to take hold of. The reluctance left her. She unbuckled her seatbelt and took my hand, allowing me to guide her out of the car.

As she stood up and closed the door, I was finally able to take her in from head to toe. She had the type of body that no man could forget after witnessing it with his own eyes. She had the audacity to have on a floral sundress. It draped the ground, making her appear royal. Her natural curves were dick-hardening. Her kinky-curly afro fell to her shoulders and surrounded her face like the sun, with highlights of blondes and light browns. I looked down at her 5'6" frame, fighting to remain cordial so my lust wouldn't scare this beautiful stranger away.

As we approached the porch, the front door opened, and she took her hand out of mine.

When Ricky noticed Ocean, he reacted dramatically, as I suspected he would. "Oop! Now, who is this?!"

I chuckled as Ocean's eyes ballooned at the sight of Ricky. I always found it humorous when people first met him or when people from back in the day ran into him. He was no longer the thug that sold nickel bags on the corner when we were fifteen. Instead of the gold rope chains, waved-up fade, and baggy jeans, he now had long pointy nails, a bright pink wig that fell down his back and wore form-fitting jeans and a crop top. However, his beard was full, a mustache lined his upper lip, and he was 6'4" in height.

"This is my driver for the day," I told him as I led Ocean up the stairs. "She needs to use the bathroom."

With a pleased smirk, he looked Ocean up and down. "Oh, okay. C'mon in, honey. Don't be scared. I'm Ricky."

"Hi. I'm Ocean," she greeted. She was still wearing a curiously intrigued smirk as she looked at him while slowly climbing the concrete steps.

"Ooo, that's a ca-ute name!" Ricky exclaimed. "And you got *curves,* baby," he went on as she brushed past him in the doorway. "Gawd damn, you got a fat ass. Is that real?"

She giggled. "Yes."

"Well, alright, girl! I know that's right!" Ricky retorted with excessive animation.

"It smells good in here, Ricky. What you cookin'?" I asked, walking in behind the two of them and closing the door.

"Mi cooking oxtails an' butta beans like mi grandma use tuh dweet."

I grinned. "Oh shit, yuh betta 'ave enuff fi mi."

Ocean's bucked eyes bounced between me and Ricky's exchange.

"Of course, mi bredren," Ricky told me.

"You're Jamaican?" Ocean asked me as we all stood in the living room.

"Yes. My mother was born in Kingston. I was born here."

"Our mothers came here together," Ricky added, returning to his normal accent as well. "They taught us patois, but we rarely speak it. Mostly, when we're around family."

Ocean nodded with a smile. "That's cool. I've always wanted to go to Jamaica one day."

"One day? You've never been, boo?" he asked her.

"No. Never really had the chance."

"You gots to change that. *Gurrrl*, Jamaica is beau—"

"Before you talk her ear off, tell her where the bathroom is, Ricky," I interrupted.

When Ricky got comfortable, his lips couldn't stop moving.

"I'm sorry, Suga," he told Ocean, pardoning his rambling. "The restroom is right down that hall to the left, honey. The door is open."

"Thank you."

Eyeing Ricky as he watched Ocean walk out of the room left an entertaining grin on my face. Ricky used to pretend to be straight when we were shorties. He felt like he had to in order to survive as a young hustler in the streets. But the older he got, the harder it became for him to hide his true self. At nineteen, he started to dress in feminine clothes and rock female hairstyles. He explained to me that he was referred to as an androgynist drag queen because he used a combination of masculine and feminine physical characteristics. His fashion blurred the lines of gender boundaries, and he was sexually ambiguous with fashion, gender, and sexual identity.

Since he and I were cousins, despite the homophobic masculinity taught to me in the streets, I still rocked with him, whether he was sporting a pink wig or his waved-up fade underneath, especially since I knew he was still the gangsta from the block that could rock an opp that tried to mess with him.

And he was still hustling.

Ricky reached into his bra, pulled out a wad, and handed it to me.

I frowned. "I don't want this sweaty-ass money."

"Take it or leave it."

Sucking my teeth, I swung my backpack around to the front. I then unzipped it, reached in, and handed him half a kilo of cocaine, which he would cook into crack and sell to his long line of dope fiend customers in his southside neighborhood. I then looked at the wad in his hand and angled my head toward the opened bag, signaling for him to drop it inside.

Rolling his eyes dramatically, he did so and then tossed the pack on the couch.

"You got time to eat?" he asked.

"Of course. I always got time for some authentic food from the crib."

Just then, Ocean appeared, making her way up the hallway.

"You hungry?" I asked her as Ricky walked toward the kitchen.

She shook her head bashfully. "No, that's okay."

"Girl, you better try these oxtails and butter beans," Ricky replied, entering the kitchen. "This is the closest you're going to get to Jamaica for now."

I looked down at her, and it appeared as if my direct eye contact had taken her breath away. "At least taste it," I suggested, hoping she would.

She tried to hide her blushing but failed. "Okay."

I liked how she listened to me. Her submission was so attractive. I guided her into the dining room with a soft hand on the small of her back. Along the way, I took in a deep whiff of her floral perfume.

"So, is that how you and Ricky know each other? Because your mothers came to the States together?"

"We're cousins. Our mothers were sisters."

"Yeah, we cousins, boo," Ricky added. He then appeared from the kitchen, holding two steaming bowls. "So, don't worry. He ain't gay. He likes the girls and not the ones like me."

Ocean giggled as Ricky sat the bowls in front of us.

"Oop! That's a nice ring, boo," Ricky said, staring at her left hand.

That was my first time noticing her wedding ring. I should have been disappointed. However, I wasn't even sure what I wanted to do with her. I just knew I was highly attracted to her and fascinated with her body. But something about her told me the last thing she needed was another man harassing her because of her curves. She looked like she needed more. She obviously was deprived of attention. For some reason, I didn't want to be yet another man letting her down. She didn't come off as needy, desperate, or thirsty at all. It was the need to be held that coated her eyes.

"You married or stuntin'?" Ricky asked.

I listened closely, watching her response and mannerisms.

"Stuntin'?" she questioned him.

"I wear a ring all the time because I get more attention that way," Ricky explained with a shrug. "People want what they can't have."

"Oh. Well, yes, I'm married."

There wasn't an ounce of bliss in her eyes as she spoke. Obviously, she wasn't happily married.

Ricky's eyes floated to mine as he sat down. "Umph," he said, keeping eye contact with me. "What a shame."

CHAPTER 4
OCEAN GRAHAM

L uckily, that was the end of the conversation about my marriage. I hated to even tell the truth because I felt as if I were, in fact, stunting. I didn't feel married in reality anymore. I felt married to a ghost, a memory of a man who used to be in my life.

In the past hour, I had fallen in love with Ricky. I had seen drag queens like him on television, but never up close. He was a riot. He'd had me laughing from the moment I walked through his door.

> ♫ Me step inna di club a dance rub a dub
> An di gyal a come wine up on me
> Mi stan so tall back against the wall
> And now she start climb up pon me ♫

I had told Ricky that I loved dancehall music, so he turned some on while Lyfe and I ate. As soon as he started twerking, I got jealous.

"Ooo, I wish I could twerk," I pouted as I finished my bowl.

I hadn't even been hungry, but those oxtails had been such a hit that I couldn't stop eating them.

Ricky instantly stopped twerking and whipped his head toward me. "You got all that booty and can't twerk?"

I shamefully shook my head.

"Stand up," he said, gesturing with his hand.

I bashfully did. He then reached for my wrist and pulled me toward him. "Okay, now, put your feet shoulder length apart and arch your back."

Ricky watched me closely as I followed his directions.

"Girl, arch that back!" He spit directions like a dance teacher. "A *deep* arch! That dip you put in your back when you about to get some dick!"

I obeyed, putting the deepest bend in my back.

"There you go! Then throw that booty. I mean *throw* that mother-fucka like you're trying to get it to touch your back."

Knowing that Lyfe was watching gave me a twinge of nervous-ness and embarrassment, but I had been having such a good time with him and Ricky that I pushed the timidness away and lived in the rare moment of fun and great company.

"Just like that!" Ricky exclaimed with excitement, encouraging me. "Now, keep doing it! Make that ass touch that back over and over again."

I threw my butt up to my back repeatedly to the beat of "Dutty Wine".

"*'Di dutty wine! My girl, dutty wine! Whoa! Di dutty wine! My girl, dutty wine'*," Ricky rapped along to Tony Matterhorn as he joined my attempt at twerking while showing his own masterful skills. "*Yaaassss!* Just like that!"

Ricky's mannerisms were so comical that my laughter took over my efforts. Besides, dancing for that short time had me already out of breath. I stood upright, giggling. When I turned, my eyes landed on Lyfe's focus on me. The way his glare lustfully narrowed in my direction made my buried nerves sprint to the surface.

I immediately shied away from his gaze.

Thankfully, Ricky then recaptured my attention. "Girl, you did good."

My cheeky grin felt so infectious. "Thanks."

Then Lyfe stood, saying, "Ah ight, cuzzo, we gotta ride out."

Ricky and Lyfe said their farewells as Ricky walked us to the door. As he opened it, I was actually sad to leave because I'd had such a good time.

"Thank you for the food," I told Ricky as I followed Lyfe out of the house. "It was *so* good." The braised beef was fall-off-the-bone tender and full of amazing flavor. I could still taste the deliciousness.

Smiling, Ricky leaned against the doorway, put his hand on his hip, and cockily replied, "I know it was. Get my number from Lyfe, and let me know if you want some more. I got you whenever you get the taste for it."

I smiled. "Thank you."

His ever-present smirk deepened while staring at me. "Mmm humph. You be careful out there rolling with this motherfucka here."

"She ain't got nothing to worry about," Lyfe replied from behind me.

I fought the chills that wanted to cover my skin. The little hood girl in me who fantasized about being the wife of a dope boy was begging me to let her come out and play. But that little girl had gotten me into way too much chaos when I was younger, so I told her to shut the hell up and go sit down somewhere.

"And I can take care of myself," I sassed them both.

Ricky's head dramatically tilted. "*Okay*! I know that's right. I like you," he told me with a wink. "Bye, y'all."

"Bye."

"I'll holla, cousin," Lyfe farewelled as Ricky closed the door.

Walking to the car, I checked my phone. Unfortunately, Irv still hadn't returned my call. Worried, I sent him a text message.

> Ocean: Hey, baby. Is everything okay?

As I popped the locks on my car, I noticed Lyfe heading for the back seat.

"You might as well sit in the front. I know you won't bite," I teased.

And instantly, I regretted saying that. His eyes narrowed lustfully once again as if my teasing had just stirred the beast.

"Do you really?" his bass assaulted my loins.

My cheeks flushed as I tore my eyes away from him and climbed into the car, feeling my love button knocking at my panties. She needed some attention, had needed it for quite some time. With this swagnificent man in her presence all day being all dominant and sexy, she was willing to pay him to give it to her.

As I put my seatbelt on, Lyfe climbed into the passenger seat.

My phone vibrated. I held my breath until I looked at it. I let out a sigh of relief when I saw it was Irv.

> Irv: I'm sorry, baby. My signal sucks on this stretch of highway. I'll hit you back as soon as it gets better.

> Ocean: Okay. Miss you.

Lyfe's voice cut into the quiet in the car. "You need to leave?"

Suddenly, I felt riddled with guilt, as if Irv was looking or could see the adulterous thoughts in my head.

"No," I quickly replied, locking my phone. "Where to next?"

He gave me the address, and I entered it into my Google Maps app. I then backed out of the driveway.

"So, you're married, huh?" Lyfe asked in a joking tone.

I nodded slowly. "Yeah."

"Does he know you're driving me around and learning how to twerk?" he continued to tease.

I cackled. "No. Actually, he has no idea since he hasn't called all day." I fought hard to hide the disgust that I felt. "He's usually always gone on the road. He's a truck driver."

Lyfe nodded slowly. In order to get off of this depressing subject, I asked him, "So, have you ever been to Jamaica?"

"My mother could never afford to go back once I was born. When I was a shorty, I always wanted to save up enough money to buy her a ticket back home."

I smirked admirably. "That's so sweet."

"She died before I could do it, though. So, I've never been able to bring myself to go without her."

My heart went out to the dread laced in his tone and expression. "I'm so sorry to hear that."

"Yeah, I'm sorry too. I fucking hate cancer." He turned and looked at me and asked, "How did your mom die?"

"She died from a lot of things."

His eyes narrowed at me, clearly confused.

"She was a drug addict for years until the day she died from complications caused by extensive, severe drug abuse."

"Damn. I knew you had been through a lot."

"How–" My words lodged in my throat when I saw the red and blue lights behind me. I suddenly couldn't breathe. My eyes widened with fear as they landed on the bookbag in Lyfe's lap. As soon as he saw the fear rise in me, his large hand gently lay on my thigh. Under his soft touch, my skin wanted to burst into orgasmic flames, even under the threat of danger.

"You're good," he insisted.

And when he told me that, I believed him.

Yet, as the siren blared and I pulled over, I still felt some apprehension. I kept my hands on the wheel at ten and two. I gnawed on my plump bottom lip as I watched the officer leave the squad car and walk toward mine. However, instead of routinely coming to the driver's side, he approached the passenger's.

Lyfe let the window down just as the officer's shadow cast over the car.

"What up, my dude?" My eyes bucked when the officer greeted Lyfe so casually.

"What up?" Lyfe returned.

"Took you long enough." The officer bent down and leaned on the window seal. Once his eyes landed on me, they bucked a bit in delight.

"Told you I was eating," Lyfe replied to him.

"Oh yeah?" The officer grinned devilishly, looking directly at me. "Eating what?"

"Cut it out," Lyfe told him without a hint of humor.

"My bad." He forced his lewd expression away and asked me, "How you doin', Miss Lady?"

"I'm good," I said shortly.

I never gave the police pleasantries.

"Be right back," Lyfe told me and then opened the passenger's door. He climbed out, taking his backpack with him.

My eyes ballooned even more. I tried to watch discreetly, peering out of the side of my eyes, fighting to see their exchange.

I inhaled sharply when I saw him open the bag, reach inside, and hand the officer a rectangular-shaped package wrapped in Saran wrap.

I knew exactly what it was. I had been too close to drugs for the majority of my life.

He even serves to the police? Who the hell am I driving around?

LYFE MILLER

"Wow, are they having a party or something?"

Ocean looked at the brownstone in Bronzeville with owlish and amazed eyes. I hadn't expected for there to be so many cars in the driveway when Brad had asked that I bring him an ounce ASAP. Even with the windows up, I could hear the explosive bass coming from behind his home.

"Must be," I replied, staring at two thick, white women climb out of the car in front of us. They then hurried toward the house, totes in hand.

"It looks like it's lit," Ocean replied as she continued to stare at the home with interest.

"Brad is always throwing parties," I said as I opened the door. Then I hesitated and looked back at the curiosity in Ocean's fascinated eyes. "You wanna come in with me?"

She tore her eyes away from the home. "N-no. That's okay. You'll only be a minute, right?"

"I mean, if they are kicking it, we can stay for a little while. My other customers can wait. You really look like you wanna see what's going on in there."

Her lips curved upward shyly, and I loved it. I liked how innocent she looked when she tried to hide her smile.

"I do," she admitted.

"Then come on."

She was no longer masking her grin as she turned off the engine and got her purse from the back seat. She then collected the keys and climbed out of the car. I hurriedly took an ounce from my backpack, slipped it into my pocket, and then threw my backpack into the back seat. I wasn't worried about anyone breaking into her car. Brad lived in a bougie neighborhood where only the wealthy resided.

I met Ocean at the driver's side door, and she began to follow me as I walked up to the entrance of the home.

I could feel her excitement. I had only known her for a few hours, but it was obvious that she needed to have some fun.

The door to the colossal brownstone was already open. I pushed it open wider, guiding Ocean in by the small of her back. I really liked putting my hand right there because my palm would rest on the curve of her ass. It felt so soft.

As we crossed through the foyer, the music became louder and louder. We entered the very crowded living room. The area was an open concept. Therefore, I could see that the living room, kitchen, and dining room were filled with people. There had to be at least one hundred people in that space alone. Women were running around in skimpy swimsuits. Ocean's eyes widened as she took in the sight of women as curvaceous as her, pouring themselves drinks in thong bikinis at the makeshift bar at the island that separated the kitchen from the dining room. I snickered to myself as she tried not to gawk at the bare-chested men alongside them.

"You want a drink?" I asked her as I looked down at her adventurous staring.

"Sure."

I watched as she gawked appreciatively at the men surrounding us. They were returning the same glances to her. I couldn't blame them. With a floor-length maxi dress on, she exuded more sex appeal than the women flouncing around her nearly naked.

I took her hand as I led her to the bar. I wanted to claim her. I was feeling territorial. It was a stinging in my chest that spilled down to the pit of my stomach. I was peeing on my territory, even though she wasn't mine.

I felt her stiffen as she looked back at me. I thought she had found offense at my intimate gesture, but then I felt her relax and allow me to hold her hand.

"Lyfe!" Before we could arrive at the island, I heard Brad shouting my name excitedly.

I turned just in time to see him approaching from behind. He slapped my shoulder as a greeting with a huge grin plastered on his face.

"Thanks for coming on such short notice. I ran out, and my lady can't party without it. Who am I to tell her no?" Brad joked obnoxiously, adding to his frat boy persona.

"You know I got you." I looked down at Ocean, who was watching our exchange. "Ocean, this is Brad. Brad, this is Ocean."

"Wow," he said as he slowly took Ocean's outstretched hand. "You are stunning."

She smiled bashfully. "Thank you."

Her humility was so refreshing. So many women who looked like and were built like her had attitudes that made them very ugly. But not Ocean. Life had obviously left her with an amount of humility that was hard for others to ignore.

"Nice to meet you," she said as she took his hand.

"Pleasure is all mine," Brad told her as he let her hand go. He looked up at me, his goofy arch reappearing. His eyes danced around wildly. Beads of sweat rested on his brow. His chest rose feverishly. He was obviously already high.

I reached into my pocket for the ounce and handed it to Brad. He had already paid me via Cash app, so once he took it, we were squared away.

"You guys staying?" he asked me.

"For a second."

"Great! Get a drink. You can have whatever you want." Then Brad began to lead the way through the crowd of people standing around the island. "Watch out! Coming through!"

Respecting his status as the homeowner, everyone moved out of his way and allowed the three of us to pierce the congregation of partiers.

"Pick your poison," Brad told me as we approached the bar.

I looked down at Ocean. "What do you want?"

She scanned what looked like hundreds of bottles of alcohol that covered the island.

"I'm a light drinker. That mango rum will be fine with some pineapple juice."

I nodded in approval and started to pour her drink. I could feel her standing close behind me as I asked Brad, "What's the special occasion?"

Brad shrugged with a shit-eating grin. "It's a Friday! My girlfriend invited some of her friends over. I invited some of mine. Then they invited some of theirs, and it turned into this!"

I chuckled, handing Ocean her drink. I then poured my own poison of 1942 straight.

"Come out to the pool, man. That's really where the party is."

I nodded as I returned the bottle of Don Julio to the collection. I then followed Brad out of the balcony door. Ocean was behind me. I wasn't holding her hand this time because she had hooked her finger through my belt loop. The way she stayed under me was so intoxicating.

♫ Sack coming in and the money don't fold (Fold)
Gotta put a stamp on it (Stamp on it)
Just hit a play, scrape it off the plate (Skrrt)
Gotta put the cap on it (Cap on it) ♫

As we stepped out onto the patio, I heard her gasp. Brad's vast backyard was breathtaking. But the center of attention was his pool with a jacuzzi attached to it. People were playing around in the water on huge floaties as a deejay spun "Put a Date on It."

"*'Nigga, put a date on it. Everybody sittin' at the table round here, yeah. There's a lot of plates on it'.*" My eyes widened with delight as Ocean rapped along to YoGotti's lyrics while dancing where we stood.

I hadn't outgrown my love for hood chicks. At thirty years old, however, I sought out the ones who knew how to be versatile, someone who knew when to turn the hood on and off so that we could go more places in life than the block.

"Hi, Lyfe!" I followed the sound of Brad's girlfriend's high-pitched voice. She was waving frantically as she floated on a huge yellow duck. "I'm so happy to see you!"

I chuckled, waving. "Hey, Samantha."

Brad hurried toward the pool, ounce in hand.

"Figures he'd have a white girlfriend," Ocean mumbled before she took a sip of her drink.

45

I laughed because I had felt the same way when I met Brad. He was a very dark-skinned dude, but his persona was lily-white.

"Who is this guy?" Ocean asked.

"He's a prosecutor in the district attorney's office."

Ocean's mouth dropped cartoonishly. "Well damn."

"I met him through another customer. But he didn't become one of my customers until he got with Samantha because she's addicted to it. Now, he's doing coke, trying to keep up with her."

"Umph," Ocean snorted.

"Lyfe!" Brad bellowed. He was now sitting on the edge of the pool. His girlfriend had swum up to him. She had already formed a few lines of coke on his thigh. "You guys getting in?!"

As Samantha started to take the lines, I looked down curiously at Ocean. Before I could ask if she wanted to get in, I noticed her unwavering focus on Samantha as she took the lines off of Brad's thigh.

"You good?" I asked her.

Her eyes darted away from them and up to me. She seemed a bit shaken up as she replied, "Y-yeah, I'm good."

"You wanna get in?"

"I would love to. It looks fun." She stared with high anticipation at the water. "But I don't have a swimsuit."

"Are you wearing panties?"

CHAPTER 5
OCEAN GRAHAM

I t was such an innocent question, but it sounded so seductive coming from his lips with that erotic voice. I swallowed hard, forcing down the longing bubbling in my throat. But as I tore my eyes off of the water and looked up at Lyfe, the lust boiled over inside of me, trying to escape out of my antsy, needy, pulsating clitoris.

"Y-yes," I stuttered in a whisper, feeling the hairs standing on the back of my neck.

"Then c'mon."

Before I could argue with him, he took my hand. He began to walk with intent toward a vacant outdoor sofa. He then started to strip right there in front of me.

I was mesmerized by every inch of his body as it was revealed, too taken aback to argue with him about getting in this man's pool in my bra and panties. But then I remembered that this day was the most entertaining one I'd had in so long that I didn't even want it to end. So, I pushed back the reluctance and started to take off my maxi dress.

"Wow, your body is phenomenal," someone said behind me.

I looked back to see a white guy wading at the edge of the pool, looking up at me.

His grin suddenly disappeared as he looked behind me at Lyfe. "No offense."

"None taken. I don't blame you. Her body *is* phenomenal."

I whipped my head back around to see Lyfe staring down at me. Before I could respond to the flirtation his words had, my eyes fell on his chest. His bare chest glowed as he stood in the path of the sun. His thick thighs bulged out of the boxer briefs that left absolutely *nothing* to the imagination. I should have had some class about me, but his impressive bulge left no ability to be graceful. It was thick and monstrous as it rested against his thigh.

I swallowed hard and tore my eyes away from it in order to spare what little dignity I had left. But looking up into those bedroom eyes was just as intimidating.

The cocky smirk on his face revealed that he had watched my classless staring for every second. But it seemed as if my body was making his eyes embarrass themselves as well. They studied every inch of me slowly as we stood in front of each other, with such thin layers covering our intimate parts.

"Gosh, would you guys fuck already?" Brad's high-pitched timbre pierced the air.

Laughing embarrassingly, I tore my eyes away from Lyfe.

However, I had quickly come to regret that. Suddenly, I was being tackled. Though his bear hug from behind was gentle, his body was so large that he was able to easily grab me, lift me into the air, and carry me toward the pool.

"Argh!" I screamed with a laugh as we became airborne.

We hit the water with a hard thud. Yet, the warm water felt great. I was able to stand up, wiping the flowing water from my face. I could smell Miss Jessie's products as they leaked from my hair.

Finally, I saw Lyfe in front of me, wiping water from his face with a huge grin on it.

"You not mad at me, are you?" he asked.

"No, I'm gonna get you back, though. Now, I have to wash my hair when I get home."

As I ran my fingers through my hair, I heard a woman behind me say, "Your hair is beautiful."

"Yeah, it is." Lyfe took his fingers to my scalp, running them through my coils.

Despite the pool being heated, I shivered from his touch. I blushed, hating that he had been making me do that all day. "Thank you."

"You guys are a beautiful couple. How long have you been married?"

My eyes whipped toward her, growing with confusion. I then saw her staring appreciatively at my ring.

I opened my mouth to correct her, but then Lyfe replied, "Two years."

I felt his arm slide around my waist under the water. He brought me toward him, pressing my breasts against his chest. He brought his face toward mine. My eyes grew with wonder until his lips softly and quickly pressed against mine.

"Best two years of my life," he then told the woman as I clambered for my next breath.

"*Awwww*," she gushed. "I just love it."

My questioning eyes met his mischievous ones. His hands then went into the water and brought them up with a thrust, throwing water into my face playfully.

I squealed, doing the same to him.

"Lyfe, here, man!" we heard Brad exclaim.

Lyfe and I turned toward Brad as he handed us the drinks we'd left by the outdoor sofa. Lyfe tread the water toward the edge. But his arms were so long that he didn't have to go far before he was able to reach the cups Brad was handing to him.

♫ *You don't love me, don't tell me you love me*
'Cause I can go fuck on your friend
I can hook up with your buddy
I ain't got time to pretend♫

I didn't live in the hood anymore, but it was definitely still in me. I loved trap music. So, as soon as I heard "No Love," my hand went into the air, my hips started to sway in the water, and I started to rap along to Da Baby.

"*'I'm tryna get me some cuddy. And I ain't really tryna be friends. I'd rather get to the money'.*"

"Ayyye," I heard Lyfe croon deeply. "*'I tried to talk to the ho. Told her my dreams, and she looked at me funny'.*"

I turned around, and our smiles met. I was still dancing in the water as he handed me my cup. As I took it, he turned me around and started to dance against my backside.

My body stiffened, but only a bit because the alcohol had started to take its toll on me. I had never been a heavy drinker. Alcohol wasn't my vice. So, it didn't take much for it to start to affect me. Therefore, my nerves quickly went away, and I started to enjoy the feeling of his hardening member against my butt cheeks. I figured that this might be the only time that I got to be this close to such a perfect specimen, so I started to dance with more effort. I put my hands on my knees and slowly rotated my ass against his pelvis. He grabbed my waist, pressing my ass against him. I could feel the perfect inches of his manhood as he began to rotate his hips in rhythm with mine.

I leaned my head back against his chest. My eyes landed on the sky. As I stared into the perfect clouds, I realized how good I felt.

This was truly one of the best days of my life. I couldn't remember being any happier. My wedding day didn't even match this bliss because, on that day, I was full of wonder. But, in that pool, I felt alive, at ease, worry-free, and happy.

I just prayed that I had the courage to continue to make my days like this from that day forward.

LYFE and I played with one another in the water for nearly an hour. We were like children. And it had been since I was a very small child that I could recall having that much carefree fun. But there was nothing childish about the sexual tension between me and Lyfe. As we danced and played in the water, the lust between us was nearly suffocating. It caused me to rely on my drink to calm my nerves more than I had previously planned to.

"I have to use the restroom." I lightly pushed away from him, ending one of our many dances. I needed distance between us so I could think clearly and sober up.

"Want me to come with you?" Lyfe asked.

"No. I'm good."

I desperately needed some space. The liquor and fun were causing me to forget that I was a married, faithful woman. I also wanted privacy so I could check my phone to see if Irv had finally returned my call.

I climbed out of the pool and tiptoed toward the sofa, being careful that I didn't trip and fall on the wet pavement. As we had been in the pool for the past hour, I had met so many people from even more walks of life. The pool was populated with lawyers, doctors, party promoters, and even some strippers. Brad knew a wide variety of people, and it was obvious that he was known for throwing a great party.

As I approached the sofa, I caught a glimpse of Lyfe watching me from the pool. He was biting his bottom lip while watching me walk, with seduction dancing in his eyes. I fought to keep my eyes off of him. Now that I was thinking of my husband, I felt guilty for how I had been carousing with Lyfe in the pool. If Irv had even caught a glimpse of that, he would have been heartbroken. Since meeting Irv, my attention had never been on another man. Of course, I had found other men attractive, but I had never even come close to the seductive and intimate exchanges that Lyfe and I had been having in that pool.

As I looked at my phone, which had been hiding under my folded dress, for the first time in an hour, guilt started to creep into my intoxication. So, I kept my eyes off of Lyfe as I dried off with a towel Brad had left for us and slipped into my dress. I then hurried into the house, keeping my face in my phone.

However, I did not have a missed call or text message from Irv. Not even an email or smoke signal, so that guilt washed away as I made my way into the living room.

"Excuse me," I spoke to the first person who walked by me. "Can you tell me where the bathroom is?"

"Yeah, sure," the guy told me. "There is one down here, but I keep hearing complaints that it's always occupied. There is another one up those stairs, down the hallway to your right."

"Thank you." Feeling the explosive pressure in my bladder, I hurried toward the stairs. I climbed them quickly, hating that I had even looked at my phone. Irv was ruining my day. I had been on cloud nine, but now I could feel disappointment creeping into my spirit. I didn't understand why I hadn't heard from my husband all day. From experience, I knew that there were stretches of the highway that had horrible reception, but I was starting to question that he hadn't been in a good spot to call me at any point of the day.

I refused to lose the excitement and happiness of the day. It had been too long since I had had this much fun, so I pushed Irv's disappearance to the back of my mind. I then climbed the steps hurriedly because I wanted to get back to the party. I found the hallway that the guy had directed me to and scurried down it. I saw the door that I assumed was the bathroom and was about to rush inside since the door was cracked. However, I was startled when I heard a high-pitched moan over the bass from the deejay's speaker that was creeping into the house.

I peered in out of curiosity. I was startled to see a woman straddling a man as he sat on the closed toilet. They were clearly in a passionate position, so I was no longer alarmed. However, I continued to watch them because they were giving a great performance. They were kissing passionately, breathing into one another's mouths as she rode him violently. His fingernails were digging into her butt cheeks as she slammed her ass against his pelvic.

Their pornographic show was starting to turn me on. I bit my lip as I leaned into the doorway, secretly watching them like a voyeur. I was so jealous of her sexual pleasure. The way that she cried out as if the dick was so good had me creaming in my sopping wet panties. The woman bit her lip as she looked toward the ceiling. The gaze of ecstasy that poured from her eyes drew jealousy from me.

I missed hot, passionate sex like this.

"Ocean?"

I nearly jumped out of my skin when I heard Lyfe calling my name. I spun around with guilt in my eyes and hurried toward him.

His eyebrows curled curiously as he noticed how flushed I looked. "You good?"

"Y-yeah," I rushed to say. "The bathroom is occupied. That's all." I noticed that he was fully dressed as well. "We're leaving?"

"Yeah. We gotta ride out. I need to meet up with my connect. I've been waiting on him for days. I gotta re-up before he disappears."

"Oh okay." I didn't try to hide my disappointment.

Lyfe chuckled at my pout as I headed toward the stairs. "Stop being a baby," he teased me.

"I was having fun," I whined.

"Well, don't make this the last day we hang out, and we can have more fun like this."

"I'm married," I reminded him with a raised brow.

"If I cared, I wouldn't have suggested it."

Stopping on the stairs, I looked back at him. The way his eyes lowered into lewd slits kept my backtalk at a minimum.

You're married. You don't make bad decisions anymore. I told myself as I returned to trotting down the stairs. *You're a good girl now.*

CHAPTER 6
LYFE MILLER

"Seriously, Lyfe, this was *the best* day of my life," Ocean swore with a stunning, cheerful expression. Her demeanor had done a complete three-sixty since I climbed into her car earlier that day. Her entire body was smiling; her voice, eyes, and movements were beaming. It was a smile that was contagious. It went viral, piercing my beard and conjuring a grin out of me as well.

I cocked my eyebrow. "Your life?"

"*Yes*, my life. I haven't felt so carefree *ever*. Thank you so much."

My brow rose even higher. "You're thanking me for paying you to drive me around so I could sell drugs?"

She giggled. "Yes!"

"Pull over right here," I instructed her, pointing to an open parking spot ahead. "I'm glad you had a nice time."

"I will never forget this day," she said as she parked.

My eyes squinted slightly as I looked at her.

She recoiled under my eyesight. "What?"

"I can just tell that you really are happy. It's genuine."

The corners of her lips touched her ears, showing her perfect white teeth. "It is."

I turned toward her, saying, "Well, that means we have to do it again."

With that smile angled toward me, I could no longer deny it. I had to admit to myself that she was the most astonishing woman I had ever met. And it had nothing to do with her modelesque beauty or the exaggeration of her curves. It was her soul that made her astonishing. It was her ability to surrender and allow me to take her on this journey today.

I brought my face closer to hers, and her eyes widened. Yet, she didn't push me away. So, I dominated our space, taking her chin into my hand and bringing her closer to me. We met over the console, and I pressed my lips against her mouth. I penetrated her lips with my tongue, and she inhaled sharply. I held my breath, reluctantly waiting for her to push me away. As we played and danced all day, deep respect for her husband was still dancing in her eyes as she tore them away from me each time. I tried to gauge her. But she did not push me away. In fact, she exhaled slowly as her body seemed to relax in my grasp.

Our chemistry became an explosive inferno. This kiss was nothing like what they do in the movies or what women read about in romance novels. It was flooded with authentic animalistic passion. It tasted like we were meant to be.

Then her hands pressed against my chest. Disappointment flooded my hardening dick.

She was pushing me away.

Her forehead softly leaned against mine as she said in the utmost disenchanted tone, "I'm married."

I sighed, hating her loyalty to whoever the lucky man was. "I know."

For a reason unknown to me, I didn't care that she was taken. Her demeanor, her need for this good time, and her willingness to surrender to a stranger let me know that her husband wasn't fulfilling his duties. She was married on paper, but she was not married emotionally. I had never been the type of man who was willing to be a side dude, but I could not let go of the opportunity to experience this woman.

"And, I told you, if I cared—"

"I care," she said with sweet sternness. "*I* care."

I wanted to insist, to pressure her. However, the usual beast within me cowered. The beast didn't recoil because he was scared of her or her husband. He retreated *for* her because he knew she needed me to retreat, and I wanted to give her whatever she wanted.

"Okay," I said, sitting back. "I'm sorry."

"Don't apologize." Her lips slowly began to arc. "It was... nice. You kissed me like you wanted me to feel it."

I swallowed the urge to make her feel even more. I nodded sharply. "I did because I could tell you needed that."

The way her eyes narrowed seductively, the way she fought for her next breath, made my lips fight to curl upward, despite my trying to remain cool.

I felt myself blushing, and in my hood, men weren't supposed to blush. I had matured beyond the corner boy raised by the neighborhood hustlers, but some of that street doctrine still ran through my veins. So, I opened the door, running from how this perfect stranger was softening me up.

"I'll be right back," I told her.

Ocean still appeared flustered as she nodded and slowly sat back in her seat.

As I climbed out, I bit my bottom lip, fighting the erection that was growing despite her rejection.

OCEAN BROWN

I licked my lips, tasting him. That kiss... damn... it was the sweetest passion I had ever experienced.

I wanted him. I *deserved* him. After months of being neglected by my husband and my body being deprived of consistent intimacy, I had earned hours of being tangled in the sheets with Lyfe.

I winced, the pain in my womanly fold throbbing with an immense desire to be touched by him. I sat back in my seat, spent, as I looked at my phone. Still, Irv hadn't called. I wondered why the hell I was so committed to a ghost.

Sucking my teeth, I scooped up the phone. Instead of calling or texting Irv again, I called Ivory.

"Hello?"

I exhaled, releasing all of the desire and anxiety swirling inside of me. "*Girl.*"

Hearing my tone, she replied eagerly, "What?"

"You would *not* believe the day I've had."

"What happened?" she rushed.

I began to fill her in, telling her everything. I told her how jaw-droppingly sexy, tall, and thick Lyfe was, how much swag he had, and how he handled me with mature and gentle dominance. I told her about how much of a riot Ricky was and how good those oxtails were. I went on and on about Brad's party and how my underwear was still wet from dancing in the water with Lyfe. And I gushed to her about the kiss we had just shared.

"Give him some pussy," Ivory demanded so casually that it was funny.

I giggled at the way she'd told me what to do with *my* body.

"I'm serious," she went on. "*Fuck him.* Buss that coochie wide open, girl."

"I can't."

Ivory groaned. "Urgh, miss me with this committed bullshit," she sneered. "If your husband was worth being so damn faithful to, you wouldn't have had this much freedom and opportunity to do everything you did today without him knowing."

"That's—" My words stopped abruptly as soon as my eyes traveled to the house that Lyfe had disappeared into. My eyes narrowed as I attempted to focus on the familiarity of the figure standing in the doorway, holding the screen door open as Lyfe talked to him.

"Ocean?" Ivory called out.

I blinked, trying to see yards away and through the trees that surrounded the porch. As they continued to conversate, Lyfe and the gentleman started to walk out onto the porch. No sooner than they stepped out of the shadows, I inhaled sharply, ducking down in my seat.

"Ocean, you okay?!" Ivory blurted.

"I gotta go!" I rushed as my heart started to beat thunderously. "I'll call you back."

I hung up before she could reply. I then waited with overbearing anxiety for him to look this way, but he never did. He shook up with Lyfe and headed back into the house he had left out of as Lyfe lightly jogged back toward the car.

I was putting the car in drive before Lyfe could even open the passenger door.

"Ah'ight, let's bounce," Lyfe said as he slid into the seat. He closed the door as I left the parking space, throwing his backpack into the backseat. "You hungry?"

"Mmm humph." I couldn't muster actual words. My mind was going one hundred miles an hour, racing with unanswered questions.

I could feel Lyfe's questioning glare anchored on me. "You good?"

I forced myself to speak beyond my wonder. "Y-yeah, I'm good."

"No, you aren't."

"Who was that guy that you were talking to?" I asked.

"My connect."

My eyes narrowed with growing curiosity as my head whipped toward him. I forced myself to give my attention back to the road. I had to focus since my body was trembling, leaving me barely able to maintain control of the wheel. My thoughts were frantic.

"Ocean, you are *not* good," Lyfe said sternly. "What's wrong?"

"He's your connect? Seriously?" I couldn't wrap my head around any of this.

"*Yes*," Lyfe pressed.

I stared out of the windshield, gawking blankly. It was a miracle that I was driving responsibly, considering the way the spiraling thoughts in my mind were blinding me.

"For how long?" I inquired.

"Why?" Lyfe chuckled. "You aren't the police, are you?"

"Just tell me," I gritted.

When he heard the urgency in my voice, his humor faded. "For like five years. Why?"

My jaws clenched as my hands gripped the steering wheel so tightly that my knuckles pressed through my skin.

"What?" Lyfe urged.

"Your connect is my husband."

CHAPTER 7
LYFE MILLER

"Huh?" I blinked slowly, confused like a lost child in an amusement park.

"That was my husband. That was my *fucking* husband!" She gripped the steering wheel tighter. Her brows furrowed wildly as anger tattooed her face.

"The husband that's a truck driver that's supposed to be on the road right now that hasn't called you all day?" I verified.

She nodded slowly, gnawing on her bottom lip. "Yep."

I should have also verified that he was the same dude that shared the house, which we had just left, with his girlfriend, but shorty looked like she was presently too fragile to take more bad news.

"Your husband's name is Irv?" I needed clarification.

She closed her eyes for a millisecond as if me knowing her husband's name had dug the knife of betrayal deeper into her heart.

She nodded her head with tight jaws.

I collapsed into my seat, taken aback. "Shit."

Irv had never mentioned having a wife. I had broken bread with

63

him and his network many times over the years. I had met the girl-friend who he lived with a year ago. I had even messed around with a few of her female friends. This man had an entire life with that woman and in the game that Ocean clearly knew nothing about.

I felt sorry for Ocean. I hadn't even known her for a full twenty-four hours, so I couldn't say that I knew her at all. However, I could sense that she deserved better. By the look in her eyes, she had been completely caught off guard by all of this. She wasn't one of those women who ignored signs. She was too street-smart for that amount of naivety. Irv was obviously very good at living a double life.

"You can drop me off at home," I told her.

Obviously, the game we had been playing all day was over. The happiness she had been feeling since leaving the party had vanished. Reality had set in. The heartbreak was all over her face.

"Why?" she shockingly answered. "I thought we were going to eat. I'm hungry."

"I didn't think you would still want to go."

She sighed, saying, "Well, I definitely don't think there's anything waiting for me at home, so..." Her sadness took the rest of her words. She just shrugged and shook her head with violent disgust dancing in her eyes.

IRVIN BROWN

"I'm killing him." My jaws increasingly tightened as I paced the floor. The vision of Lyfe kissing my wife in that car had been stalking my brain ever since I'd witnessed it. It had taken everything in me to keep my composure as I made that transaction with Lyfe. I had walked him outside to ensure that it was indeed Ocean. I only needed to see the license plates to verify it.

"Why? You don't even love her, and you have a woman." Ron looked at my rage with confusion as he sat on the couch, clutching a Blue Moon. The only reason he'd gotten away with questioning me was because he was my right hand and best friend of twenty years. He was a brother in all aspects of the word, the closest thing I would ever get to it since I didn't have any siblings.

"But that's my wife. I can't let the streets think shit is sweet. If I let word get out that I let niggas get away with fucking my wife, they will definitely try their hand at Bridget. And I will start a war over *that* pussy."

Ron shook his head, disagreeing. As I angrily paced the floor, I had to admit that killing Lyfe over Ocean was dramatic. Everyone knew she was my wife, but they also knew the woman that I was in love with was Bridget, the woman I lived with more days than I ever had with Ocean.

I'd met Ocean driving around in the hood one day. When I laid eyes on her, I was in pure disbelief that a woman so beautiful was so tattered and worn. I took her in and cleaned her up physically and emotionally. The entire time, I was molding her to be my loyal and obedient wife. And that is exactly what she turned out to be. Because I had saved her, she treated me like her messiah. She rarely asked me any questions and believed in me, which was why I had been able to live a double life for so long.

Because of her past, I never told her how I made a living. I had loved her too much to tell her I was one of the men who was putting poison on the streets. I made up having a career as a truck driver. Her being so young, naïve, and fresh, she believed me.

Then I met Bridget a year ago. She captured my heart and never let it go. I was like putty in that woman's hands. I was ruining my marriage and Ocean. I knew she needed stability to maintain her happiness. Yet, I was so sprung that I was distancing myself more and more. I was falling out of love with the woman I had created.

Yet, my ego was still getting the best of me. I was no longer in love with Ocean. I was no longer committed to her, but I didn't want anyone else to be able to enjoy the dope, humble, and loving woman she had grown to be.

I had been toying with the thought of leaving her. Bridget was demanding it, and I was so in love with that woman that I was willing to give her what she wanted. But I was man enough to know that Ocean didn't deserve that level of hurt and betrayal. I feared she wasn't strong enough to handle it. But now that she was fucking other men, I guessed she would be strong enough to handle me leaving her now.

I stopped pacing, the feeling of jealousy boiling over in my stomach. "Fine, he can have his life. But since he's fucking my wife, he isn't going to be taking care of her with my product," I told Ron. "Tell one of the lil' homies to go get my shit."

OCEAN GRAHAM

I was in pure disbelief, wondering how I could have missed that my husband was living a double life. I had never known Irv to be around drugs of any kind. We were comfortable, but we weren't rich. We didn't have the type of money that a connect would have, that I knew of.

I couldn't go home. Physically or emotionally, it wouldn't be good for me. Being alone with this heartbreak and deceit would be dangerous for me. I had so many questions for Irv, but I feared the answers. I feared the lies he would tell me. I even feared the truth. So, I preferred to say nothing for the moment.

"Where do you want to eat at?" The sadness and disorientation in my voice were embarrassing. I was literally lost.

I heard him tell me the main and cross streets to head to, but I had no response.

The rest of the ride to the restaurant was quiet and eerily still. For the twenty-minute ride, I was completely mute, my thoughts consuming me. I didn't understand how I could be married to a man and have no idea what he was doing. I wondered why Irv had felt the need to even lie to me about it. A part of me wanted to think that he had done it to protect me. However, the extent of his lies was so intense that for whatever reason he had behind it, they were still heartbreaking.

Upon arriving at the restaurant, we climbed out of the car silently. I could feel the weight on my shoulders as we entered the restaurant.

"Why wouldn't he tell you he's a distributor?" Finally, after we were seated by the hostess, Lyfe broke our silence. "You don't seem like the type who would have left him because he was selling drugs. You kicked it with me all day."

"Because I... " I paused, waiting to feel the usual hesitation to tell my truth. But it never surfaced. "I'm a recovering addict." I was honest. Something that I rarely was with strangers. Yet, Irv's deception left Lyfe's kiss on my mind heavily. Now, more than ever, I felt like Irv did not deserve my loyalty. However, I didn't want to burden myself with the guilt of further intimacy with Lyfe before I found out the truth from Irv. So, I needed Lyfe not to be this amazing, stunning man sitting in front of me. I needed him to stop looking at me with those eyes. I needed the admiration to go away, and for him to look at me like I was the filth I used to be so, he would stop rocking my world.

His eyes bulged in surprise, and so many questions danced in them.

"When I met Irv, I was addicted to heroin." As expected, his eyes expanded wider as his head cocked to the side in pure disbelief. "I had been since I was fifteen," I explained.

His brows arched dramatically. "Wow. Fifteen?"

"Yes. I had watched my parents do drugs all of my life. I swore I would never do drugs. I didn't want to end up like them. I never wanted to do the things that heroin made them do, like neglect their child and go to shameful extremes for a high. But they left me all alone. They didn't care about my well-being. I had to figure out how to eat, how to get school uniforms. There was no family to take me in. My grandmother was too old and living in a nursing home. I was more afraid of being a ward of the state, so I stayed all alone in our section-8 apartment, which my parents rarely even came to. So, I was in the streets, trying to make money to survive. There were very few things I could do to make the amount of money I needed. I would steal from stores, but that only got me so much. I had to sell my body. I didn't have a choice. I couldn't be sober doing it. First, it was weed. But soon, that high wasn't enough to mask the shame and disappointment in what I had to do and who I was subject to doing it with."

With each word, Lyfe shrank with immense compassion for me.

"Once I was hooked on drugs, all I thought about was getting high. Wrapping the tourniquet around my arm, putting the lighter to that spoon, and sticking that needle in my arm was a seductive fantasy that I made come true every day. I was like that for five years. Then, I met Irv. I was literally standing on a corner hooking when he drove by. He said he saw the beauty in me beyond the grime and filth I was consumed in and made a U-turn." Even while drenched in heartache, I smile weakly at the memory. "From the moment I got in his car, he rehabilitated me. He sent me to rehab. He ensured that I went to school and got my GED when I was done with rehab. At first, since he was thirteen years older than me, I thought he looked at me like a daughter or younger sister that his heart just went out to. But then, he admitted that he was falling in love with me. I was so taken aback that this man was falling in love with me knowing all of the filthy and degrading things I had done. Irv isn't the best husband. But he loved me despite my damage, and that selflessness and unconditional love made me fall in love with him too. Before he told me he had feelings for me, I believed that no one could truly love me. And things were good between us for a while. But our marriage hasn't been the same for quite some time. Then, our baby was stillborn, and that's when our marriage started to take a turn for the worse. I feel like the baby dying was my fault because of all of the abuse I had put on my body in the past. Then, as the days ticked by, me and Irv became more and more distant. That's why I fill my days with working and driving Uber. I can't let that guilt, being alone in a lifeless marriage, or the memories of my past push me to use again in order to forget about it or not feel it."

Lyfe sat back. He was silent for a while, seemingly ensuring that he'd fully ingested every word I had said.

After a moment, he suggested, "Maybe he didn't tell you he was selling drugs because of your past with them."

I shook my head confidently. "I'm an addict, but I'm strong, and I'm not naïve. He knows that he could have told me and that I would have been okay. My rehabilitation is a big deal to me. I never wanted to be like my parents, and when I was going down that road, I hated myself for it. I didn't want to live anymore. Once I was clean, I planned to cling to it for the rest of my life. Every minute that I am focused on working or anything else productive is a minute that I am not thinking about getting high. That's why it's important that I stay busy on the good things."

"I feel you." Lyfe leaned forward. When he gently grabbed my hand, I tensed up, but he held on tightly, not letting it go. "A lot of us were put into positions by others who left us to make some fucked up decisions. You should never feel like you are less worthy of real love or loyalty because of that. You think I wanna sell drugs? Hell no, especially when I hear stories like yours. I don't want to be responsible for a fifteen-year-old girl being high off of something I put on the streets. But life didn't deal me a better hand, so I have no choice."

When I saw familiar desperation in his eyes, when I heard the same despair in his words, I knew he was telling his raw truth. "Why don't you have a choice?"

"I have full custody of my brother. He's seventeen, and he's autistic."

At the beginning of this conversation, I was intent on ruining the chemistry between us. Now, I was obsessed with it. My attraction to him multiplied at that moment. I was thoroughly impressed with the man sitting across from me.

"Back when he was younger, my mother couldn't afford the therapy he needed, so he was very dependent on her," Lyfe explained. "Then she died, and I became all he had. I was fresh out of high school with no job experience. None of the jobs I was getting was earning me enough to take care of two men, in addition to getting him the help he needed. So, I started selling drugs to take care of us and to get the help that he needs so that if, God forbid, I died too, he will always be able to take care of himself."

My heart went out to him. Now, I was holding his hand just as tight as he had been holding mine. "Wow," I breathed.

His eyes shied away from my admiration. "Yeah, my brother is my entire life. That's my right hand. But he is a lot to handle and takes a lot of my attention. I had to learn to be a father at a very young age. That's why I've never been in a serious relationship or have had any children. I have to focus on my brother. Outside of hustling, he requires my full attention."

Esteem danced in my eyes as I stared into his. He began to massage my hand with his thumb as he continued to hold it. Finally, his sweet spheres didn't shy away. They stayed anchored on mine, holding them hostage.

"You deserve better than a man who would hide an entire life from you. A lot of immature men mistake submission for stupidity."

I replied with a short laugh. "Irv is forty years old, though."

Lyfe shrugged a shoulder. "That doesn't mean he isn't immature."

Just then, the waitress at Texas Roadhouse walked up to the table. As she rattled off her greeting, I heard my phone buzzing in my purse. I reached inside as Lyfe gave the waitress his drink order. My heart started to palpitate violently when I saw that the notification had been a text message from Irv. I unlocked my phone and opened the message with a trembling hand.

With every word I read, my eyes got bigger and bigger. Once I got to the end of the message, I jolted to my feet. "I have to go!" I blurted.

The waitress looked at me with concern. Lyfe's eyebrows curled as he watched me frantically gather my things.

"What's wrong?" Lyfe asked.

I darted away from the table, feeling my world crumbling. "We have to go!"

CHAPTER 8
LYFE MILLER

The waitress looked between me and a bolting Ocean, her head and eyes turning right to left like she was watching a confusing ping-pong match.

"I'm sorry," I told her as I threw a twenty-dollar bill on the table. I then jumped to my feet. Remembering that my backpack was underneath the table, I reached down for it. I then threw it over my shoulder and chased after Ocean.

"Ocean, hold up!" I called after her, jogging through the restaurant.

I finally caught up to her at the exit. As she barged through it, I gently grabbed her elbow and spun her around.

"What's going on?" I asked.

She was panting fearfully, looking up at me with distressful eyes. "He's divorcing me."

She snatched away from me, storming through the exit. I followed her closely, hearing her say, "He saw us. He sent me a text message that said he saw us kissing, and since I've been unfaithful, he's leaving me. He told me not to come home."

I cringed as I noticed her eyes tearing up.

"So, where are you going?" I asked as she charged toward her car.

"Back to that house to talk to him."

"That's not a good idea, Ocean," I tried to convince her.

Her eyes squinted tightly. "Why not?"

"Because... Because..." After all she had told me, I figured she was too fragile for more heartbreaking truth at that moment. She couldn't handle learning about Bridget.

Finally at the car, she looked back at me, up into my eyes, waiting for me to say something.

"He's not there," I lied. "When we were leaving, he had already told me he and Ron were making a run a few hours away in Indiana."

"Ron?" Her eyes bulged. "His best friend? He's in on this lie too?"

I gritted, instantly regretting that I had driven the knife in deeper without even trying.

"Look," I said as I grabbed both of her arms gently. "Why don't you just come back inside, put something on your stomach, and think all of this through?"

Her hand went to her head. Her fingers combed her coils as frustration blanketed her expression. "I can't eat right now. I don't have an appetite anymore."

I swallowed the seed of anger in my throat. I detested that motherfucker for doing this to her. He had full knowledge of her fragility and was still killing her softly with more lies and further manipulation.

Though she had kissed me, he had walked out on their marriage a long time ago.

It was evident in Ocean's eyes that she was fighting with the decision of what to do. She chewed on her bottom lip, anxiety running rampant in her eyes.

Just as I opened my mouth to convince her, my body lurched forward in response to an unexpected hard thrust against my back. Caught off guard, I fought to keep my balance and my body from colliding into Ocean's. I then felt a hard tug on my shoulder. I whipped my head around just in time to see a hooded man snatching my bag from my back and then sprinting away.

I reacted instantly, pulling my gun from my waist and taking off after him.

"Lyfe!" Ocean called me frantically.

My long legs soared over the pavement, through the parking lot and a brush of high grass that separated the restaurant from a Walmart.

Fearing that this motherfucker was about to get away with the only way that my brother and I ate, I aimed and fired, my legs never stopping.

Pow!

One shot grounded him. He flew forward and landed with a hard thud on his face. Within seconds, I was standing over him. Blood poured from the wound in his back as he lay trembling on the ragged pavement of the Walmart parking lot. His quivering fingers clawed at the pavement as he fought for his life.

Consumed with rage, I used my foot to roll him over. His lifeless body rolled over onto its back. I gritted when I recognized Doe, one of the lil' homies that served on one of Irv's blocks.

Both parking lots were lively on that Friday afternoon. Thankfully, we were in the rear, but I wondered if nosey eyes had seen us.

Hurrying, I snatched the bag from his arm. I threw it over my shoulder, looking around for a discreet way to escape without being seen. The run and sudden ambush had me gasping for air through heavy breaths.

"Lyfe!" Ocean's fearful voice pierced the air.

My head whipped around as I attempted to find her. I then recognized her car alongside the Walmart amidst the setting sun. Her slanted eyes were watching me fearfully. She looked like an angel in disguise as her head jolted out of the window.

I took off toward her car. As I ran toward it, her BMW came speeding in my direction.

As I met the car, the passenger's door swung open. I rounded the hood, jumped in, and slammed the door shut.

"Go!" I ordered.

"What the fuck was that?!" she exclaimed breathlessly.

"Your husband!"

Confusion etched her face as she sped through the parking lot. "Huh?"

"That was one of Irv's crew members. He wouldn't have randomly tried to rob me. How would he have known where I was? That was your husband's doing. He followed us or had someone follow us and had me robbed; he just wasn't expecting me to kill shorty, I'm sure."

"Shit," she sighed.

"Go this way," I hurriedly ordered, pointing to the right. "Take me to my crib."

"Okay. I'm so–" Ocean's attention was taken away when a large blacked-out van pulled alongside us.

Suddenly, the world was moving in slow motion. My head turned toward the van just as the windows started to roll down. I looked ahead and then behind us, realizing we were blocked in at a red light. Thankfully, we had room to merge into the turning lane.

"Move over to the turning lane. Hurry up!" I barked as my life flashed before my eyes.

No sooner than Ocean turned the steering wheel, explosive shots started to ring out from the van.

"*Arrrgh!*" Ocean screamed frighteningly.

I was proud of her for ducking while flooring the gas and maneuvering over into the turning lane, just missing an Escalade that was flying by.

"Shit, shit, shit!" Ocean chanted above the barrage of bullets flying at the car.

I ducked while maintaining focus on the road so I could direct Ocean.

"Make a right at this corner," I blurted. "Then turn into that alley!"

I had been shot at before, but that was when I was younger, when my mother was still alive. Then, I didn't feel much fear because it was a norm in the hood. Many of my homies had been shot and killed merely because they were in the wrong place at the wrong time. Our life expectancy was short, even at the tender age of fifteen. I was never scared or even cared as long as my mother was still alive to take care of my brother.

But, now, she was gone, and our worthless father had never been in the picture. The severity of Landon's disability barely allowed him to survive my mother's death. He would never be able to survive mine. That realization had my heart pounding with fear that was unfamiliar to me.

I looked back in time to see the van making a U-turn in the middle of the busy four-lane street. Horns blasted warnings as cars swerved out of its way, nearly losing control.

Relieved, my body finally relaxed. "We're good. They went the other way," I told her as we inched down the alley to a stop.

Pulling my eyes away from the back window, I saw Ocean clutching her chest, attempting to catch her breath.

Now that the shots had stopped, I realized that I had just nearly ruined my brother's life, a life that was way too fragile for any further heartbreak or the confusion of another loved one being snatched away from him unexpectedly.

"What kind of man am I married to?" Ocean mumbled.

Yet, I was too busy unraveling to answer her. Thoughts of Landon fending for himself, being lost and confused in a world that he couldn't navigate, caused panic to consume me.

"Let me out," I said, clambering for the door. "Unlock the doors." I was so frantic that I couldn't find the power switch for the locks.

Her brows furrowed. "Where are you going?"'

"Let me out," I insisted.

"You're going to leave me? What if they come back for you... or for me?"

I couldn't let this premature attraction to Ocean lead to my brother being left in this world alone. I wasn't done preparing him for my absence.

I had to go.

Finding the power switch, I hit it and pushed the door open. I grabbed my bag from between my legs and hopped out. As I slammed the door, Ocean painfully cursed me, "Fuck you then!"

Before I could respond, she sped off.

I looked at the BMW barreling down the alley in pure disbelief at the way my chest was aching with disappointment to see her go. My morals started to play a brutal game of tug of war. Part of me wanted to ensure her safety, to comfort her. Yet, the best of me knew that wasn't my responsibility. My priority was Landon, his therapy, and his growth, so that once these streets were successful in taking my life, he would be able to survive without me.

OCEAN GRAHAM

This hurt.

It actually hurt.

As I sped out of the alley, I felt the stinging pain of tears coming to my eyes, and I was shocked. Ultimately, Lyfe was a stranger to me. Yet, I felt completely abandoned by him.

The heartbreak of the entire day was too much to handle. I began to hyperventilate with tearful sadness. I clutched my chest as tears clouded my vision. I inhaled sharply as I nearly hit a pedestrian crossing the entrance of the alley.

"Damn, bitch!" the young woman cursed me as I slammed on the brakes.

She stabbed her middle finger into the air while sneering at me with eyes that were giving me death threats.

I accepted all of her anger, allowing her to pass before I sped out onto the street.

I felt myself on the verge of a breakdown. I took deep breaths, trying to desperately maintain control. It was essential to my sobriety that I was able to control my emotions. For most addicts, the core of drug addiction stems from emotional immaturity and instability. The main reason why I became dependent on drugs was that they helped me forget the painful emotions that were unbearable to live with every day. People with addictions lack the ability to find productive outlets for their feelings and to refrain from self-medicating them. Since getting clean, handling and controlling my own emotions was an essential skill that I had been attempting to master in order to remain sober. My main positive and safe outlet had been Irv.

Realizing that that security, my outlet, was no longer an option initiated the thunderous pain of a monstrous and cruel heartache. It was intolerable. Approaching a red light, I squeezed my eyes closed, gripping the wheel as I mentally held on tightly to the ability to withstand this without relapsing.

"God, please help me," I prayed as tears slid down my face. "Lord, please– *Argh*!" My prayers were interrupted by a startled yelp as a pounding round of knocks came from the passenger side of the car.

Whipping my head toward the sound, I gasped when I saw Lyfe peering into the passenger window.

I hurriedly unlocked the doors as the streetlight turned green.

As he jumped in, car horns started to blare obscenely at us.

"I'm sorry," he said, closing the door.

The explosive cacophony of horns continued to fill the air around us. Yet, for some reason, my foot could not move over to the gas pedal.

"W-what...what are you doing?" I stuttered as obscenities from other drivers behind me pierced through my windows. "I-I thought you...you were leaving."

Lyfe's eyes expressed sympathy as he focused on my tears. He lifted his large hand and gently wiped a falling tear. "I can't leave you like this."

CHAPTER 9
LYFE MILLER

When I took off running down that alley after her car, I couldn't believe I cared that much. I didn't know her. The day I had spent with her was fun but also toxic since it had led to the destruction of my livelihood. Knowingly, Irv would *never* serve to me again, and I would have to find a new connect. Now, I was at war with whoever wanted to retaliate against me for Doe's death.

"I don't know what to do," Ocean whined as we rode through the city. "I want to go home."

"He told you not to go home," I reminded her gently. "And he just shot at us."

She cringed at the recollection. "But I, at least, need some clothes. Do you think he's trying to kill you, or me, or *us* over a kiss?"

"I'm not sure if it was him in particular," I told her.

She looked over at me with hopeful eyes. "You don't?"

"Oh, he definitely sent that motherfucka to rob me. Probably because he was feeling some type of way about me kissing his wife.

Doe was young as hell, though. Most likely, whoever was driving that getaway car shot at us in retaliation for me killing his homie."

Ocean seemed only a bit relieved as she continued to chew nervously on the corner of her bottom lip.

"Still, you shouldn't go home," I advised her.

"You don't think so?"

"Hell no. Clearly, Irv is pissed off, and you definitely have no idea who the man you married really is. I wouldn't go home just yet. He may not have told those motherfuckas to shoot at us, but he definitely sent them to rob me. He's feeling some type of way. I would definitely let things die down at least for one night."

Staring out of the windshield, Ocean nodded slowly. Even in her sadness, I saw beauty. I shamed myself for even thinking of that, shaking my head as I thought strategically.

"Since we don't know where his head's at, let's ditch this car real quick," I told her. "Make a left."

"Okay," she replied, her voice nearly in a whisper.

Her face was masked with anxiety. My heart went out to the worry in her eyes. I hated that the safety and happiness in them had been sucked out. She had an allure that made those Instagram models look below average.

Because of her exquisiteness, she deserved to be *maintained*, not contaminated by a man's bullshit.

OCEAN GRAHAM

I sucked my teeth when Ivory didn't answer the phone for the third time.

Currently, I was sitting in the back seat of Ace's truck. He was Lyfe's friend, whose home he had directed me to drive to. I didn't know what was going on when he and Ace disappeared into a room and started talking quietly. I assumed Lyfe was telling Ace what had happened. As I waited, I could feel myself plunging into a panic attack.

To maintain a healthy level of emotional stability, I took soothing, deep breaths while praying and meditating.

After their conversation, Ace and Lyfe emerged from the room twenty minutes later with serious and focused expressions. Lyfe and I then followed Ace out of the back door and into his truck. Now, he was taking us to Lyfe's house. Lyfe told me that we would figure things out from there.

"What's wrong?" Lyfe asked me.

I looked over at him, wondering why he cared. All day, he had been catering to me as if he were obligated to. Even when he had gotten out of the car in the alley, I was hurt, but I understood completely. This once blissful day with his Uber driver had turned into utter chaos. It baffled me why it was still in his heart to take care of me. Those unanswered questions had me falling into an undeniable fascination with him, even in the midst of my heartache and drama.

"My homegirl isn't answering the phone," I replied.

I stared out of the window, longing for more friends that I could rely on. I had known Ivory for quite some time, but we hadn't been close the entire time because of the lifestyle I'd had when we were teenagers. We had gone in two completely different directions in high school. She had graduated from high school and gone to college. It wasn't until I'd gotten my life together and gotten on Facebook that I was able to reunite with her. Everyone else from my past was left back there since they were directly associated with my past addictions or were still lost in the streets. Most, if not all, of the girls I used to hang with back then were either dead, in jail, still heavily using drugs, or lost in the wind. When I would bump into old friends that were still struggling, I gave them my number so that I could help them as Irv helped me. However, none of my offers had been accepted.

I had associates I met through my job. Yet, they remained just associates. I didn't spend much time with them or share my life with them.

I noticed that Ace was pulling into an alleyway behind 87th and Morgan. Being attentive, I watched where he was going. He soon pulled over behind a brick house and popped the locks.

"Ah'ight, bro. Thanks," Lyfe told him as they shook up.

"No problem. Holla at me later." Ace looked into the back seat. "Nice to meet you, Miss Lady."

"Nice to meet you too." I opened the passenger's door and climbed out.

Lyfe met me at the door, assisting me out of the large pickup truck before closing the door behind me. He then led me toward a privacy fence. He opened it and revealed a beautiful, manicured lawn. The grass was lined perfectly. The garden behind the house and along the fence was breathtaking. It was bright and colorful, with a combination of tulips and wildflowers.

"Wow, this is your home?" I asked, filled with awe.

He chuckled as if he had gotten this question before. "Yeah."

"I'm surprised that a man would have such a nice lawn."

He laughed again as he led me over the concrete path alongside the grass. "That's Landon. He's obsessed with gardening."

"Really?" When I realized how shocked I'd sounded, I quickly followed up with an apology. "I'm sorry. I just wouldn't expect a teenager to be so good at it, especially a teenage *boy*."

"People with autism have specific interests, things that they are particularly genius at. Gardening is one of Landon's."

I nodded, continuing to take in the impeccable landscaping.

Finally, we reached the back door. After unlocking it, he allowed me to enter first. The house was as impeccably neat as the garden. Considering that the residents of the home were two guys, I had expected clutter. Instead, I was met with a warm, decorated home that had been clearly cleaned by someone with OCD.

"You have a very nice place," I said, stepping into the kitchen. Yet, this floor had an open concept. So, from where I stood, I could see the kitchen as well as the living and dining rooms.

"Thanks," Lyfe replied. "But I have nothing to do with it. I can't clean on the level that Landon needs. I have a housekeeper, and Landon is always cleaning. Landon needs things to be spotless and in order. He hates dirt and clutter."

As I stepped further into the kitchen, I noticed a row of shoes perfectly lined against the wall.

"Should I take my shoes off?" I asked, looking back at Lyfe.

"Please?" he asked with a boyish grin. "Landon is here."

I obliged as I snickered inwardly, finding it funny that such a large, grown man was abiding by the rules of his little brother. But it was adorable to me, and I admired Lyfe for considering his brother's extreme needs.

As I slipped off my flip-flops, I heard a light trot down the stairs that were adjacent to the living room.

"Hi, Lyfe," an older woman greeted him.

Since I knew his mother had passed away, I watched the older woman walk through the living room with a smile, wondering who she was.

Once she saw me, her eyes slightly bulged with interest, but she gave me that same welcoming expression. "Hi. I'm Esther, Landon's caretaker."

"Hi. I'm Ocean."

Her eyes bulged again once she heard my name. "Interesting name. It's beautiful, though."

I nodded with an appreciative smirk. "Thank you."

Esther gave her attention to Lyfe. "Landon's already done with his homework for the day, and he aced his test."

Lyfe scoffed humorously. "Of course, that nerd did."

"You leave my friend alone," Esther replied, playfully smacking Lyfe's arm. Her hand looked so tiny against his huge bicep. "Well, we're off to therapy. We need to hurry. We're her last session for the night," Esther announced. "Landon!" she called. "Are you ready?"

Soon, I heard heavier footsteps on the stairs this time. Once Landon rounded the stairs, it was apparent that he was the younger version of his older brother. It was as if their mother had created a clone of the exact same person. Landon had Lyfe's exaggerated height. Yet, he was a few centimeters shorter. They had the same dark toffee complexion, and Landon was just as attractive.

Yet, it was obvious that he had many differences from Lyfe. He kept his distance from us and made very little eye contact. He fidgeted with his hands and kept his eyes lowered to his feet. He was very meek compared to the swag and dominance of his brother.

"What's up, Landon?" Lyfe greeted him.

"Hi," he replied with his eyes still lowered. Landon's voice was that of a little boy, barely ten years old.

"I heard you aced your test, my dude."

Landon broke out into a huge grin. He then looked up into Lyfe's eyes very briefly, and I saw the stunning resemblance of their orbs. "I did."

Lyfe nodded. "Good job."

Landon's eyes lowered immediately. I noticed him glance down at my feet. Apparently, the sight of my bare feet gave him relief, which was visible in his expression.

"This is my friend, Ocean," Lyfe introduced me.

His eyes continued to avoid mine, but his brows curled. "Ocean? That name doesn't make sense. Your name can't be a body of water."

I giggled. "I get that a lot."

As Esther and Lyfe laughed along with me, Landon's facial expression remained stoic.

"Because it's a very odd name," he said flat out.

Esther forcefully interjected, "*Well*, it's time for us to go, Landon."

"Bye, Lyfe," Landon replied immediately. He then made an about-face and hurried toward the door.

He only stopped to put on his gym shoes. He never turned back to wave at Lyfe or to wait for Esther.

Esther shuffled to put her shoes on and then hurried out behind Landon.

"C'mon," Lyfe told me, gesturing for me to follow him. "You can relax in the living room. You'll be good here. Irv doesn't know where I live."

Hearing that, I was even more comfortable as I followed him to his big, plush sofa.

"I hope Landon didn't offend you. He just got into therapy a few years ago, so he's still learning how to interact socially."

"He didn't offend me at all," I assured him as I sat on the couch. I sunk in. It was so cozy. I imagined that sleeping on it was incredible.

Lyfe grabbed the remote off the cocktail table and turned the television on. "Have you ever been around anybody who's autistic?"

"No, but I have definitely been around people with different behavioral and emotional... *issues*."

Lyfe laughed as he surfed the channels. "Don't be comparing my brother to none of them crazy motherfuckas in the streets."

"No, I'm not doing that at all." I chuckled. "I'm just comfortable around all sorts of people. Very little offends me."

He looked back, smiling at me. "Good."

And, suddenly, all of the weariness washed away for a second.

I glanced down at my phone to see if I had missed a return call or text message from Ivory.

I hadn't.

I was used to her disappearing. She was my girl, but she often vanished, usually when she was with a guy. When she was on a date or involved with a man, she became completely engulfed in him.

I guessed Lyfe had seen the irritation on my face because as I tossed my phone back onto my lap, he said, "You're cool. If your girl doesn't call you back, you can stay here."

My eyes darted up at him. He was padding toward me, and then he sat next to me. With his arm behind me, draping the back of the couch, I felt so safe in his huge shadow. Memories of our kiss lingered behind the dramatics of the day. Goosebumps rose all over my brown skin. The reminder of the taste of his lips made me flush.

I asked, "Are you sure?"

I was honestly surprised that after all the mayhem my husband had caused him, he was willing to allow me to stay in his home.

"Of course. You helped me out all day. And I don't like the fact that if you leave, you aren't sure what Irv will do. I prefer you stay here."

Looking deep into his captivating orbs, I exhaled discreetly, feeling as if I was finally in the company I'd needed for a long time.

CHAPTER 10

OCEAN GRAHAM

"Don't do it. Don't do it, Ocean. Don't do it." I quietly chanted as I stared into the television. I wasn't paying any attention to the newest episode of *Married at First Sight*. Over the voices of the new happily-married strangers played a more entertaining sound. A few feet away, Lyfe was in the bathroom. After a while of calming down from the hectic and dramatic day, he excused himself so that he could get comfortable. He had disappeared into the bathroom, and then I heard the shower running. As hot steam began to pour into the dining room, I realized he had left a small crack in the door.

I stared at the television, chewing nervously on the corner of my bottom lip. I was battling with my bad-girl urge to tiptoe over to that door and get a more revealing peek at what I had been admiring all day. Unfortunately, this was just another form of self-medicating. Instead of focusing on everything that had unfolded that day, I had redirected that frustration and anger to obsessing over seeing Lyfe's nakedness.

"Yolo," I whispered as I pushed off the couch. *You only live once.*

Although I knew only Lyfe and I were in the house, I was nervous. Fearful goose bumps rose to the surface of my skin as if someone could see me. I tiptoed across the hickory wood floors toward the bathroom. The closer I got, the harder my heart pounded in my chest. The exhilaration was a high that I was familiar with, that I had chased for years.

Once at the doorway, I peered inside and was filled with disappointment when I could only see the sink and toilet. However, when I peered into the mirror, there he was. My eyes took in pure angelic magic. Luckily, the shower was surrounded by glass doors, exposing his mahogany, chiseled flesh. Soap-suds bubbled all over his body as he lathered with a macho scent that floated through the crack in the door along with the steam.

I was mesmerized, completely overtaken by the statuesque image before me. He didn't make me smile. He *was* a smile. Everything about him was pure, swagnificent, dominant, masculine joy. I had crept over to the bathroom to simply be a voyeur, but I had gotten so much more. I had been rewarded with pure romantic pornography. My eyes had been blessed with the rare view of a masculine masterpiece. He was perfect, from the curls collected atop his perfectly lined fade to the size of his arms, the mass of his chest, the flawlessness of his ginger skin, to the thickness of his toned thighs.

Like a pervert, I watched him cleanse off the day with my mouth agape. I could feel myself slightly drooling. Then he began to wash off the suds.

Once my eyes traveled down, I swallowed hard, unable to take in what I was seeing. His dick was a work of art. It was a collector's item.

"Gawd damn," I breathed in a mumble.

He bent over and turned the water off. I inwardly gasped and hurriedly floated across the floor on the tips of my toes. Once at the couch, I plopped down, trying to appear like I wasn't flushed and turned on. I perfected the shape of my curls with my hands and straightened out my dress.

Soon, the bathroom door opened, and his excellence appeared, surrounded by a cloud of mist. I stared owlishly at the droplets of water trickling down his body. He was wrapped in a towel that barely covered his massive lower half. He held on to it while hurrying a foot away into his room.

"Whew!" I exclaimed under my breath. I squeezed my thighs together, smothering my pulsating clitoris.

I actually began to fan myself while focusing on the television. I wanted him to take me so I could blame him for the act after it was over. I hoped he would. I almost prayed for it as he emerged from the bedroom.

To my dismay, he was fully dressed. Yet, he was only wearing red basketball shorts and a white tank top. Trying to prevent gawking at him, I looked down. My eyes landed on his feet.

Wow, even his feet are pretty.

I longingly gazed at his sculpted back as he stood in front of a drawer at the island. He then pulled something out and began walking toward me.

"Here, I want you to have one."

Deeply puzzled, I sat up and reached for the large sheet he was handing me. "What's this?"

"Two years ago, I did a fundraiser for The Color of Autism Foundation. All generous donors received prints of this from me."

As he explained, I took in the photographic image, which was breathtaking in perfection. It was vibrant in color and nearly 3D as it bounced off of the eight-by-ten print.

"This is Landon," I whispered while staring at it. "Wow, it looks so real. It looks like a photograph. Who painted this?"

"Me," he answered proudly.

My brows rose with shock and awe. "Oh wow," I replied as my eyes smiled. "You're *very* talented. Is this a hobby of yours, or are you an artist?"

"I wouldn't consider myself an artist. I am dope at sketching, watercolors, and spray painting, though," he boasted with a teasing smirk. "I used to paint and sell the canvases years ago. But the struggle was real. Money was slow. When my mother died, I had to focus on faster money, so I let the passion go."

Still staring at the print, I told him, "That's a shame. You are really good."

"I still draw and paint sometimes. A lot of my work is on my Instagram."

"Oh, cool. Let me check them out. What's your IG handle?"

As he sat beside me, I lay the print next to me on the other side. The fact that he had thought enough of me to gift me this caused my heart to swell and my sweet center to gush.

"Give me your phone," he softly ordered.

Everything he said was so dominatingly seductive. With each gentle command, I was willing to jump in obedience and even ask him, "How high?"

LYFE MILLER

I wanted to bend that big, beautiful, soft, curvy ass over, push my dick into her, and take away the stress of her day with every good stroke.

We talked on the couch until Landon returned from therapy. As soon as I heard the key in the lock, I tensed up, knowing Landon would feel uncomfortable with Ocean's lingering presence. He didn't like new people, especially new people in his personal space. I was very careful about who I allowed in our home because of that. But I was still a man, so he had had to deal with the presence of a woman or two.

As I assumed, when he walked into the house, he overtly showed discomfort with Ocean sitting on the couch.

"What up, bro? How was therapy?" I asked him.

"Fine," he spat as he darted toward the stairs.

"Esther went home?"

"*Yes*," he forced with an attitude.

He was being such a brat, refusing to make eye contact with me as he stormed up the stairs.

"Did she take you to get dinner?" I called out.

"Yes. That's why we're an hour and thirteen minutes late."

I chuckled. "Okay, dude."

"I'm going to play my game. *Bye.*"

I shook my head as he disappeared up the stairs.

"It's okay," Ocean said with a yawn as she slightly patted my thigh. "I can go to a hotel. I don't want him to be uncomfortable."

"Why waste your money? Plus, he needs to learn how to deal with people hanging around."

"You've never had a woman around him?"

"I've had company here, but not often because I don't trust a lot of people to understand him. But I have never been in a relationship or had a woman living here."

Her eyes swelled. "Wow. I remember you telling me that you've never been in a serious relationship."

"When I was younger, that wasn't my focus, of course. Then when my mother died, my focus was completely on him. I didn't have room for anyone else who needed my attention."

She slowly nodded. "I can understand that," she muttered over a long yawn.

I chuckled. "Sleepy?"

"I would love to lie down. It's been a *loooong* day."

"It has been." As I stood, she looked up at me with big, doe eyes. I then took her hand, saying, "Come on."

She obeyed with questions in her eyes. I led her into my bedroom. Once inside, she looked around, clearly impressed at how immaculate my private space was.

Admiring the paintings on the wall, she asked, "You painted all of these?"

"Yep."

My bedroom walls were adorned with images of my mother, African-American art, and royalty, all painted by me.

"Gosh, you're a great artist," she gushed.

Looking down at her, I realized I was still holding her hand. The lust dancing in her eyes as she returned my gaze made my manhood even more erect than she'd had it for most of the day.

The hesitation she'd had in her eyes all day was now gone. It had been replaced with longing, need, and animalistic desire.

"You can sleep in here," I told her, regret seeping into my erection.

"You sure?" she asked.

"Yeah."

"Thanks." Longing boiled over in her gaze as she submissively looked up at me.

"My t-shirts are in that top drawer. You can sleep in one."

She nodded slowly, continuing to give me those tantalizing, cat-like eyes. "Cool."

"I'll sleep on the couch."

Disappointment painted her eyes. "Okay," she mumbled.

I then grabbed the back of her head and placed a soft kiss on her forehead. "Good night. Get you some sleep."

I couldn't look at the want and discontent in her eyes. I made an about-face and left, closing the door behind me.

The desire to wreck that pussy had not left.

Not at all.

However... For some odd reason, I didn't want to do anything to her that would make her feel worse. I actually had feelings for Mrs. Ocean Graham.

≈

Hours later, at two in the morning, I was wide awake with a dick so hard that it hurt.

Ocean had been sleeping for hours. That had been confirmed by the constant, soft rumbling coming from the other side of my closed bedroom door.

My phone began to vibrate on my lap. I picked it up, answering in a whisper, "You outside?"

"Yeah," she purred.

"Bet."

I hung up and tiptoed toward the door. I unlocked it quietly and slipped outside. It was two in the morning and still seventy degrees. The weather was beautiful.

Tif's truck was running at the curb. I hit a light jog toward it and climbed in.

"Hey you," she hummed.

"What up?"

She smirked with flirtation. "It's obvious what's up with this two-in-the-morning call."

I chuckled. "Aye," I replied with a shrug of my shoulder. "It's been one of those days."

Tif leaned into my space, seductively licking those talented lips of hers. "You need some release, baby?"

"Hell yeah."

On cue, she leaned over into my seat and reached inside my shorts. I reclined the seat as she pulled my hefty length out. I wasn't worried about anyone seeing us. The windows on her truck were blacked out.

"*Sssss*," I hissed as my dick disappeared down her throat. "Shit," I sighed when she started to slob and hum on it.

Tif was superb at oral. Yet, I was prematurely tumbling toward an orgasm because Ocean had had me on edge all day.

"Get up," I said, tapping her on the shoulder. "Sit on it."

She looked up at me with a wet mouth as she jagged my manhood slowly. "Let's go inside."

"You know how my brother is. What if he wakes up?"

Tif's eyes narrowed at me slightly, but she sat up. As she began to lift her form-fitting t-shirt dress around her waist, I took a condom out of my pocket and slid it on. She then climbed over into my seat and straddled me. As she slid down my manhood, I reclined the seat further.

It was wrong for me to lie. Unfortunately, that's how I kept women, whose characters I didn't trust around Landon, at bay. Tif was too immature and uncaring to ever be in his presence, so I could get away with fucking her outside while Ocean slept in the house.

Tif wasn't special to me. We weren't even dating. We had been only sneaking links since I'd met her a few months ago. After our initial conversation, it was obvious that she was a young woman who only talked about materialistic, superficial things. So, I had placed her in the booty-call category.

I only dealt with her dense mindset and immaturity on a late night when nothing else was available. This had been one of those nights. Lying on that couch with Ocean in my bed with a hard dick was intolerable after the day we'd had. It had taken everything in me to keep from slipping into that room and bringing her out of her sleep with long, deep strokes.

Yet, raising and caring for Landon had given me a level of maturity that taught me to think beyond sex. Fucking Ocean that night would have made us both feel good, but she was too overcome with emotions to enjoy the aftermath. And I didn't want to be some dick she would regret the next day. I also didn't want to be responsible for her feeling any guilt.

"Mmm," Tif moaned as she bounced on my shaft. "I missed this dick."

Tif was able to take all of me like a champ. She slid to the base of my length and lifted to the tip of it. Then she slammed down slowly while bracing herself with the palms of her hands on my chest.

I gnawed on my bottom lip, feeling her dripping center grip my dick tightly. But when I looked up at her, I didn't see who I wanted to see. It dissatisfied me and turned me off. So, I tore my eyes away from her in order to maintain an erection. I looked up at the sky through the open sunroof, envisioning Ocean, and was baffled that a stranger suddenly meant the world to me.

CHAPTER II
OCEAN GRAHAM

It took me a moment to recall where I was. As I woke up, I stirred, squinting my eyes as I attempted to adjust to the sudden jolt of sunlight. I then remembered that I was in Lyfe's bed, and the realization of all that had happened the day before hit me.

"Urgh," I groaned with regret.

When Lyfe had initially rejected me, I'd assumed he was trying to be a gentleman. But, now, it felt as if he purely wasn't interested because of all of my drama. Sulking, I quietly started to strip out of Lyfe's shirt, get dressed, and pray that he wasn't awake. It was time that I stopped hiding and faced my reality. After dressing, I made up his bed. I then folded his T-shirt and lay it atop the sheets.

Peering out of the door, I was satisfied to see that Lyfe was still asleep. Yet, I could hear the television on upstairs, so I knew Landon was awake. I padded toward the coffee table without a sound and slipped the drawing Lyfe had gifted me off of it. Then I inched toward the door.

I was able to gently open it and slip out without waking Lyfe or alerting Landon. Standing on the porch, I unlocked my phone, went to the Uber app, and requested a ride. I descended the stairs and walked a few houses away, just in case Lyfe woke up and realized I had snuck out. I was embarrassed, so I was tucking my tail and running.

While I waited for my Uber, I saw that Ivory had finally decided to return my call at three that morning. Looking at the app, I realized my Uber was five minutes away. I anxiously looked at Lyfe's house, praying that he wouldn't wake up before I was able to leave. I would have loved to maintain some type of connection with him. He had been such a cool and supportive person. I wanted to at least be as much of a friend to him as he had been to me. I owed him that after he had looked out for me. But humiliation was forcing me to sprint in the opposite direction of him.

We hadn't even exchanged numbers.

As I waited, I called Ivory back.

"Hello?" she answered groggily.

"I'm sorry. I forgot it was like eight in the morning."

"Hey, girl. It's okay. I'm sorry I missed your calls yesterday. I was boo'd up with Romell."

I sneered as my eyes rolled toward the beaming sun. Romell was a jerk that used Ivory, lied to her all the time, and played her constantly. But every time he called, she ran to him like a puppy. She was so thirsty for male attention that she would take any treatment to get it. That was the only part of her life I had outdone her in. Being a prostitute at such a young age taught me a lot about men and how they think. I knew the worth of my body for damn sure, so I never let a man use me. I always made sure I walked away with something, whether it was a financial come-up or an emotional one. Yet, I never judged Ivory's walk since mine was so imperfect.

"I called yesterday to see if I could stay over for a few days."

"Why?" She gasped with excitement. "Did you finally leave Irv?"

"Actually, he left me."

"The hell?!" she spat. "It's the audacity for me! The nerve..."

"He saw me and Lyfe kissing," I revealed with regret.

She began to stutter in shock, "W-what... *What*? How?"

"Apparently, he wasn't on the road picking up a load. He was in a house on the south side serving Lyfe."

"*Serving*?! Wait! What?"

I sneered, "Exactly."

"He's a drug dealer?" Hearing her disbelief made me feel better. At least someone else had been as manipulated by this man as I had.

"He's definitely Lyfe's connect."

Ivory gasped again. "*Noooo*!"

"*Yes.*"

"Where are you now?"

"Well, since you wouldn't answer the phone last night—"

"Sorry. I was fucking, girl," she so easily dismissed.

I kissed my teeth. "*Anyway*, I stayed the night at Lyfe's house."

Instantly, she perked up. "*Ooo*, how was the dick?"

"We didn't have sex."

Ivory groaned. "Why not?"

"Probably because since my husband saw us kissing, he had someone steal the work that Lyfe had copped from him, and someone shot at us."

"What in the entire fuck?!" Ivory screamed into my ear. "Oh my God! Where are you? Come over here *right now*."

"I have to take an Uber to my car. Then I'll be over."

"Okay. I'll cook us some breakfast so we can eat while you spill the tea."

Then, thankfully, the Uber pulled up. I hurried toward it, telling Ivory, "I'm getting in the Uber now. I should be there soon."

"Okay, girl."

I hung up and took one last glance at Lyfe's house. Admittedly, I felt another wave of heartbreak. Yesterday, before the chaos had unfolded, I was looking forward to him becoming a part of my life in some way, shape, or form. But as my Uber drove away, I realized that maybe his purpose in my life had been temporary, a brief season to show me the true caliber of the man I was married to and to show me the happiness I should be striving for. And, if that were the case, I appreciated meeting Lyfe and would never forget him.

He was the most perfect stranger I would never see again.

I FINALLY ARRIVED at Ivory's house. With a deep breath, I turned off the engine and gathered my phone and purse, feeling the weight of the world on my shoulders. As my hand grasped the door handle, my phone rang. Recognizing the familiar number, I inhaled sharply and answered quickly.

"Hello? Irv?" I rushed.

"Yeah," he spit dryly.

Hurt, I mimicked him, "*Yeah*? That's all you have to say to me?"

"You're lucky I have the decency to call you in the first place."

I gasped. "Excuse me?"

"You're a whore." Tears welled in my eyes as he continued to heartlessly spew obscenities that he once would have never used toward me. "You are still the whore I met when I saw you on that corner selling your body for twenty dollars so you can get high. Nothing has changed."

His audacity was daunting. With each word, my tears formed into spewing rage.

"As a matter of fact, a lot has changed," I snapped. "I'm not that immature teenager you met five years ago. You can't pull the wool over my eyes anymore. Let's talk about the fact that Lyfe was even able to kiss me because you have been so neglectful of my needs that you haven't been around to have sex with me, love me, or comfort me because you've been living a lie! You're not about to talk down to me to deflect from the fact that you've been manipulating me for five years. Since when are you the connect? I thought you were on the road picking up a load, Irv?"

"I was making money for us." His words were so emotionless, as if his lies weren't as dreadful as they felt.

"You never needed for anything. You worked because you wanted to. Of course, I wasn't going to tell you that the drug game was how I was making my money because that was the source of all of your demons." His soft, emotionless tone was more hurtful than his lies.

"You still lied!" I shrieked. "What about all of those times you couldn't talk to me because *supposedly* there wasn't any service on the highway? Why couldn't you talk to me for real? What else are you hiding from me? If you can lie about a career, you can lie about any damn thing!"

He scoffed as if I were being ridiculous. "Lying about how I make my money and you kissing another man is not the same thing. How long have you been fucking him?"

"I never have. I met him yesterday."

Irv blew an annoyed breath. "Figures."

"Stop insulting me. What did you expect? You haven't been here for me, Irv. But we can fix this. We can work this out."

I honestly wanted my marriage. He had lied to me, and I had

been in the arms of another man. I would never forget the way that Lyfe had made me feel that day. Yet, that had been *one day* versus years of unconditional love. I didn't have a lot of examples of a good marriage, but I did know marriages came with arguments and heart-breaks. I couldn't expect perfection. What he'd lied about, I could understand because of my past. And I hoped he could look past what I had done. Lyfe was a perfect stranger, but he was not my husband. He was not the man who had looked past my faults and loved me into rehabilitation. I wanted to give Irv the patience and under-standing he had given me.

"I want a divorce." Irv's words were a near-fatal assault on my heart.

Tears welled in my eyes as they bucked with shock and complete awe at his sudden coldness.

"I'm selling our place. I already put it on the market this morn-ing. You'll be hearing from my lawyer."

I blinked in slow motion, staring out of the windshield in pure disbelief that my husband was talking to me this way. He had rescued me out of the ashes. Yet, now, he was throwing me back to those same ashes with no apprehension.

"You just need some time," I told him, clinging on to hope. "We'll talk about this another day and time."

I refused to believe that we could be over like this. There was no way that this man could have such a kind heart that he had lifted me out of the ashes like a Phoenix just to leave me five years later.

However, his cynical chuckle said otherwise. "Tomorrow, next week, or next year, I will still feel the same way. You'll be hearing from my lawyer."

His overt crassness made my stomach knot up. My eyes bulged. Before I could respond, I realized that his end of the call had gone completely dead. I tore the phone away from my ear and looked at the screen.

He'd hung up on me.

I broke down. I began to bawl as I grabbed my things and slowly climbed out of the car on weak legs. I hurried over the curb and through Ivory's yard. I then rushed up the stairs. I didn't care if anyone lingering outside on her block on the Southwest side saw me crying. I was rushing because I felt the urge to regurgitate.

I rang Ivory's doorbell, thinking this couldn't be real. I understood the hurt Irv must have felt seeing me in the arms of another man, but for him to be so cold was deathly heartbreaking and confusing.

Finally, Ivory's front-door locks began to turn. She opened the door, holding her long cotton robe tight in front of her slim-thick frame. Her jet-black, satiny hair was pulled back into a tight ponytail. Her long lashes fluttered feverishly as her light brown eyes adjusted to the sudden burst of sunlight.

She gasped at the sight of my tears. Using her small yet long arm, she reached for my elbow and pulled me inside her house.

"It's going to be okay," she insisted as she took me in her arms.

"He's so pissed at me."

"You talked to him?"

"He just called. He was so cold," I cried as I lay my head on her shoulder. "He hates me that quickly? I know I cheated, but he's treating me like I've never been anything to him, never even meant anything to him."

"He's just hurt and upset right now. It'll pass. You have nothing to feel ashamed of. You kissed Lyfe because Irv hasn't been doing his part. And he hasn't been doing his part because he has been lying to you."

"Exactly. He wasn't even apologetic about it." I pushed back, trying to get myself together. I used the neckline of my dress to dry my tears. "I'm sorry for coming over here like this."

"It's fine. And you can stay here as long as you need to," she offered as she stepped back, granting me entry.

"Hopefully, it won't be that long. We just need a few days to calm down so we can figure this out."

A WEEK LATER

CHAPTER 12

OCEAN GRAHAM

Unfortunately, my initial assumptions of Irv just needing more time couldn't have been further from the truth.

The past week had been stressful. Initially, I had called myself giving Irv some time and space. However, after days went by without a single word from him, I reached out to him.

I immediately regretted it, though. Every word he'd said over the phone or via text was fueled with hatred. It was as if he despised my very being.

I had taken it upon myself to go home to get some clothes and to talk to him face-to-face. What once felt like a warm and loving domicile felt cold. Everything was how I had left it. So, clearly, Irv hadn't been home either. I sat there for hours, waiting to see if he would come, but he never did. I wanted the courage to stay there and wait him out. However, the loneliness was scarier and louder than my demons. I couldn't take that on top of the heartbreak, so I rushed back to Ivory's place with my tail tucked between my legs.

I was in my office at work, going over a few applications from potential renters for a new development we were managing in the South Loop. From time to time, I found myself gazing at the drawing Lyfe had given me. I had chosen to hang it in my office at work. Every time I looked at it, I was reminded of the stranger who had come into my life and turned it upside down. Despite the drama that had ruined that perfect day, I still smiled whenever I thought of him, which was often.

A knock on the open door of my office pulled my attention away from the paperwork.

I looked up to see a casually dressed man peering inside.

"Hi, may I help you?" I greeted.

"Ocean Graham?"

"Yes, that's me. How may I help you?"

I was excited to have a prospective resident to focus on. I needed any and everything to keep my mind off my breaking heart until Ivory arrived for our lunch date.

The gentleman took a few steps into the office and handed me a manila envelope.

No sooner than I took it from him, he announced, "You've been served."

My eyes darted up at him. However, my curiosity landed on his back because he was quickly shuffling his way out of my office. My eyes narrowed as I tore the envelope open. I wondered what bill collector could have been suing me. I even thought back to any professional issues I may have had at my job or as a rideshare driver that would have warranted being sued. But there was nothing that came to mind.

When I saw the words "Petition for Divorce" on the heading of the paperwork, my world stopped. Breathing ceased.

This was *real*. This was actually happening. Irv was not having an extended temper tantrum. He was not being a crybaby because his ego was broken. He was truly leaving me.

I couldn't allow myself to break down, though. My fingers clawed at the wood of my desk as I attempted to hold on to whatever sliver of control over my emotions I could. But I couldn't look past the fact that all of this was so sudden and cold. If anyone knew my innermost demons and how I got to those dark places, it was Irv. Why he would choose to deal with things in such a callous way was beyond me. It was as if he wanted me to relapse.

Yet, this was what rehab had been meant for. The world and my loved ones could not tiptoe around me, keeping all negativity and heartbreak at bay because of my addiction. I had to learn to deal with things like this without running to drugs to cope. This, however, had been one of the hardest things to suffer while being sober.

Naturally, I wondered if this had to do with our child's death. I wondered if he blamed me as well.

Just wondering if that were it brought painful tears to my eyes. Just as they had begun to fall, I heard Ivory's concerned tone. "Ocean?"

I looked up, wiping my tears away. She was entering my office with orbs heavily doused with concern. Despite the worry lines on her forehead, she looked beautiful enough to temporarily take my attention away from my own miseries. Her light skin had been tanning in the summer sun. Her silky, long hair was pulled into a high bun. She was casually dressed in a Rosa Parks t-shirt and jeans. She didn't even have on an ounce of makeup. But the magnificence in her natural beauty was effortless.

Since I'd had this expression of sadness and despair for a week, she had grown used to it. Ivory sighed deeply and sat down in the chair in front of my desk where so many residents had sat to sign their new leases.

"Everything is going to be okay," Ivory softly encouraged me.

That familiar sting of tears introduced itself to my eyes. I looked up at the ceiling, making a desperate attempt to stop them.

"No, it's not," I told her.

"What did he say now?" Ivory asked with a slur of hate.

I didn't answer verbally. I couldn't. I simply tossed the papers across the desk.

Ivory's brows curled tightly as she scooped them up and scanned them. A few seconds ticked by before she gasped. "He seriously filed for divorce?!"

Pained, my eyes squeezed together tightly. "He sure did."

"He is taking this too far. Over a kiss? Unt uh! *Hell no!* C'mon." Then she stood and gestured for me to follow.

I shook my head, feeling sick to my stomach. My world was crumbling, and I was too weak to hold it together. "I don't feel like eating anymore. I don't even have an appetite."

"We aren't going to eat. We're going over to that house to see what is *really* going on."

LYFE MILLER

"I don't want to go to the grocery store with you."

I tilted my head to the side, looking at Landon as I stood at the front door, slipping into my Jordans. "I know, Landon."

Pacing, he looked at nothing in particular as he continued to argue with me. "There are *way* too many people in there. I don't like that."

"You said that your therapist is a smart lady, right?"

Landon nodded confidently. "She has her PhD from Harvard, which holds a record number of honors and awards with forty-nine Nobel Laureates, thirty-two heads of state, and forty-eight Pulitzer Prize winners. So, Dr. Val is *very* intelligent."

I chuckled inwardly, not wanting to offend his sensitivity with me finding humor in his knowledge of all of these random facts.

I had always thought myself to be a pretty smart man. I had graduated from high school and had even taken some college courses before figuring out that college couldn't teach me the talents in art that God had already naturally blessed me with. But Landon was like a fucking encyclopedia. A lot of the things he talked to me about went completely over my head.

"Well, she obviously knows what she's talking about then, right?" I asked him.

"Yes," he answered with a hard nod.

"Well, your therapist said you need to venture out into more populated places so you can get used to being in social settings."

He then shook his head. "I still don't want to go."

"Well, you *have* to go, bro, so c'mon."

I opened the door and held it ajar, leaning against it with my hand in the pocket of my shorts. I then gave Landon a stern glare. He knew that expression well. He was more than aware that when I gave him *that look* and stopped talking that he had no choice but to comply.

He began to flap his hands, which was self-stimulation for him. He then reluctantly slipped into his sneakers.

Finally, we left out of the front door. It was now July, and the sun was shining so bright that my eyes squinted tightly, trying to adjust to it.

Since I'd killed Doe, I had been laying low while keeping my ear to the streets. I had heard that the person who had shot at me and Ocean was another one of Irv's young homies who was waiting in the getaway car for Doe. I had also heard that Irv's only objective was to take his work back, not kill me. Still, I had been laying low as a precaution all week, and my guard had been at its highest.

I had also finally managed to stop thinking about Ocean. When I woke up and saw that my bed was empty, I wasn't surprised. So much had happened the day before that I couldn't blame her. Yet, I would've liked for her to have left a number or something so I could've kept in contact with her. I had typed my handle into her Instagram so she could look at my paintings, but I hadn't gotten a glimpse of hers. I had no way to contact her, and she hadn't followed me on Instagram. For the first few days, I was bothered by that. In one day, I developed an interest in her that wouldn't allow her to leave my thoughts. But she had disappeared. This was the first day that I hadn't been obsessing over her.

"Lyfe." The way Landon said my name, I knew he had one of his nerdy facts to tell me.

So, I reluctantly asked, "Yeah?" I then got ready to be schooled by my younger brother.

By the time he finished one of these conversations, I always felt like the younger, *dumber* brother.

"Did you know that if unwound and linked together, the strands of DNA in each of your cells would be six feet long? We have one hundred trillion cells in our body, which means if all of your DNA was put end-to-end, it would stretch over one hundred and ten billion miles, which is hundreds of round trips to the sun."

I laughed to myself as we descended the stairs. "No, I didn't know that."

"So, racism doesn't make any sense."

"Why is that?"

"Because we're all 99.9 percent alike. Of the three billion base pairs in the human genome, only 0.1 percent is unique to us. While that 0.1 percent is still what makes us unique, it means we're all more similar than we are different."

Landon's other specific interest was DNA. He was like a fucking scientist when it came to genomics.

As he continued to fill my ears with scientific jargon that I couldn't wrap my head around if someone paid me to, I noticed one of the homies walking my way.

"Oh, what up, JC?" I turned to Landon and told him, "Go ahead and get in the car. Let me holla at my homie real quick."

Landon nodded and walked toward my truck. I popped the locks just as JC walked up to me.

Since JC was a part of Irv's crew, he and I had hung out a few times. He often rode down on me since we lived in the same hood. Still, my guard was up until he met me at the curb and extended his hand so we could shake up. As we did, he greeted, "What's the word?"

"Shit. I was about to head to the grocery store with Landon."

"Oh, okay. I saw you when I was riding past, so I rode down on you. I heard about that bullshit with Irv."

I grimaced, shaking my head. "Man, I feel like everyone in the streets knows at this point."

JC copped his weight from Irv as well, but he and Irv weren't friends. He and I were cooler than he and Irv were, so I was comfortable talking to him about this.

"You know how people talk."

I nodded, ensuring him, "I had no idea she was his wife."

JC waved his hand dismissively. "Irv doesn't care about his wife. He rarely even talks about being married, and Bridget has him sprung."

I nodded feverishly in agreement. "Exactly. That's why I don't get why he sent Doe and his homie at me."

"He thinks you're screwing his wife. He had to do something as a man."

"Nah, a real man would have let that ride since he obviously doesn't want his wife. His ego just has the best of him right now."

JC nodded. "Facts. You coulda let Doe get away with taking that shit, though."

I had never told anyone that I shot Doe. The police had no leads in the investigation. However, since the streets talked so much, it hadn't been hard to put two and two together.

"He was just doing what Irv told him to do," JC added.

"I didn't even know it was Doe until I had already shot him. Doe was in the streets. He knew what could potentially happen to him when attempting to rob somebody."

JC slowly nodded. "You're right."

Looking behind JC, I noticed Landon becoming fidgety in the car. "Aye, let me go before Landon gets agitated."

"Fa sho."

JC and I shook up again. We then parted ways. I headed to my truck, hoping I wouldn't have to talk Landon into going with me all over again. Just as I stepped off the curb, I heard an eerily familiar explosive pop. Instinctively, I ducked and went into my waist for my gun. However, it was too late. I could feel the paralyzing, sharp pain starting at my back and shooting throughout my body.

"Urgh!" I bellowed out as my body collapsed. I fell onto my back.

Looking up into the sky, I blinked slowly. The realization that the streets had finally got me swallowed me.

As the pain consumed me, I fought to maintain the ability to breathe. Then a shadow cast over me, blocking the sun. JC was standing over me, aiming his Glock at my head with a menacing glare.

"Doe was my family, motherfucka. That was my brother. My mother never gon' be the same."

I had no idea that they were even related. I wanted to say that, but when I opened my mouth, instead of speaking, I coughed, and blood splattered against the Air Force Ones on JC's feet.

"Oh God! Oh God!" Landon's unraveling took me and JC's attention away from one another. Landon was in a frenzy behind him in the grass alongside the passenger's door. "You're going to die too! You're going to die!"

I watched weakly as Landon's outburst made JC lose control. He was no longer cool. He began to fidget with the gun still in his hand.

"You're going to die too!" Landon screamed. "You're going to die like Mom! You're going to die!" He then began to smack his palms wildly against his head.

"Landon," I tried to call for him, but my voice was weak as life slipped from me.

I fought through the lightheadedness to lift my head. That's when I noticed JC becoming fidgety as well, taken aback by Landon's outbursts.

JC started to inch toward Landon. I used the little strength that I had to anchor my eyes on his trigger finger, which was unstable. He rushed toward Landon, spewing angrily, "Aye, motherfucka—"

That was all JC had been able to say before I lifted my pistol, aimed upwards, toward the back of JC's head, and fired.

Landon jumped out of his skin and covered his ears with trembling hands as a hole was blown into the back of JC's head. JC's body tilted lifelessly onto my truck before falling forward, landing partially in the grass and in front of my truck near me.

"Landon," I finally found the energy to call his name audibly.

"You're going to die too! You're going to die too!" he chanted erratically while pacing wildly.

"Landon," left my dry and trembling lips in a mumble as I felt myself losing air. "Call the po..."

OCEAN GRAHAM

"That's the house right there."

Ivory parked a few feet away from the house I was pointing to with determination in her eyes.

As I grabbed the handle of the passenger's door, she grabbed hers too.

"I'm good going in their alone," I told her.

Since Irv had been so careless and cold toward me, I didn't know what I would be walking in on. I couldn't take him embarrassing me in front of Ivory.

She sucked her teeth. "Girl, please. I'm not letting you go in there alone."

I grimaced, a part of me feeling like her urge to accompany me wasn't selfless but more so out of nosiness. As my eyes rolled toward the sky, I caught a glimpse of the house and saw the screen door open.

I hurriedly sat back, reached over, and pulled Ivory down to duck with me.

"What?!" she snapped.

"He's coming out!" I snapped, peering over her dashboard at the house. My heart pounded so violently that it shot a sharp pain through my body. Anxiety was swallowing me as I stared out of the window with huge, doe eyes.

Staring along with me, Ivory inhaled sharply as a woman followed Irv out of the house. She was high-yellow, and her hair, though stringy, fell down to the arch of her back. She was obviously Mexican or maybe Caucasian. As Irv took her hand and guided her down the steps, I noticed that the woman was also very pregnant. I let out a heartbroken moan as I took in her bulge. It was a large size, so she had to be at least five months along.

"Oh, hell no!" Ivory snapped.

I cringed with embarrassment as she lunged toward the handle of her door and opened it. I was able to snatch her back by the hem of her shirt before she could dart out.

"No, Ivory," I begged.

"Why not?" she snapped.

"I just... I..." I couldn't find the words. This was all too much. "He's not about to embarrass me in front of her."

Ivory's eyes glared as we discreetly watched Irv walk this woman to his Ram. Looking at her, I could tell she was young. I could also see the struggle beyond her beautiful features. There was a look people in the streets had even after they had left them. She still had that hard-life appearance. He opened the passenger door for her and helped her inside. Once she was inside the car, he even leaned in and kissed her belly.

"Umph," I moaned as I squeezed my eyes shut. I fought to keep the contents of my stomach from rising up my throat and exploding out of my mouth.

Ivory slurred, "That son of a bitch has some sort of a savior complex."

I tore my eyes open and looked at Ivory.

"That bitch clearly used to be a dope feign," she explained. "No offense, but did you see her? She looks like an addict. Maybe *that's* why he's been so cold to you. He has some kind of savior or hero complex. He needs to save his woman, to fix her. He might only feel good about himself in his relationship if he's fixing his woman, making her over. You're fixed now, so he doesn't want you anymore."

Watching Irv's Ram pull away, it all began to make sense. But that did not prevent the tears from falling.

It was hard to determine which deception hurt worse: his infidelity or the fact that his side piece was having the baby that I couldn't. The vision of him kissing her belly played in my mind behind my closed, tearful eyes. Realizing that she was having his child inflicted a pain that was crippling and unbearable.

"I'm so sorry, Ocean," Ivory said as she rubbed my leg. "You can stay with me as long as you want."

I cringed, finally coming to grips with the fact that my marriage was over.

"It won't be long," I assured her. "I'm sure my company will give me one of their vacant units." As I spoke to her, I stared at the Ram as it decreased smaller and smaller in size as it drove away, symbolizing my stability and sanity also growing smaller and smaller... until it completely disappeared.

FIFTEEN YEARS AGO

CHAPTER 13
OCEAN GRAHAM

♫ Bitch, I'm paid, that's all I gotta say
Can't see you, lil' nigga, the money in the way
And I'm, I'm sitting high, a ganster ride blades
If you ain't gone ride fly, then you might as well hate ♫

I will never forget this day. It was the first time I had committed a crime, when I realized that I could no longer depend on my parents to eat.

I was only twelve years old at the time. It was a nice summer day. School had been let out. I hadn't gone that day though because my parents hadn't been home to make me. I didn't want to go because I was tired of being bullied about my clothes having that ratchet stench. I had hidden in the house all day until I heard other kids outside. Now, I sat on my porch watching everyone play. It was a guy sitting in front of my house in his car blasting "Stuntin' Like My Daddy" from his Charger. Some older girls were on a porch a few houses down, dancing pervertedly to the beat.

Most girls my age were wearing pigtails while riding their bikes on the sidewalks and waiting impatiently for the ice cream truck to ride down the block. Other girls were in a group jumping rope. Their parents were most likely watching them from only a few feet away on the porch as they hung out with their friends. Others were in the house because they trusted their obedient children not to leave off the block.

I watched a beautiful summer day play out before my tired eyes. My mother and father had been partying until five in the morning with their friends in our home on the East Side of Chicago.

Even though we had a residential address, the four walls that I slept in could barely be called a home. My mother had finally gotten Section 8 the year prior, so we had been able to move out of the slum row houses we once lived in. There wasn't much furniture in our new home at all. Our living room only had folding chairs in it until my father brought in a couch he had found in an alley that someone was throwing away. Anything else they had sense enough to buy would only get sold whenever their habit outweighed their need to have belongings. The same went for my things. What they purchased for me when they were sober often disappeared whenever they needed money to get high. I would hide the things I really liked, like my favorite pair of pants and my favorite shirts.

I slept on a thin mattress under the window in my tiny bedroom. Anything that belonged to me was housed on the floor alongside me.

The kitchen only had a very dirty microwave that didn't even rotate when it was in use, so everything I heated up was never heated properly. We used to have curtains, but they disappeared one day and were replaced with newspaper. I often heard people refer to my parents as Bobby and Whitney. When I was young, I never understood what that meant. But once I got older and learned the tragic tale of Whitney Houston being hooked on drugs alongside her bad-boy husband, Bobby Brown, I soon understood the correlation. My parents were in love with each other just as much as they were in love with crack cocaine. I just wished they'd had an ounce of that love for me.

Since they had been using our living room as a drug den, along with their dope fiend friends, all night, I had barely gotten any sleep. After the sun rose, the house eventually quieted down. I then knew that they had smoked all of their drugs and had escaped into the day to panhandle or steal so that they could buy their daily supply. I should have used the quiet to get some rest, but the hunger pangs were so strong that they were unbearable, leaving me unable to sleep. And the roaches kept me wide awake. Our home was infested with them. In the daytime, it gave me the creeps to see them crawling all over the walls and on my covers. If I sat still for too long, they would even crawl on me. So, I'd retreated to the porch.

But watching the other girls in our neighborhood only left me feeling worse. Many of them were struggling financially as well, since we all stayed in the same impoverished neighborhood. But others had parents with good enough jobs or hustles to keep their hair done and clothes clean. Some of the kids were dirty and smelled just as bad as I did. I often saw their parents with mine, so I assumed that they were on drugs too.

"Mmmph..." I clung to my stomach, moaning as another hunger pang surged through my body.

I hadn't had anything to eat since the day prior. Most of the time, I would eat the leftovers of what my parents left lying around, but that was mostly sweets. On other days, I would just deal with it until they remembered they had a daughter at home that they needed to feed. But that day, I didn't have either option. I had searched our house high and low for any form of substance. But what my parents and their friends hadn't demolished, the roaches had already claimed for themselves.

"Hey, Ocean."

I pulled my eyes away from the girls shaking their butts to Lil' Wayne and saw Reggie approaching my porch with his little sister. Reggie attended my school, and we were in the same grade. His sister was two grades behind us. Reggie didn't bully me like the other kids, but I assumed it was because his parents did drugs with mine.

"Hey, Reggie. Where y'all goin'?"

"To the store," he answered, pausing in front of my house.

When I saw the hole in his shoes, I felt relief that another kid was literally in my shoes.

"I'm gonna walk with y'all," I told him, standing from the porch.

I didn't really want to walk. It always hurt my feet when I walked for long periods of time because my shoes were too small. But I was so hungry and hoped that since Reggie and his sister were walking to the store, they had money to buy snacks they would share with me.

As we started walking, Reggie asked me, "You ditched school today?"

Instead of answering, I was too busy looking at the short white stick between his fingers. It looked like a cigarette, but since my mama smoked those, I knew it wasn't one.

"What is that?" I asked him.

"A joint."

I inhaled sharply. "You're doin' drugs, Reggie?!"

He frowned with disgust. "It's not drugs like that. I'm not a crackhead. This is weed."

"How did you get it?" I pried.

Reggie reached into his pocket and pulled out a lighter. "I stole it from my uncle when he came over."

When he lit the joint, my eyes bulged. "So, you smoke weed?"

He frowned like my question was idiotic. He then shrugged. "Yeah. Everybody does."

He hit it. I didn't like how the smoke looked pouring from his nose. It reminded me of how my mom and dad looked when they would hold the pipe to their lips and take a big pull on it. But, unlike my parents, Reggie didn't start nodding right away like he was sleepy.

"You wanna hit it?" he asked me.

I looked around, slowing my steps. I had always wondered about getting high. When my parents did, they looked so at peace and happy. And when they weren't high, they were irritable and mean. I had started to wonder if getting high would make me happy too. But, if it was going to make me treat other people the way my parents mistreated me, I never wanted to be *that* happy.

"Do you?" Reggie pressed.

"Yeah," I answered slowly. "But I don't want anyone to see me."

Reggie quickly took my hand and dragged me between the two buildings we were about to pass. He then handed me the joint and told his sister, "Say something if somebody comes."

His sister feverishly nodded and obediently began to be on the lookout.

I stared at the joint, nervous and scared.

"Hurry up before somebody sees us," Reggie urged.

I had never smoked anything in my life, but I had seen my parents smoke a million times. So, I just did what I had seen them do. I inhaled and then held it, allowing the smoke to pour from my lips.

I then gave the joint back to Reggie. He and I handed it back and forth to each other while his sister looked out for us at the entrance of the gangway.

Once it was gone, we kept walking to the store. Slowly, my feet began to feel heavy. Everything Reggie did and said cracked me up.

But, most of all, I noticed how good I felt. I wasn't sad. I wasn't concerned about where my parents were. I was actually happy. Despite how my clothes smelled, how dirty they were, or how bad my feet hurt, I was playing as we walked to the store. Reggie chased me and his sister as we raced ahead to a spot to see who had won. It was the most fun I had ever had.

I wanted to cling to that feeling forever.

Once at the store, I followed Reggie and his sister, feeling my mouth watering with anticipation of what they would buy. Now, my hunger pangs had magnified. I was so hungry that it felt like my stomach was trying to eat itself to keep my body from starving to death.

"What are you doing?" My eyes narrowed as I saw Reggie put a bag of chips down his pants.

His head whipped backward as he quietly snapped, "*Sshhh!*"

"Are y'all stealing this stuff?" I asked, beginning to freak out as he stashed another bag of chips.

"Yeah," he answered like it was no big deal.

"Aren't you going to get in trouble?" I whispered frantically. "You can go to jail."

Reggie simply shrugged. "Me and my sister do this all the time. We don't have any money, so what else are we supposed to do?"

Looking further up the aisle, I saw his sister sneaking a pack of cookies into her pocket.

"Get you something," Reggie told me.

"Unt uh," I refused, shaking my head vigorously. "I don't want to go to jail."

Reggie sucked his teeth. "Whatever, *Scary*. Don't be asking me for none of my stuff then."

My heart broke. I was devastated.

I stood frozen in place as Reggie and his sister left the aisle. As I lost sight of them in the store, I felt like I was losing my ability to put something on my stomach. My hunger was more powerful than my fear at that point, so I followed Reggie's lead. I made sure that the store clerks behind the bulletproof glass weren't paying me any attention. I then began to put as much food and snacks in my shirt and pants as I could without it appearing obvious. Reggie and his sister had gone for the snacks and sweets, but I was going for the gusto. I took packs of Ramen noodles and juice, things that could be a real meal when I needed one.

Once I was back at home, I felt like I was having a smorgasbord. I had never had that much food in front of me before. I ate until it hurt to keep swallowing. I hid the rest of the food under my pillow and enjoyed the mellow feeling the weed had given me. It was forcing a smile on my face that hadn't been there in a long time. I didn't have a TV, so I just looked out the window, watching the neighborhood because I had been using that as my favorite and only television show.

From that day forward, I was hooked on doing what I had to do to survive and chasing that euphoric feeling I had gone to bed with that night.

PRESENT DAY

CHAPTER 14

OCEAN GRAHAM

"**O**cean, things appear to be very cut and dry. Your home in Bronzeville was purchased before the marriage. Your car is in your name. The property you found out about is actually in the name of Bridget Martinez. Other than splitting the assets in the shared bank accounts, this divorce should be fairly easy *unless* you plan to fight him for something."

Irv and I had barely talked since our last conversation. It felt like he had been just looking for an excuse to get rid of me, and seeing me kiss Lyfe was exactly that. From that day forward, he had completely washed his hands of me. He had no interest in my life, my needs, or my pain. It was as if I had never existed to him. I was starting to think that Ivory was right; Irv *did* have a savior complex and had moved on to his next needy bitch since he had already rescued and fixed me.

Part of me wished I had been more broken, so he would still love me. I wanted to reveal my weaknesses to him so he could see that my soul would never be completely healed. However, with my sobriety had come self-esteem, and I would be damned if I broke myself down to make him love me.

Sitting across from my divorce attorney's desk, I didn't have the energy to fight for anything.

"There was no prenup to ensure that he owed you anything if the marriage ended because of infidelity." As my eyelids lowered, she asked, "Is there anything you want to fight him for, like cars or property? Is there anything you feel like you deserve?"

I slowly shook my head, telling her, "No, there isn't anything I want."

She raised an eyebrow, pressing me, "Are you sure?"

Nodding, I assured her, "Yes."

I didn't have the power to contest anything, and there was nothing for me to fight Irv for. He had given me everything I could ask for: a chance to become a better person. He was the sole person responsible for getting me clean, educated, and employed. I owed him my life, but I hadn't even been able to give him a child.

"Ocean?"

Blinking back the approaching tears, I looked up at Sharon. Her gray eyes were full of compassion as she watched me inhale sharply to gather myself.

"You're going to be okay," she assured me.

There wasn't an ounce of my being that believed that. I had been barely holding on for the past two weeks, fighting to self-medicate by pouring myself into my work instead of the substances that my mind had been fantasizing about.

Since things were fairly simple with this divorce, Sharon assured me that it should be finalized quickly. As I left her office, that was the only thing that gave me comfort. I hurried out of the building and to my car. I was eager to get back to work so I could sign the contract for my new place.

As I had assumed, my supervisors were eager to give me a property to live in. I had found a cute condo in Hyde Park. The amenities were the best, however. It was one of the newer developments in the neighborhood. Therefore, the amenities included a grocery store, cleaners, and restaurant in addition to the usual luxuries. The only thing I wasn't looking forward to regarding the move was having to communicate with Irv about getting the rest of my things out of the house in Bronzeville.

The last thing I wanted to do was uproot my stability by moving into a new place. I would have preferred to live in my comfort zone, but Irv had left me no choice.

AN HOUR LATER, I walked into Ivory's apartment. The smell of weed crept on me like an intruder that knew I was in fear.

Sucking my teeth, I held my breath. Weed wasn't my hardest addictive substance, but it was what had led me to experiment with much more harmful drugs.

I hurried to Ivory's guest room just as I had heard her question from her room, "Ocean?"

I closed the door, pretending not to have heard her. I then lay on the bed, fighting the strong urge to ask her to hit that weed. I knew that the temporary high would make me feel so much better. I longed for the euphoria. Yet, that bliss would only open up the gates to a greater high that I would always seek and that nothing would help me obtain. I would chase it until I was knee-deep in addiction and ruin.

I couldn't have expected Ivory not to indulge in her own home just because I was sober. It was up to me to be strong no matter what environment I was in. Yet, it frustrated me that I was in that environment at all. I should have been in my own home, where I had a loved one who cared as much for my sobriety as I did. However, instead, that loved one had found a replacement for me and threw me back into the streets he had taken me out of.

"Ocean?" Ivory's voice was closer now, on the other side of the door.

The door then opened, and she poked her head inside the room.

"Oh, hey. I was just making sure it was you," she said. "How was the meeting? Did you get him for everything he owns?" Her eyes widened with anticipation of my drama as she leaned against the doorframe. She then brought a blunt to her lips.

Sucking my teeth, I asked, "Really, Ivory?" looking at the blunt.

Her eyes rolled to the ceiling. "Girl, I'm in the doorway."

"I can still smell it."

"You've been around weed." She continued puffing, totally disregarding the way I was barely holding on to my sanity and sobriety.

Ivory had always been so nonchalant about my addictions and past, to the point that she was so comfortable cracking jokes and triggering me.

"So, spill the tea," she pressed. "What happened?"

Swallowing my frustration, I told her, "Nothing happened. The divorce should be final soon. I'm not getting anything. He owned everything before we were married. We are only splitting the assets in our accounts, and it isn't that much."

She frowned. "Damn, you can't even get the house out of that cheating bastard?"

I cringed, hating that she was easily bringing up deceit that I was trying to forget. I parted my lips to answer, but she'd kept talking.

"Romell is coming over tonight," she announced with a thirsty glow in her eyes.

I rolled mine mentally. Of course, he was coming over. Romell only took her two places: for granted and to the bedroom. That's it.

"He asked if he could bring his buddy with him." She raised her eyebrows as her smile widened.

"I'm good, Ivory," I refused. "I don't feel like entertaining a man tonight."

"Who said you had to entertain him? All you gotta do is open your legs."

I frowned, offended. "Damn, I don't even know him, but I'm fucking him already?"

Ivory shrugged. "Don't act like you're uptight with that thang."

I needed this place to stay, so I bit my tongue. Yet, it was apparent with each of Ivory's "jokes," there was offensive intent behind them. It had been easy to ignore previously, but now that we were living together, it was so obvious that she looked down on me for the things I'd done.

She went on, ignoring how uncomfortable I was. "You need some dick, girl."

"No, I don't. I need some peace and to get my mind right."

She sneered. "You have really turned into a lame."

I lightly scoffed. "Ivory, you know it's important that I watch what I do, who I hang with, and where I go. It's important for my sobriety. I'm barely holding on as it is."

Her head tilted dramatically as she rolled her eyes. "You're not about to go get a crack pipe and put it to your lips."

I grimaced discreetly. She was so naïve. Little did she know that that would be the first thing I would do if I listened to the demons in my head.

"Come on," Ivory begged. "I already told—"

I blocked her out. I grabbed my phone and focused my attention on it. She was frustrating me, but since I needed the free place to sleep for the next week until I received the keys to my new place, I had to humble myself.

As she rambled on and on, I went to my Instagram app. I quickly noticed that I had a DM, so I tapped on the message icon to read it.

As my eyes scanned the words, I sat straight up on the bed.

"What's wrong?" Ivory asked.

I looked up, not realizing that my thoughts were all over my face.

"I got this weird message from somebody," I replied.

I then read it again: *First, you disappeared on me without even saying goodbye. Then you don't even try to contact me. I didn't make enough impression on you that day for you to at least wanna know how I'm doing? I got shot. I deserve a wellness check or something.*

My eyes darted up to the profile picture of the person who'd sent me the DM. I squinted, not wanting to believe it was *Lyfe.* But when I clicked on the username, and the profile appeared, it truly was him in all of his swag and royal hood glory.

Though I had scanned his Instagram profile the night we met, seeing the photos of him again felt like seeing his beautiful face for the first time.

It was still as impressive.

I gasped audibly. "Lyfe got shot!"

"I thought you hadn't given him your contact info."

"I hadn't. I guess he figured out my Instagram handle since I liked a few pictures of his paintings that day."

Ivory's voice sounded as if she were smiling as she replied, "*Oooh*, that means he was looking for you."

I kissed my teeth, narrowing my eyes at her. "Would you focus, please? He got shot!"

Ivory smirked with humor. "You think it was Irv?"

"That's not funny, Ivory." I stood up as I typed vigorously in the

DM thread, giving Lyfe my number and demanding that he call me right away.

"Where are you going?" Ivory asked while I slipped my feet back into my flats.

"To go see Lyfe."

Though my mind had been buried with heartbreak and wonder regarding my marriage and Irv, I had often thought of the perfect stranger I'd spent that blissful day with. Ever so often, behind the tears and lingering thoughts of relapsing, I wondered what Lyfe was doing. I thought of him and lusted for his touch and that kiss. I longed for the bliss he had given me that day and the purity of it. Yet, I knew that beyond that bliss, I needed his intimacy. Being around him with this weak heart, I would take it and use it to make me feel better before I was emotionally ready to deal with the consequences that came with it.

Lots of rehab had taught me to stay away from situations like that.

CHAPTER 15

LYFE MILLER

By the grace of God, the bullet JC had shot into my back had missed my spine by an inch and my heart by centimeters. However, it had hit a main artery. Thankfully, my neighbor had been in her window looking for the mailman as I walked away from JC, so she had seen the entire incident unfold and had called the police.

JC didn't survive. He was dead on the scene. When I woke up from surgery, I was greeted by homicide detectives. However, all they did was take a statement. I hadn't been charged with his murder, and it didn't appear that I would be since my neighbor and Landon had witnessed that I had shot him in self-defense and to protect Landon.

"Has your nurse washed your wound today?"

My eyes rolled with humor as I nodded my head. "Yes, Landon."

I cut my eyes at him to see if that answer was good enough for him to leave it alone and go back to playing his Nintendo Switch.

Of course, it wasn't. "She needs to do it twice."

Sitting beside him on the bench in my ICU room, Esther laughed.

"The nurse on the night shift will do it before he goes to bed," she told him.

I cringed when I saw Landon wringing his hands. I was more concerned about his mental health than my physical recovery. I hated that he had seen me get shot. Now, on top of all of the other anxieties he had, he was plagued with worry about me.

"They can't use hydrogen peroxide or alcohol," he told me, his eyes focused on a particular tile on the floor. "That can slow the healing process."

"Landon, the nurses know what they are doing," I assured him.

"The proportion of error reports submitted by nurses ranged from 67.1 percent to 93.3 percent last year. So, they don't *always* know what they're doing."

Ever since I had been shot, Landon had been fixated on how to treat gunshot wounds. It was his way of ensuring that even though I had survived the surgery, I wouldn't die. He had been researching it day in and day out and getting on my gawd damn nerves with all these facts and statistics.

A knock at the door interrupted Landon's medical-jargon rambling.

I hoped that it wasn't the nurse to poke and prod at me again. I prayed that it was finally Ocean.

As the door slowly pushed open, her beautiful face peered around it. Her eyes cautiously searched the room. When her beautiful orbs landed on me, I knew I was hooked on this girl.

I had been consumed with thoughts of her since waking up from surgery. Beyond being stalked with thoughts of her beauty and yearning to feel the inside of her, I suddenly felt like life was too short to let the opportunity of me seeing where things could go with her pass me by. I had always been so absorbed with the responsibility of taking care of Landon that I had never even considered adding anything to my plate. And there had not been a woman that crossed my path that made me want to try. But after meeting Ocean that day, I envisioned her beyond sexually. I had daydreams of her in my kitchen cooking breakfast. I imagined her stomach round as it held my growing fetus.

A bolt of lightning had struck me at some point during our adventurous day. Her smile, her laugh, the way she moved; it was as if I was seeing the world in a whole new light. Unbeknownst to me, I had been searching for her my whole life. I only knew it because, now that I had met her, my life suddenly looked new and brighter, with so much more meaning. Now that I'd found her, I was fixated on seizing her and never letting her go. I needed to be there for her, to support her, to make her smile every day until she no longer felt the wounds of her past.

I hadn't had a way to contact her, so I had gone through my likes on Instagram because I remembered I had shown her my work on my profile. I had hoped she'd liked one or was following me. After clicking on every woman's profile who had liked any of my posts that looked like her, I finally found her and DM'd her immediately.

But I still questioned my obsession with her. I questioned the feeling of home that thoughts of her gave me. It all felt good but unreal... until our eyes met as she inched into the room.

The moment that our attention locked on one another, I knew fate had found me.

"Hello," Ocean greeted softly.

"Hi," Esther returned. She then noticed that Landon had chosen that moment to stop piercing the air with his random facts and put his undivided attention into his Nintendo Switch. She slightly nudged him, saying, "Don't be rude, Landon. Say hi. Do you remember her?"

147

"Of course," He frowned, keeping his eyes on his game. "She's that woman with the weird name."

Luckily, Ocean didn't find offense in Landon's attitude. She chuckled softly as she walked toward my bed.

"Come on, Landon. Let's go to the cafeteria," Esther said as she stood. "I'm hungry, and you should eat before therapy." She then reached for Landon's hand, which he snatched away from her.

I knew he didn't want to go to the cafeteria, but more than that, he didn't want to be in the room with Ocean. So, he stood and reluctantly followed Esther out of the room.

Suffocating tension swelled between me and Ocean as they exited the room. Flirtatious expressions danced in our eyes as we fought not to stare at one another's artistry.

"So," I said as the door closed behind them. "I gotta get shot for you to contact me?"

She smiled nervously while lowering her head in shame. Then she slowly reached for my leg as she stood at the foot of my bed. She softly touched it while looking up at me.

I was having an internal war between my mind and dick. My dick was winning as my eyes focused on the way Ocean's curves were emphasized in the black slacks she was wearing. She looked so professional in them and the matching blouse, which had me longing to reenact an office-girl fantasy.

I guessed I wasn't doing a good job of masking that I was lusting after her because she blushed, and her eyes shied away from mine.

"I'm glad you're okay," she said gently.

"Me too." I chuckled, trying to laugh away the nervousness that her beauty gave me.

The day I met her, I knew I had been enticed by her. But having her in my presence again let me know she was so much more than that. She wasn't just beautiful; she took my breath away. There was a presence that she brought into the room that I needed and wanted to be around.

"How are you doing?" I asked her.

Her head dramatically leaned to the side. "I should be asking *you* that."

"I'm fine," I assured her.

She looked me over slowly with beautiful eyes that weren't even flawed by the concern and stress in them. "I can't believe Irv did this. I'm so sorry."

"He didn't do this."

She appeared very hopeful as she replied, "He didn't?"

"My guy, JC, did this. Well... I guess he wasn't my guy after all." Her eyes narrowed with confusion, so I explained to her, "Doe was his brother."

"Oh my God," she sighed, shaking her head.

"How are you?" I pressed again.

"I'm okay."

"Just okay?"

"Yeah, I guess," she replied with a sad shrug. "Irv and I are getting a divorce."

Even though I did not fully know her, I cared about her. I constantly received confirmation that I wasn't just attracted to her. Because, at that moment, I felt bad for the pain I saw in her eyes.

"Because of a kiss?" I asked.

An expression of pure disgust covered her face. "He used that as an excuse. I found out that he's having a child with some chick he's held up in that house with."

I fought to hide the relief I felt. I was happy that she finally knew the truth. I was even happier that she had found out without me having to be the one to break her heart.

149

"I went back to that house you took me to and saw them coming out the door."

"*Them?*" My heart began to pump with anticipation.

"Yeah. He and that woman were leaving the house they obviously share." She sneered.

Now, I was hopeful. "Did you confront them?"

"No. I couldn't bring myself to," she admitted, looking ashamed. "It hurt just watching them. And considering the way he's been so cold to me, I couldn't take the risk of him embarrassing me in front of her. But it's obvious that they are together because they were being intimate with each other. He even kissed her stomach."

I sat up a bit, causing myself to flinch in pain. She watched me cautiously, but when I held her hand, she relaxed and softly sat on the bed next to me.

"I'm sorry," I told her.

"What are you sorry for?" she asked me with a slight smile.

"I feel like all of this is because of me."

"It's because of you that I finally know the truth about him. So, *thank you*, actually."

OCEAN MILLER

"I'm proud of you."

I blinked slowly, relishing in the moment that his words designed. "Really?"

Focusing on him was a mistake. His beauty pulled admiration and lust from me that I felt deep down to my bones. Looking at him engulfed me in masculinity and security.

"Why?" I pried.

"I know I don't know you that well." As he spoke to me, a finger on the hand that was holding mine traced my palm. "But after spending time with you that day and remembering the things you told me, I know you really loved him and respected him even more. You had much respect for him because I had to take that kiss from you."

I hated how my heart fluttered with every word he said. I despised how my body was responding to him so easily from the moment I walked into the room. Even in a hospital gown and looking disheveled from being in the ICU for a week, he was still bewitching.

When I'd called, and he asked that I visit him, I headed his way with no question. There had been so much drama in my life since me and Lyfe's day together. Yet, thoughts of him had still superseded it all. Before walking into that hospital room, I thought my focus on him was silly and a rebound. Yet, now, being in his presence validated that something real was between us. I felt like I was already his.

"You took it, huh?" I challenged him with a raised brow.

He was beautiful when he arrogantly smirked. "Yeah, I had to *take* it."

I blushed, saying, "I don't think you had to do too much persuading."

"I didn't?" he challenged my brashness.

"No. I wanted it," I admitted.

I hated that he was in a hospital bed *and* I was fighting to survive a broken heart, yet, at that moment, all I could think about was him ripping my clothes off and taking me.

Lyfe looked directly into my eyes, challenging my audacity to be as cocky as him with our sexually-charged banter. "Did you?"

I nodded with a flirty smile. "Yes."

"Why?"

"You made me comfortable. You made me feel free. You made me feel loved without even knowing me."

It felt so good being in that room with him. I had naïvely assumed that the bliss I had felt the first day I'd met him was because of the adrenaline of all of the spontaneous things we had done. On the ride to the hospital, I naively doubted that the sexual tension and happiness between us would reappear. But, now, we were just having a conversation, holding hands, and still, I finally felt that bliss again.

"I want to keep making you feel that way." The coy smirk had disappeared. The confidence was still there, but it had been paired with sincerity I couldn't ignore.

I gasped discreetly, completely taken by the way he had won our game of chicken. I tried desperately to cling to the ability to control this conversation like a grown woman, not some smitten teenager. "Do you?"

"Yes. I like you."

I giggled; that infatuated little girl coming out anyway. "No, you don't."

He bit his bottom lip seductively and nodded. "I do."

"Why?"

From the moment I had allowed some neighborhood boy five years older than me to take my virginity for ten dollars because I so desperately needed it, I had never heard a man tell me he liked me. Men wanted to fuck me. And even when I'd met Irv, he took me, claiming me. But I had never been told that I was liked with so much compassion.

"Why wouldn't I?" Lyfe protested.

"Because of all the things I told you about my past. I could so easily go back to being that person I was then."

I felt as if he had forgotten who I used to be, that he had let the fun and partying allow him to forget the things I had told him in the restaurant.

Lyfe shrugged a shoulder. "Everybody has a past—"

"Not everyone has one as filthy as mine."

"But everybody's is dirty. And your past made you the woman I'm attracted to right now. Without the drug use and street life, you wouldn't be this down-to-earth, street-smart, humble, and caring woman I'm interested in. I want you, all your flaws, and all your ugliness. I want you just like you are, and I wouldn't want you any other way."

I was in awe and full of admiration, so much so that I couldn't speak or hide that I was dazed. He clearly noticed it, smiling adorably while squeezing my hand.

"Don't disappear on me again," he told me. "I know you have a lot going on, so no pressure. Let's just get to know each other, be friends, and see where the universe takes us."

I was more than happy with that, so I sat with Lyfe for an hour until Esther and Landon returned. Then I excused myself because I didn't want to further make Landon uncomfortable with my presence. Once in the car, I headed south, feeling a rush of excitement. I wasn't investing too much emotionally into what Lyfe had told me. I wasn't even stable enough to at the moment. But just hearing him say those words and being with someone who I felt really saw me and still cared for me gave me the energy I needed to face my day and demons.

♫ *I know that ya' into me*
You 'bout it? Then let me see
Ride, don't be scared of me
I'm rowdy as they can be ♫

I turned the corner, snapping my fingers to "Buss It" and singing along to Air Lennox's lyrics while preparing myself to face the biggest demon of my present.

Once the house was in sight, I swallowed any lingering fears, but it was easy because what I was about to do had nothing to do with me or Irv. This was about Lyfe. Since he'd had the courage to rock with me despite my past, then I was going to rock with him.

After parking, I turned off the car and hopped out. I knew Irv was there since his Ram and Range Rover were parked in front.

"This asshole has just moved in with this chick," I grumbled as I marched through the lawn.

Once I was on the porch, I laid on the doorbell ignorantly. In between ringing the bell, I could hear music playing and voices inside. Soon, the door flung open, and a glaring woman appeared. I had seen her from yards away the first time, but I was sure it was her, although her baby bump was hidden by the loose-fitting off-the-shoulder shirt that swallowed her upper body.

Her pale skin flushed red as she glared at my presence. Ivory had been right; I knew a junky when I saw one, reformed or not. This woman was fresh out of the streets. I could see the filth and addiction all over her. I wondered what corner Irv had gotten her off of.

"I need to speak to Irv," I spit. "Tell him to come to the door."

Her light grey eyes fell into even more narrow slits as her perfect, pouty lips parted. Yet, before she could spew whatever fiery words she had for me, Irv appeared behind her.

"Who is this?" the woman spat.

I swallowed hard, realizing she had no idea who I was.

Not a clue.

"A friend," he lied. And as her scorching words got ready to flow out, Irv cut her off. "Let me handle this, baby."

I refused to allow him to see that his words had stung. I was more ornery than hurt, so I refused to make him feel as if he had won.

Every part of my being wanted to dog walk this heifer, but she had not owed me her commitment or respect. Therefore, she wasn't the one who deserved to be beaten within an inch of her life. That was all for Irv. Yet, there was a bigger task at hand that required me to be smart about this. So, I remained quiet until she walked away.

Irv stepped out onto the porch with murder in his eyes. I stepped back only a bit to keep him from colliding with me. However, I held my ground, standing toe-to-toe with him, facing my sorrow head-on.

"Put the word out that Lyfe is to remain untouched," I ordered bluntly.

He blinked, completely taken aback by my demand. "Oh, so you're bossing up for your new boyfriend now?"

"No one is to touch him! Do you hear me?" I growled with no fear. "If anyone else fires even a BB gun at him, I will turn state's evidence on your ass. I will blow up this entire *secret* organization you're running, and I'll finger you for the attempt on my life that you ordered—"

"I didn't tell them to shoot at you. I told you that."

My jaws tightened as I threatened him further. "As far as I know, you did, and that will be my story. You tell your crew that this beef with Lyfe is over. It's done. Or you'll be in prison, far away from your next helpless charity case that you're using to build your nonexistent self-esteem." When his lips parted, the fire in his eyes told me he was about to kill me with his words, but I cut him off. "And I'm *taking* the house in Bronzeville. I deserve it. I earned it while living this lie with you for five years. I hope you got all of your shit out of there because I'm *going home*." I took a step forward, closing the space between us. I then glared into his eyes, facing the powerful force that had torn my world apart. "And if you try to stop me, I will tell your new bae *everything* since you obviously lied to her about being married. I will even tell her how you have a kink for saving women in distress. So as soon as she gets herself together, you won't want her anymore either.

Contrary to what you may think you made out of me, I am still *very much* that gutter street rat that did what she had to do to get what she wanted. So, do *not* try me, Irvin."

Without another word, I spun on my heels in the middle of his astonishment and stormed down the stairs. I hurried to my car, ready to rid myself of his cancer, lies, and manipulation. Thankfully, in reply, all I heard was the front door slamming behind me. A slow, pleasing smile spread across my lips as I hopped into my car.

Finally feeling a small, minute glimpse of a promising future, I sighed with relief, turned on the engine, drove off, and turned up the radio.

♫ *I know that ya into me*
You 'bout it? Then let me see
Ride, don't be scared of me
I'm rowdy as they can be (Yeah)
I like all the ways you do
Ooh, boy, you're killin' me (Ooh, boy)
I know that you feelin' me (Bussit)
Bussit to the tenth degree ♫

CHAPTER 16
OCEAN GRAHAM

"Fuck," I groaned when I heard the deep voices on the other side of Ivory's front door. Grimacing, I pushed her spare key into the door and reluctantly walked in.

As I had assumed, Romell was in the living room on the couch next to Ivory. Another guy was sitting on the loveseat, looking up at me with expectation already in his eyes.

My eyes glared at Ivory as I gave everyone a dry, "Hi."

"Hey, boo," Ivory was all too excited to greet me. "This is Romell's friend, Johnny," she introduced as she tilted her head toward him.

I forced myself to at least look him in the eyes, but he didn't give me that same courtesy. His lustful eyes were tracing my curves as he said, "What's up, Ocean? I heard a lot about you."

Johnny was cute, but his mannerisms screamed immature and perversion. So, I forced out another dry, "Hi," and headed to my room.

I have to get out of here, I thought to myself. I needed to separate myself from Ivory. Her naivety was unhealthy for me and my sobriety. She thought it was a game because she hadn't had to live it or even see it because she was privileged. She grew up in a diverse neighborhood where the worst crime was kids egg-bombing homes as a prank. She had no idea the detriment behind the vices that she kept throwing in my face.

As I walked into my room, Ivory burst in behind me.

"Stop being so mean," she whispered, pushing the door closed slightly.

"I told you I don't feel like entertaining a man tonight, Ivory."

"Please? Just for a little while," she begged. "If they feel like Johnny is a third wheel, Romell will leave."

"I don't have time. I went to that house and told Irv I was taking the house in Bronzeville."

Ivory's eyes grew wide with excitement. "Good for you."

I blushed. "Thanks. So, I need to pack so I can go back home."

"You have plenty of time to pack. You can spend one more night with me." When I rolled my eyes, she continued to beg, "Please? Have some drinks with us. It's a celebration, anyway. You took your house back!"

Despite my reluctance, her excitement was infectious. I was proud of the way I had stood up to Irv.

Smiling, I gave in, "Fine."

"Cool!" she exclaimed with a little hop.

"I'll be out there in a minute. I need to change my clothes."

Happy with that, Ivory skipped out of the room. I shook my head, hating that I had given in. Yet, it had been a progressive day, and it deserved to be celebrated. But I was intent on moving out the following morning. Me and Ivory's friendship was best from afar.

I peeled out of the slacks and blouse. I then slipped into some leggings and an Adidas T-shirt.

I wasn't at all interested in Johnny. Admittedly, like a schoolgirl, my sights were on Lyfe. I was so interested in building this friendship with a soul that had captivated me. He had gotten my attention before, but after visiting him in the hospital, I was smitten. While going through a heartbreaking divorce and learning how to deal with my feelings without getting high, the last thing I could do was self-medicate by falling into a premature love affair with Lyfe. But I was definitely excited about our budding friendship.

"Right on time, Ocean!" Ivory exclaimed as I came out of the bedroom.

Noticing the shot glass in her hand, I leaned my head to the side, giving her a warning glare.

She smirked with shameless guilt. "It's rum punch. Nothing too hard."

"Oh. Okay," I replied as I padded toward the couch.

I took the shot glass from her, encouraging myself, *Have some fun, girl.*

Since I had gone to rehab, I had been so careful that I was becoming a prude to others. I didn't want to put a damper on the night, so I forced myself to let my hair down. I needed to realize that it was okay to have fun without regression.

"To my friend, Ocean, for closing a very heartbreaking chapter in her life and bossing up!" Ivory exclaimed as she jolted her shot glass in the air.

I smiled shyly as Romell took his shot, and Johnny nodded in my direction, a creepy grin still planted on his face.

"Let's turn up!" Romell shouted as he grabbed his phone. Apparently, he was connected to Ivory's Bluetooth speaker because "Whoopty" gradually became louder.

♫ *Whoopty, bitch, I'm outside, it's a movie, huh (whoopty)*
Blue cheese, I swear, I'm addicted to blue cheese
I gotta stick to this paper-like loose leaf
Bitch, I'm 'bout my chicken like it's a two-piece ♫

Of course, Ivory put all of her attention on Romell, so I was stuck acting as if I didn't see Johnny practically molesting me with his eyes. I had even sat away from him on the accent chair adjacent to the couch. However, he left his seat and walked toward me.

He was actually a very cute guy. It wasn't just his obvious swag either. He had a pretty-boy face that was giving me some roughness, with a beard and colorful tattoos that covered the front of his neck. His light brown locs fell to his shoulders. His chestnut eyes popped off his pecan skin.

His six-foot frame cast a shadow over me as he stood in front of me.

However, as I looked up at him, I understood why Lyfe was so captivating to me. Johnny's beauty wasn't even skin deep. It was surface at best. Looking at him, I could feel that his exterior was where his beauty stopped because something ugly was underneath.

"You want a drink?" he asked me. "You're the only one without a cup."

I shrugged. "Sure." I needed a drink if I was going to participate in this forced double date.

"C'mon," he said as he gestured with his hand. When I appeared confused, he added, "If I'm going to pour you a drink, you have to come with me."

As he walked away, I followed him to the kitchen. Ivory's living area had an open concept, so I could see her flirtatiously grinning in Romell's face like a Cheshire cat as Johnny and I entered the kitchen.

I leaned against the island as he asked me, "What you drinkin'?"

"Rum punch."

"Punch?" he asked with a teasing frown. "Lightweight."

"Yeah, I'm not much of a drinker."

Johnny nodded as he grabbed the store-bought rum punch I had picked up a few days ago. He then poured a nice amount into a plastic cup. He handed it to me as he sat the bottle down so close to me that he had to lean against me while facing me to put it back. His chest brushed against mine as he looked down at me.

"You're pretty," he told me.

I lightly lay a hand on his chest, softly pushing him back a few inches. "Thank you." I then smiled to wipe away the tension.

He scoffed, wearing a smirk, saying, "You ain't gotta be like that."

"Like what?" I challenged.

"Uptight."

"How am I being uptight?" I argued.

"You pushed me away."

"You were in my personal space, and I don't know you."

He licked his lips seductively. "I'm trying to get to know you."

"And that's fine from right where you are," I replied as I pointed to where he was standing.

Johnny kissed his teeth. "Come on now. You know you're far from stuck up."

My brow rose. "How do you know what I am?"

His answer was an arrogant shrug. I slightly rolled my eyes with a humorous sneer and turned to walk away. He gently grabbed my arm, and I snatched it away. As he let go, his hand fell along my body, rubbing my thigh.

I had been around men like him many times. They assumed that because they were good-looking and their friend was getting action, they deserved their own piece of ass. Buddy had a rude awakening coming his way, however. I would have loved to be comforted, touched, and given intimacy by a gorgeous man. I deserved it after the bullshit I had been through for the past few months.

However, *I* chose when I wanted to be a hoe, not a man.

"Got you a drink, huh?" Romell asked as I entered the living room.

"I bet it's rum punch, though," Ivory teased.

"Whatever." I giggled as I returned to my seat. I then put my attention into my phone to avoid Johnny.

For the next hour, I surfed Instagram and Tik Tok while joining in the banter Ever so often.

> ♫ *That my best friend, she a real bad bitch*
> *Got her own money, she 'on't need no nig'*
> *On the dance floor, she had two, three drinks*
> *Now she twerkin', she throw it out and come back in*
> *That's my best friend, she a real bad bitch* ♫

As "Best Friend" started to play, Ivory's eyes got big, and she jumped off the couch.

"I love this song!" she exclaimed as she rushed toward me. She was wobbly on her feet because she was a bit tipsy by now. Once in front of me, she grabbed my hand and snatched me up. "C'mon, friend."

Once she pulled me onto my feet, she turned her back and started to dance on me, rapping along to Saweetie's lyrics.

Slightly feeling my alcohol as well, I danced along with her. As my eyes moved along the room, I caught Johnny and Romell watching our dance with longing and craving twirling in their eyes.

By the time Doja Cat's verse came, Romell stood up, took Ivory's hand, and pulled her toward him. He then turned her around so she could twerk on him instead. He grabbed her waist and pressed her rotating ass against his pelvis. Licking her lips, she started to slowly grind against him.

Before I could return to my seat, Johnny stopped me. "Unt uh. Come here."

He had skipped across the room so fast that he was able to pull me close to him before I knew it. Forcing myself to go along with the mood, I danced with him, face to face. But then he grabbed my waist and turned me around as well. He pressed his body against the back of mine, running his hands along my hips. He was pressing his pelvis against my ass to the point that his belt buckle stabbed into me.

I gritted, telling myself to just dance with him. It was easier than looking like the killjoy. There was nothing physically wrong with Johnny to make me reject his advances. But his personality came off so lewd to me. Yet, there were many men like him. They assumed that they deserved to treat women any way they wanted because so many women allowed them to.

The song ended, giving me my cue to end our dance. I pulled away from him and returned to my seat. Looking up at him, he gave me a smirk that I couldn't read.

"What?" I asked.

"I want you."

My eyebrows rose. "Okay?"

"What are you going to do about that?" he challenged.

I laughed. "Nothing since I don't know you."

"Well, get to know me."

"That's what we're doing."

He grimaced a bit. We began to have a staring contest, his ego against my will until he finally gave up and returned to his seat.

Beyond being irritated with his obscene advances, I was feeling my liquor and the exhaustion of the long, emotional day I'd had. As I returned to surfing Instagram, I even yawned.

"Unt uh! No yawning!" Ivory told me.

I slightly rolled my eyes. "I had a long day," I replied without looking up from my phone.

Suddenly, a text message banner appeared at the top of my screen. It was Lyfe, so my eyes lit up.

Lyfe: I miss you already.

Immediately, my skin began to tingle all over.

Ocean: I can't lie; I miss you too.

Lyfe: What are you doing?"

Ocean: Having a drink with Ivory.

Lyfe: Cool. Call me later.

Ocean: We're almost done, so I will.

Lyfe: You better.

Still blushing, my eyes looked up to see if anyone had witnessed me acting like an inexperienced school girl.

Ivory and Romell weren't paying me any attention, though. Ivory had straddled him and was kissing him passionately while Johnny watched. Repulsed at the perverted look in his eyes, I stood and began to walk toward my room.

"Where are you going, Ocean?" Ivory asked.

"To make a call. Be right back."

Before she could further question me, I hurried into my room and closed the door. I took a deep breath now that the tension in the living room was no longer suffocating me.

I inched slowly toward the bed and collapsed on top of it, wishing that I had the strength to pack my things and leave right then.

CHAPTER 17
OCEAN GRAHAM

I guessed that I was more tired than I'd thought because I fell asleep. As I began to wake up, I didn't even know how long I had been sleeping. I just knew that someone was in the bed with me. I could feel them hovering over me, touching me. I assumed it was Ivory trying to wake me up until I realized the person was pulling my leggings down.

Gasping, I rolled over onto my back. When I saw Johnny's face, I immediately started fighting. I began to swing and kick with the intent of sending him through the wall behind him.

As I tried to push him off me, he pressed his body weight against me.

"Get off of me!" I shouted.

We began to struggle as I fought to pry his grip loose from the waistband of my leggings.

"Stop acting like you don't give this motherfucka up," he threatened.

I began to hyperventilate, realizing this asshole was seriously attempting to rape me. I tried to kick, but all of his weight was on my legs.

Fear caused a lump in my throat so large that the screams of terror lodged in it.

He grabbed my right arm. He was so strong that he was able to pull it, causing my hand to lose grip on the other one that was pulling my leggings down. He then pinned my arm above my head.

"No!" I screamed. "*No!* Get off me!"

I could feel the cool air in the room touching my skin. He was successfully pulling my leggings off.

"I said no!" I screamed, releasing my free hand from his. I then slapped him, clawing at his face.

Enraged, his nostrils flared as he let go of my leggings. He then reached back and swung forward, landing a punch against the side of my face that dazed me. As I recovered, he took advantage of my delusion and used his knees to spread mine apart.

Panicking, I then frantically tried to reach under my pillows.

Finding my gun, I tried to take it off safety, but my hand was trembling uncontrollably since Johnny had managed to get my leggings under my butt cheeks.

Finally, taking it off safety, I aimed at the ceiling and fired.

Johnny jumped out of his skin as his eyes widened. Now that he was off guard, I kneed him in the balls.

"*Argh!*" he bellowed as he collapsed next to me.

Then my bedroom door burst open.

Romell appeared shirtless and in boxers. Ivory was with him. Her fair skin was flushed red. Her hair was disheveled, and her panties and bra were in disarray as she looked between Johnny and me curiously.

"This bitch is crazy!" Johnny snapped, heaving as a result of our struggle. He was still holding his crotch as he rocked from side to side.

I jumped out of the bed, pulling my leggings up. My face was stinging from his blow. "This motherfucka tried to rape me!" I screamed, waving my gun as I gestured.

As I looked at Ivory for help, her expression appeared to be questioning what I was saying.

"And he hit me," I heaved. "I'm calling the police."

"Whoa!" Ivory said as Romell shook his head with regret. "Calm down. Are you sure you aren't overreacting? You *were* drinking."

My eyes bucked. "I woke up to him on top of me, pulling my pants down! Ain't no overreacting to that!"

"I'm outta here," Johnny mumbled as he charged out of the room, pushing by Romell and Ivory.

As Romell followed him, I looked for my cell on the bed but couldn't find it. I started frantically searching for it, my heart still beating feverishly and my hands still shaking.

"Wait, Ocean," I heard Ivory say behind me.

My skin crawled, hearing the questioning tone she was still using with me.

"Stop talking to me like I'm crazy," I gritted as I tossed the pillows and sheets.

"I'm just saying, Ocean. Maybe he thought you wanted it. You *were* dancing on him, and you do have a past of—"

Immediately stopping my search, I swung around to face her with glaring eyes. "Fuck my past!" I bellowed. "I don't care if I was dancing on him! I could have invited him into this room and sucked his dick, but once I say no, it's fucking *no*!"

My oncoming tears meant nothing to her. She continued looking at me like I was still that teenager who stood on the corner of

Halsted waiting for a John to ride by so I could sell my body for money to get high.

Her judgmental eyes stared up at me as she asked, "Are you sure you didn't lead him on?"

My mouth fell open. "How could I lead him on if I was in here sleeping?!" I screeched. Yet, I didn't give her ignorance a chance to reply. "Get out, Ivory."

Her eyebrows rose as her head cocked to the side. "You forgot that this is *my* house?"

Scoffing, I chuckled dryly. "You're right. *I'll* leave."

As Ivory's lips parted to say something, I stormed away from her. I heard the front door slamming shut as I sat my gun on the dresser and started to quickly gather my clothes, toiletries, and other belongings.

"Romell?!" she called out, sounding hurt that he could have possibly left.

I sneered with disgust, shaking my head as I started to throw my things into the duffle bag at the foot of the bed, which was where I found my phone.

I heard the door opening and then Ivory calling out, "Romell?!"

I repulsively grunted as I threw the last of my things into the duffle. I then hurriedly zipped it and grabbed my gun from the dresser. After slipping on my flip-flops, I stormed out of the room and through the living room toward the door. As I marched toward the front door, still heaving in fear and disbelief, I could see Ivory standing in the screen door.

"Move!" I barked, causing her to jump out of her skin.

She spun around and then looked down at the gun. Shook her head and stepped aside, discernment dancing in her eyes as if I were some crazy basket case.

I fought the urge to mop the floor with her face as I tore through the doorway. Luckily, I didn't see Romell or Johnny anywhere as I raced toward my car. I clung to my sanity, refusing to allow my thoughts to race toward those of the past that persuaded me to believe that because of my upbringing, I deserved to be mistreated, I deserved bad luck, and I deserved to struggle.

AFTER LEAVING IVORY'S PLACE, I went straight to the police station and filed a report. By the time I was done being interviewed by the detectives, it was after midnight. Walking into my home was eerie. I was still a wreck from Johnny's attack. I was still trembling and enraged at his and Ivory's audacity. And now, I was standing in my living room, faced with the realization that Irv wasn't home to protect me, to help me through this because he had been cheating on me for God only knew how long.

"Fuck you, Irv," I gritted as I walked into our bedroom.

I was seething. Johnny had ignited a fire in me that I had been fighting hard to smother because had I allowed it to explode, I would have taken a hundred steps back in my sobriety. As I looked around my home, I couldn't take the hurt and disappointment anymore. My pain was turning into an explosive rage more and more as each second ticked by.

My blood began to boil. There was too much anger and hurt in my body for me to handle. I remembered something that I had been taught in NA. When anger boiled up, I needed to take the pot off the heat and open the lid. I needed to let that steam evaporate safely. Otherwise, it would turn into a violent tornado that I couldn't control. I wanted to scream. Even more, I wanted to *hurt Irv*.

Storming into my bedroom, I opened the closets. Anything that he had left behind, I gathered in a pile in the middle of the floor.

There weren't many of his things left since he had been slowly moving out, most likely into the home with his side bitch. But there were enough of his things still there that I knew he would want, like Jordans and other expensive sneakers, snapbacks, watches, leather coats, and high-end jeans. I extracted all of it from every closet and dresser drawer.

Once I was done, I tossed it all into a garbage bag and dragged it to the backdoor. I then opened our large barbecue grill and removed the cooking grates. After dumping his belongings inside, I hurried back into the house in search of the lighter fluid and the utility lighter. I found them underneath the kitchen sink and then stormed back outside. My chest rose high and fell low as I fought not to cry. I fought not to allow Irv and Johnny to succeed in trying to take away my worth and my sanity.

I doused his belongings with the lighter fluid. My hands were trembling as I lit the pile. They weren't trembling with fear. It was my hurt and anger fighting to grow beyond my ability to hold it back. I watched the flames explode, preparing myself for the biggest mental and spiritual fight of my life. Mentally, I was leaning on that imaginary door with all of my body weight, my feet planted on the ground, refusing to let that anger and hurt out because if I did, the only way I knew to comfort it was by getting high so that I could simply leave my reality. That was my way of coping. It felt good. I enjoyed it. I looked forward to the numbing feeling. Yet, no matter how good it felt, it was destructive. I had to remember *that*, not Irv leaving me, not Johnny trying to take my body, and not Ivory's judgment. What was most important, despite everything going on around me, was remembering that coping with it the way I knew would only lead to further pain that I would never survive.

LYFE MILLER

"Are you serious?" I mumbled to myself. I couldn't believe that I was checking my phone every five minutes.

Ocean hadn't called me as promised, and I actually cared.

I *cared*.

I wanted to blame gravity for the way I had fallen for Ocean, but this plummet had nothing to do with the universe's force. This was all heart.

Any other time, I would have just called another chick. But no one else had been on my mind except Ocean. I lay in that hospital bed in the darkness with the television watching me as I fought with my ego. I wanted to call her, but my ego kept insisting that I didn't play myself.

I groaned. Feeling my ego losing the battle.

Giving up, I began to dial her number.

As her phone rang, I felt so lame. I admitted to myself that, for the first time in my life, I was smitten. I was crushing hard on Ocean.

Meeting her had led to losing my connect and almost my life, and still, I was completely engulfed with her toxicity.

"Hello?" she finally answered with a sluggish moan that was sexy as fuck.

"I'm sorry. I woke you up?"

"No."

By the sound of her voice, I assumed she was lying until I heard Sza playing in the background.

I felt a heat of jealousy rise in my chest.

"You busy?" I asked.

"No. I was just... listening to some music and having a drink. I had a long day after I left you earlier."

The protector in me quickly rose to the surface. "What happened?"

"Nothing." She tried to sound believable, but I knew better.

"You're lying."

"No, I'm not," she tried to convince me.

"Is this how we're going to start this off?"

"This?" she questioned softly.

"*Us*. I told you I like you. I'm trying to see where we can go."

I shook my head, looking through the darkness at the ceiling in pure disbelief. I couldn't believe I was being this open. For some reason, it just came so easy with Ocean.

"Even with me and all my drama?" she asked. "I feel like since I met you, there has been one thing after another."

"Because you're going through something right now. Your life is changing, and most times, change isn't easy. A husband living a double life and a divorce is going to come with drama."

"That's not scaring you away?"

"Hell no. I'm not a weak man, and I don't scare easily. Besides, if we can make it through all of this together, we can make it through pretty much anything."

"Together?" she questioned softly.

"Yeah."

"*Mmm*," she moaned.

Hearing her sensuality made my dick rock up immediately. "Don't do that."

"Do what?"

"Moan. I'm in the hospital hooked up to all these machines and shit. You gonna have my blood pressure shoot up and alarm the night nurses."

We shared a laugh.

"I didn't do it on purpose," Ocean said. "That just sounded really good. Why can't I moan?"

"Because I'm trying to do things differently with you. I look at you like something delicate that I don't want to break. But if you keep moaning, I'm going to throw all that out of the window and take your body in the exact way I've been fantasizing about."

I heard her inhale softly. She then giggled away the sexual tension. "I'll stop then because I appreciate you wanting to take things slow. I need that."

She did need it. I felt the desire in her need to be handled in the most correct way, and I wanted to be the person to give it to her.

CHAPTER 18
LYFE MILLER

A few days later, I was released from the hospital.

"You coming to see me today?" I asked Ocean as I eagerly packed up medications and discharge papers.

"Of course. As soon as I get done driving Uber."

"I think you need to stop doing rideshare," I teased her.

"Why?"

"'Cause that's how you met me. How do I know you won't meet another man and let him take you to parties, and then you end up kissing him and getting shot at?" She started laughing uncontrollably. "I can't let you meet another man like that. That's *our* ghetto love story."

Still giggling, she replied, "There is no other man like you, Lyfe Miller. Not one."

My jaws tightened as I fought a grin that was threatening to take over my face. "There better not be."

In the last week, Ocean had helped me get through the long, boring days and nights I had spent cooped up in the hospital. I had ordered her to stay home and focus on getting comfortable in her home alone, rather than sitting up at the hospital with me. Still, we had laid up most nights getting to know one another beyond the drama that had surrounded the first day we'd met. I felt like I was back in middle school, fighting to stay awake on the phone with a girl I was telling my homies I was bound to smash soon. Yet, unlike back then, I was surprised that getting to know Ocean had been just as passionate as I'd imagined penetrating her would be.

"It's not even possible," Ocean continued flirting. "The world can't handle more than one of you."

"The world or you?"

"Both." She snickered femininely. "Definitely both."

As I chuckled away the tightness in my chest her heavy flirting was causing, my homie, Ace, appeared in the doorway of the hospital room.

I greeted him with a head nod as I told her, "Ocean, Ace just got here to take me to the crib."

"Okay. Tell him I said hi. I'll talk to you later."

"You be careful."

"Yes, sir. I'll see you later."

As I hung up the phone, Ace taunted me, "Ocean again?"

I chuckled. "Shut up, man."

"Y'all been talking a lot lately. Every time I come up here, you're on the phone with her."

I smirked as I finished packing my bag. "Is there a point?"

Ace replied with a short laugh and teasing grin as he plopped down on the bench. "The point is to fuck with you for falling for your plug's wife after only knowing her a few weeks."

I shrugged. "He ain't my plug no more."

Ace chuckled wryly. "I bet the fuck not. What are you going to do about that, by the way? That's how you make sure Landon gets the therapy he needs. I got a connect for you if you need it."

I groaned inwardly. "Thanks, man, but I don't know how I wanna move now."

"Have you been stacking your bread?"

I gave him a knowing smirk. "Of course. But you're right. I do need to find another plug. But I honestly just want to find another hustle altogether. A *legal* one."

Ace's eyebrows rose with shock.

"I never want to put Landon through this again," I explained to his silent curiosity.

Ace nodded. "I feel that."

"Besides, I'm thirty years old. I'm lucky JC didn't kill me, but I'm even luckier that nobody has killed me before all of this. The life expectancy for hustlers in the game ain't that long. I'm wearing out my welcome."

"You ain't lying," Ace replied.

Ace had been in the streets way before I had. When I was in high school, fantasizing about a career as an illustrator, graphic artist, or professional artist, he was hustling. Despite our differences, Ace and I had remained homies, even after high school. Since we had known one another for so long, he knew a lot about my dedication to Landon and why I'd had to turn to the streets in the first place. He had been the person to put me on when I needed it after my mother died.

"I definitely feel that shit," Ace added. "So, what are you gonna do?"

I shrugged, with so many options running through my mind. My passion was art and Landon. Nothing else. The only thing that had ever come close to mattering as much was Ocean, and even she was still a premature notion.

"Probably invest my savings in something lucrative," I replied. "I'm still trying to figure out what that is, though. I got enough product to give me time to figure it out."

I was shocked that I was even considering any of this. However, it didn't take much convincing after seeing the fear in Landon's eyes the day I got shot.

Ocean had me thinking seriously about the future as well. When I thought of what we could potentially be together, I knew I couldn't be the provider and stability I wanted to be for her and Landon until I was no longer hustling. My interest in her was forcing me to change for the better, to mature. She was already improving my life. I wondered what kind of superpowers she would use to put a spell on me next, once I finally was able to penetrate her.

I feared those powers. It terrified me more than getting shot had.

OCEAN GRAHAM

"Are you going to this store right here?" I verified with my passenger as I approached the address in my Uber app.

"Yes," the older gentleman in my back seat replied.

"Okay," I answered before I slowed to a stop. "Have a good day, then."

"You too, Miss."

I impatiently waited for him to exit. I was eager to reach my financial goal for the day so I could go meet Lyfe. Despite knowing this wasn't the right time, I was truly falling for the way Lyfe was handling me. Once he called last week, I realized that that was all the medication I needed. Talking to Lyfe felt like none of the bullshit mattered. His conversation implanted esteem in me that made me feel like I could handle anything.

I knew that being in his presence would be even more enchanting than the conversations that I had experienced with him the last few days. His company helped me cope with all of my drama. He had even soothed the wound that Johnny had left behind. But I refused to tell Lyfe about that incident because I was beyond tired of being cloaked with drama in his eyes.

Instead of pulling off, I pulled into a vacant parking space in the strip mall to wait for a ride request in the area. No sooner than I parked, my cell started to ring. It was an unidentified number, so I was hesitant to answer, worried that it was a spam call or one of those gawdawful stalkers constantly inquiring about my vehicle's warranty.

However, since I had been getting calls regarding my case against Johnny, I answered. "Hello?"

"Ocean?"

Crippled by the sound of his voice, I stared blankly out of the windshield. Breathing ceased as anger washed away my previous delightful mood.

"Hello?" he asked again. "Ocean?"

"I-it's me," I stuttered.

"Hi," Richard was excited to say. "How are you?"

"How did you get my number?" I spat.

I hadn't heard from him in years. I hadn't seen him since I was still in the streets.

"I saw Elaine, and she gave me your number."

I grimaced.

Rarely, I would travel to my old neighborhood. Either I was driving through and needed gas, or there was a particular store I wanted to go to. Sometimes I would see old friends I used to do drugs or prostitute with. I would give my number to some of them, who were dear to my heart but still in the streets, to call me if they ever needed anything.

Elaine was one of them. She and I used to hook together. I was only sixteen when we met, but she was in her twenties. She had taught me a lot about Johns and how to work them. She was on drugs, too, so a lot of times, we would get high together. When I bumped into her last year, she was still very much addicted to heroin, which most likely meant she was also still prostituting.

"How are you?" Richard asked again.

The excitement and hope in his voice made me want to regurgitate. "I'm fine. What do you want?"

I had absolutely no love for him. A father was supposed to protect and love their children, especially their daughters. He should have taught me how I deserved to be treated. Instead, he exposed me to the very things he should have been protecting me from. He had valued getting high over my innocence, sanity, and livelihood. And he was so much of a cowardly, weak man that he had allowed the woman who had birthed me to do the same.

From the very moment that my mother died, I automatically put him in the same category.

"Why do you want to know?"

He sighed, his voice sounding hoarse and rough. "I know I haven't been much of a father to you, but I miss you."

I rolled my eyes, seething. Yet, I allowed him to go on because the little girl he had abandoned was seeking some sort of justice for how I had been discarded.

"I've been sick. Fighting for my life really opened my eyes to a lot of things. I love you." I cringed as he went on. "I worry about you. I want us to talk more, maybe even have a better relationship. I don't have a lot of time left on this earth, I assume. The way I've been abusing my body is coming back on me. I'm trying to right my wrongs, so maybe God will forgive me for everything I've done."

I had never heard him sound this loving. Every interaction with him as a child had been either chaotic or heartbreaking because he was always high or desperately searching for the next hit. He wasn't concerned about my well-being. He never cared for me. He never fed me. This conversation was the most attention he had ever paid me as a father.

Yet, a couple of loving sentences weren't going to fix a decade and some change worth of trauma.

"So, you want to be my father *now* so you won't go to hell when you die?" I spewed.

He blew a sad and frustrated breath. "It's not only that. I truly do think of you and worry about you. You're my only child, the only family I even know of. Do you have children?" he asked, sounding hopeful.

"Richard," I groaned, calling him by his first name. "I can't have this conversation right now."

This was all too overwhelming to bear. I just wanted this conversation to end. I didn't need this pressure on top of everything else.

"I understand. I called out of nowhere. Can we talk again soon?"

"I-I...Uh...I...," I stuttered, not knowing what to feel.

Then, by the grace of God, my other line rang. I recognized it was the number of the investigators working on my case against Johnny. Glad to be forced to do so, I began to rush Richard off the phone.

"I have a call on the other line."

"Okay, but please call me back," he asked quickly. "*Please?*"

The genuineness in his tone caused a nauseated feeling to swim through my gut. I wasn't used to it. I had never heard that from the man who was *supposed* to be my father. I suddenly felt compassion for the need I heard in his voice, compassion that I'd vowed never to feel for him again.

"I have to go," I told him before clicking over. "Hello?" I answered my other call, putting forth an effort to sound unbothered.

"Hi, Mrs. Graham. This is Detective Rollins."

Detective Rollins was the lead detective I had been speaking to about my charges against Johnny. The sex-crime detectives were still investigating, and I had been waiting to hear back from them regarding Johnny's arrest. Since I had no contact information on him, not even a last name, I worried that Ivory wouldn't be cooperative with the investigators when they contacted her to get Johnny's information. Of course, I hadn't heard from Ivory since that night, and I hadn't wanted or expected to.

"Hi. How are you?" I returned.

"I'm good. And you?"

I grimaced inwardly, irritation lingering from Richard's call. "I'm... I'm okay."

"Well, I have some news regarding your case. We did get in contact with Johnny and got his statement. We also got the statement from Ivory and Romell. However, the district attorney will not be pursuing charges against Johnny."

My heart sank to my stomach. "Are you serious?"

"Yes," she answered reluctantly. "I'm so sorry."

"Why not?" I asked, disbelief swimming in my tone.

"Considering your record, she doesn't feel like we will have a strong enough case."

"Because I was arrested for prostitution years ago?!" I snapped.

"Yes. Since you were over eighteen, those arrest records aren't sealed, and the defense will more than likely do a background check and bring it up in court, including the charges for possession. For an attempted rape, they just don't feel like it's a strong enough case to pursue. I'm sorry."

I scoffed, struggling to find anything worth saying. I couldn't, so I simply hung up.

Past Narcotics Anonymous meetings had taught me that change was inevitable in life. I had to find a positive coping mechanism for that change because negative thinking led to emotional suffering and destructive behavior I couldn't afford. For years, my positive coping mechanism had been Irv. No matter how viciously he had broken my heart, I wished for him to be there at that moment to help me cope with this roller coaster of hurt that had begun so suddenly.

However, I now had to learn how to cope in other ways. I had to learn to support myself so I would never again depend on anyone else. People had the potential to abandon me at any moment. I had to learn how to depend on *me*.

CHAPTER 19

LYFE MILLER

Finally, Ocean was in my home, tucked under my arm where she had been since she'd come through the door an hour ago.

We were settled on the couch. I was sipping on some Hennessy XO. The only other thing I had craved outside of living and Ocean while in the hospital was alcohol. With all that had happened, I was eager to wash the stress down with a good cognac.

We were watching Judas and the Black Messiah, so we had been quiet. Yet, she was exceptionally quiet compared to how she had been conversing with me all week.

"What's wrong, Ocean?" my baritone, beast of a voice jolted into the quiet atmosphere. She inhaled, and her beautiful lips parted, but I quickly interjected. "And don't say that it's nothing because I already know that something is bothering you."

She blushed shame-facedly as her head lowered.

"What's up, baby?" I pressed.

Her eyes swam up to mine. A hint of desire filled them.

The sexual tension between us was smothering. No matter what was going on around us, the passion we shared was always present.

"I... Um... I..."

"Talk to me," I coached her.

"My father called me today."

During many of our conversations, she told me stories about her parents and upbringing. Most of the stories were filled with how she had been deprived as a child and her well-being put to the side because of their addictions. But, since I was well versed in the streets, I knew that much more than going hungry and being in a dirty home alone went along with having parents who were addicted to heroin. It was much more than that that would have led her to her own addictions and prostitution. But I never made her tell me any of it. I just waited for the details and took them when she was comfortable giving me the little pieces. However, it only took the few pieces she had confided in me to know that speaking to the father she hadn't seen or heard from in years would leave her speechless and consumed with cutting memories.

"No wonder you've been so quiet since you got here."

She sighed. "I'm sorry. His call caught me completely off guard."

"What did he want?"

"I thought he wanted some money, but he actually sounded like he wanted to just talk."

I raised a brow. "Word?"

"He said he missed me and wants to see me."

"Why is that making you look so unhappy?"

Exhaling slowly, Ocean leaned further into me as if she were trying to lose herself in my aura. "Because I'm confused. I don't know what to believe. You know how addicts are. They manipulate everybody, and my parents especially manipulated me. That's all they ever did. I don't trust that he's sincere."

"Maybe he's trying to change that now."

She lightly groaned. "And I would love that if it were true. It would be great to finally have a loving parent in my life. But I don't know if I can trust him. I'm scared to let my guard down just for him to turn around and disappoint me again."

"Just listen to your heart."

She frowned slightly. "I don't trust my heart when it comes to him."

"Why not?"

"As a child, all I wanted was for them to treat me like I was their daughter. That's why every time they showed me a little bit of attention, I fell for it, just to be made to look like a fool. The first person to break my heart, manipulate, or use me wasn't some neighborhood boy. My mother and father did that. Years ago, I promised myself that I wouldn't give them the opportunity to let me down again."

"And nobody can blame you for that," I assured her.

"I guess I'm just going back and forth, playing the conversation in my mind over and over again, wondering if he's finally realized he has a daughter. I don't know what to do." She growled frustratingly.

I used the arm draped around her to bring her body even closer to me. She sighed, leaning against my chest.

"I tell you what," I spoke. "Either way, you might end up with regrets. If you don't meet him, you'll regret it. If you do, you may still regret it. So, do what's best for you and make sure you're strong enough to deal with the consequences. And if you're not, I'll be here to help you through it." I lowered my head, kissing the top of her hers. The scents of coconut and peppermint oils soothed me. "Whatever you do, you have nothing to be ashamed of. Absolutely nothing."

She reached up and gently grabbed the wrist of my draped arm.

She then looked up at me, admiration flooding her eyes. "Thank you."

Before I could reply, her soft, velvety lips smashed into mine. I felt her relax as I brought her into my shadow, enfolding her into my massive frame. She clung to me as if my grasp was somehow empowering her. And in the heat of our embrace, welding sparks flew, igniting our kiss. She became breathy, inhaling my air as she parted my lips with her tongue. Sucking it, I tasted the sweetness of her soul and the innocence of her dirty past.

My hands traveled up her back and around her neck, slightly squeezing it. She moaned into our kiss, clinging to me to the point that I could feel her nipples hardening underneath her shirt.

"Fuck," I groaned.

She pushed back, looking up into my eyes, "What's wrong?"

"I want inside of you." My dick was dancing in my shorts, aching to be freed.

She pouted, saying, "I need you inside of me, but... I like how things are going. This is the most loving way I have ever been courted by a man, and we aren't even having sex. I really like it."

I hated that I cared enough for her to give her exactly what she wanted. My dick was crying with disappointment as my erection retreated. Looking into her eyes, I released her neck and began to stroke her natural coils. "We're not going to have sex then."

"Mumph," she pouted.

I chuckled, kissing the top of her head again. "Let's watch the movie."

OCEAN GRAHAM

It was so hard for me to accept this type of treatment from a man. It was romantic and kind, elements of courting that I had never experienced. However, Lyfe was... *life*. He was soulful, sincere, and a breath of fresh air. My center was throbbing as I sat wrapped in his arms. My clitoris was beating even more erratically than my heart.

Luckily, when Landon returned from therapy, Lyfe followed him upstairs. I knew he'd needed to in order to cater to Landon's apprehension and uneasiness with my presence. I appreciated it, but I did not want Landon's annoyance with me invading his comfort zone to stress Lyfe, so I got ready to excuse myself and head out. I had every intention of running home to masturbate to the memory of the blazing kiss Lyfe, and I had shared.

Until he returned from Landon's room, I took advantage of the privacy to look at my phone. There was nothing, in particular, I was looking for. I was just casually browsing my social media pages since I hadn't done that all day.

I sat up when I saw a post by Ivory on my Facebook timeline. She had shared a post of someone else's that read: *Bitches really be hoes all their life and then try to claim somebody took that raggedy pussy.*

My eyes narrowed as I stared at the name of the person who had published the shared post.

It was Johnny.

In her own post, she had written above his, I read: *He's innocent. You've been selling that thang since you were fifteen, and now all of a sudden, you're righteous? Lmao! Everybody sees through that fake shit, even the police.*

The virtual dagger stabbed me in my chest, and it hurt like hell, causing me to squeeze my eyes shut tightly. I gritted, trying to remain calm. I didn't want to be frazzled when Lyfe returned. It was as if he could see right through me. No matter how much I tried to mask my feelings, he saw them. I had purposely not told him about what Johnny had done because I was tired of being a complete train wreck around him. I had been fighting to be my best self for years. Now, I was fighting to be the best me for a man who saw me as precious, despite my flaws.

Pissed off, I tossed my phone too hard to the side because as soon as it left my hand, it bounced off of the couch and onto the floor. It collided with the snifter that Lyfe had been drinking out of, knocking it over.

"Shit," I whispered frantically as Hennessy spilled onto the carpet.

I jumped up and hurried to the island where the roll of paper towels were. After tearing a few off the roll, I dashed back over to the couch, dropped to my knees, and dabbed at what was becoming a stain.

"Great. Landon already doesn't want me here. Now, I'm making messes. He's going to *freak*."

As I mumbled to myself, I could feel tears stinging my eyes. I wasn't crying because I had spilled Lyfe's drink. Tears were threatening to fall because of what I had read on Facebook, potentially pissing off Landon had merely set them off. I was a grown woman. At twenty-seven years old, I knew not to let the words of others affect me. But when those words were right, they stung like a swarm of angry bees.

"Fuck." Flustered, I stood up and went into the kitchen in search of a cleaning agent to stop it from staining before Lyfe came back downstairs.

I quietly opened cabinets, finding nothing but plates, cups, and Tupperware. Standing in front of the sink, I squatted and opened the cabinet, assuming Lyfe's cleaning products might be there. As I searched, I regretted every time I'd sold my body. I felt like all of my sexual transactions for money in the past had followed me into my present, torturing me and taking away my feminine worth.

Luckily, I found some OxiClean stain remover. As I reached inside, I was trembling with anger so much that I knocked a few of the bottles down.

"Gawd damn it."

Picking them back up, I noticed a bag tucked in the corner. It was clear, so my eyes immediately recognized its contents.

Staring at it, my mouth started to salivate. My hands trembled violently. Tears streamed down my face as I reached into what was clearly Lyfe's stash. My fingers were shaking desperately as they wrapped around a baggie. I quickly slipped the cocaine into the pocket of my denim Bermuda shorts. I then rushed over to the spill with the remover in my hand. I felt completely defeated, like a failure. I had been clean for five long years, and in an instant, I was willing to relapse because my past had been insistent upon haunting me that day.

I hurried to clean the mess. I then returned the cleaner. My stomach was in knots as I returned to my seat. I dried my tears as I took deep, soothing breaths. Yet, nothing would take away the gnawing feeling of guilt and filth that was bubbling over inside of me except cooking that cocaine and smoking it.

"You good?" The sudden sound of Lyfe's voice jolted me out of my trance.

I forced a smile as I quickly stood. I could feel myself still shaking as I told him, "Yeah, I'm gonna go."

He was obviously disappointed as he arrived at the landing and took long, easy strides toward me. "Why?"

"To give you and Landon some privacy." Nervously, my eyes avoided his. I searched for my cell phone and keys, which I found in a crease on the couch.

"He's good," Lyfe tried to convince me.

I giggled. "You're lying. You know he's not good."

Lyfe closed the space between us, grabbing my waist and bringing me so close to him that I knew he could feel my frantic heartbeat.

"He has to get used to it," he said with a smooth rumble.

Now, I was not only trembling because I could feel the evidence of my failures in my pocket. I was quivering under his intensity.

I smiled softly. "You don't have to make him get used to it all in one night."

He looked down on me with a gaze full of sensual promises and suffocating intimacy.

"Why are you looking at me like that?" I asked.

"I really wanted to wait. I wanted this to be different. I wanted to show you something different," he confessed. "But I can't help it. I want you."

I would have thought the way that he pressed himself against me was threatening had he not had so much desire in his eyes.

I stood on my tiptoes, bringing my mouth as close to his as I could. I slid my arms around his neck, assuring him, "I know your heart."

"Do you?" he asked as he started to guide me toward his bedroom.

"Yes," I purred in a raspy whisper as he bent down and kissed me. "I know you truly care for me."

"Good," he replied just as we inched into his bedroom.

I could barely tear my clothes off as he took my mouth with his. Lyfe only let me go to lock the door. Then his hands eagerly resumed guiding me. Our heavy breathing accompanied the sound of our feet quickly sliding over the carpet as he pushed me to his bed. My butt hit his plush mattress hard. I kicked off my sandals and hungrily pulled my shirt over my head. I tossed it to the floor just as he climbed into the bed, forcing me to lie back as he straddled me.

Arching my back, I reached behind it and unhooked my bra. Lyfe paused only long enough to admire the chocolate mounds before him, smiling with delight. He then lowered his head and began to flick his tongue gently over my nipples, teetering between sucking them and playing with them with his fingers. His mouth, finally on another part of me, caused an earthquake of pressure to erupt in my center. I sat up slightly, kissing the top of his head as my hands ventured down to his shorts, pushing them down.

Abandoning my nipples, he sat up and ripped off his shirt, revealing his thick athletic form. He then gripped my jean shorts, forcing them down.

A devilish smile crept through his beard as he peered down at me with eyes that sent stimulating chills throughout my body. "You never wear panties, huh?"

As I smiled sheepishly, he spread my thick, cocoa thighs apart. His head lowered, disappearing between them. He put his face to my soft mound, taking in my sweet, feminine scent with a deep breath. I gasped when he pressed his tongue against my eager clit.

He then consumed me. My body boiled over with pleasure. He kissed and tongued my soppy center as he stroked me with his fingers. I writhed under him. He grasped my ass tight with both of his large hands. He then pushed me against his eager feeding, making me ride his face.

"Lyfe!" I moaned, my body tightening as his sucking became unwavering. An explosion erupted in my core. "Oh, gawd!" Juices gushed out of my center like explosive flames. "*Yeeees!*"

He growled into me, causing deep vibrations in my honeycomb.

"Ah!" I exclaimed.

"Mine," I heard him claim with a mouth full.

"*Mmmph!*" I was exploding so powerfully that I began to mutter gibberish and howl animalistically. My fists banged against the mattress as I fought to contain my composure while he ate the most powerful orgasm out of me.

"Fuck!" I hissed.

Deeply chuckling, he sat up, looking down at me as he allowed my juices to drip from his beard. He led his erection to my pulsating epicenter. He slid inside until his length disappeared. I inhaled sharply, mouth agape, as I adjusted to the pressure of his size.

"Fuck, it feels like I belong in here, baby." He collapsed on top of me, our foreheads meeting gently as he began to ride me. We breathed in one another's oxygen as he fucked me so sensually that it was unfamiliar to me.

"Tell mi dis pussy fi mi."

I shuddered. "Please don't do that."

"Duh wah?"

I gnawed on my bottom lip, hating how his sudden accent was ending me.

"Speak patois while you're fucking me," I whined.

"Wah mek nuh, baby?"

I whimpered, feeling my grip on reality fading.

"Because..." I panted. "Because... You're going to make me cum."

"Dat a di point."

I shuddered as his chest met my breasts so lovingly. We focused on one another, on the perfection and passion of our rhythmic motions. I buried my nose in his neck, inhaling his exotic, masculine scent. His mouth met my neck, kissing it and then my shoulder. I moaned. He panted. It was the most perfect communication I had ever dictated with another human being.

I loved how he felt. Not just inside of me but on top of me. The passion was just as addictive as any opioid I had taken. I wished to have that feeling forever, to engorge myself with it, to pull up a chair and sit in it.

CHAPTER 20
OCEAN GRAHAM

Two days later, I was clinging desperately to rationale and common sense. Lyfe's performance in the bedroom had the ability to make me lose all sense of reality. It had been two days since we first had sex, and since, I had been trying perilously not to fall prematurely in love. He already consumed me mentally. But, once his perfection penetrated and claimed me, I was smitten.

"Hello?" his deep rumble thunderously exploded through my car speakers. My clitoris immediately began to thump between my thighs.

"Hey," I spoke softly, feeling my skin flush with longing. "I'm outside."

"Bet."

My eyes narrowed as I finally looked beyond my own desire to notice how he sounded. "You okay?"

"I'm good."

"It doesn't sound like it."

He blew a weary breath. "Landon has been having a bad afternoon."

"I can just go home."

"Hell no," he refused. "That would only make my day worse."

"Are you sure?"

"Yeah. C'mon."

Weakly, I obeyed. "Okay."

Hanging up, I climbed out of my car. Two days away from Lyfe felt like an eternity. And I was aware that that feeling was so premature but so much bad had happened that I was running to the good through his neighbor's grass toward the front porch.

As I ascended the stairs, the front door opened. He held the screen door ajar, allowing me in. His fresh, woodsy scent assaulted my senses and weakened knees.

"Hi, Landon," I greeted him softly as I walked into the living room.

Stubbornly, he kept his eyes on the television as it displayed images of DNA.

"Stop being rude," Lyfe fussed at him as he shut the door. "Speak to Ocean."

He defiantly kept his eyes on the television.

I gave Lyfe a sympathetic gaze and mouthed, "It's okay."

However, I did suddenly feel guilty for being there. Yet, Lyfe insisted that Landon had to get used to sharing him.

"I'll be in your room," I told Lyfe.

It was the middle of the week, and I had early appointments the following day. So, Lyfe and I's plans were to Netflix and chill.

As I disappeared into his bedroom, I heard Lyfe tell Landon, "Head up to your room. You need to study."

"I don't want to!"

I cringed as I peered into the living room from Lyfe's bed. Lyfe was standing over Landon as he sat on the couch with an irritated scowl on his face.

Frustrated, Lyfe stuffed his hands into the pockets of his basketball shorts and tilted his head to the side. "I don't care if you don't want to. You don't have a choice."

Landon groaned so loud that I heard it in the other room. "Yes, I do!"

Lyfe's lips parted to retort, but he stopped when Landon started to wring his hands and slightly rock.

Lyfe softly blew an irked breath. Then he shook his head in defeat and made an about-face. He marched into the bedroom with me and closed the door behind himself. His irritable scowl had the nerve to be adorable.

I insisted, "I can go home."

"No, the fuck you can't. I have to unspoil him."

"Why does it have to be at my expense?"

His dominant orbs bore into mine, spewing masculinity. He then leaned in and slightly grabbed my neck. "Because it's you that I want."

I whimpered, melting.

"Gimme kiss," he ordered. Yet, before I could oblige, he took my lips with his, sucking them quickly and softly before freeing them and my neck.

I swallowed hard, fighting the urge to disregard Landon and our plans and take his dick into my mouth right then.

Lyfe left the bed, and my heart instantly dropped because I wanted him near me. But when he quickly took his remote from the nightstand and returned, I was pleased, as if I was just as spoiled as Landon. I knew then that I was helpless. Lyfe had me wrapped around every inch of his 6'4 frame.

"How are you?" he asked as he turned on the TV. "Have you heard anything about the divorce?"

"No. It's pretty cut and dry, though. We don't have anything to fight over. He hid his entire life from me, so he most definitely has hidden his money. Besides, I don't want anything from him."

"He most likely has all of his drug money hidden in a stash in cash," Lyfe suggested as he flipped through the apps on the smart TV.

"Right. We're going to split the assets in our joint accounts, and that's about it." I shrugged.

"You still handling everything okay?"

I chuckled dryly. "Are you referring to his baby mama or him lying to me about who he really is?"

"All of it."

"I honestly can't think about it if I want to stay sober. I just have to move on. I know that doesn't sound healthy. I should probably start back going to meetings, but...." My words withered away in shame. Realizing that I was speaking such embarrassing truths to such a perfect man began to choke me.

He looked away from the TV and gave me his undivided attention. "What?"

"Nothing."

Sighing, he lay the remote down next to me. "You don't have to be ashamed."

"It's hard not to be."

"I get it. But I'm not judging you. We all have a past."

My head tilted dramatically. "You used to be an addict and a prostitute?"

Lyfe waved me off. "You were a child. And even if you weren't, I still sell the drugs that you were addicted to. So, who am I to judge?"

Suddenly, heavy footsteps interjected our conversation. Lyfe sighed with relief as he realized that Landon was going upstairs to his room.

"I'm not, Irv," he told me. "I don't see your past as weak or anything that I have to fix. Your wounds make you a stronger person, and I'll kiss every one of those motherfuckers if you let me."

I gushed, lowering my head onto his shoulder.

"I've been thinking about calling my father," I admitted.

I had been going back and forth with this decision for days. My father had been calling, but I didn't want to answer until I knew what I wanted to do. Lyfe had been so supportive, insisting that whatever I decided to do was the right decision because it would be what I needed. Yet, I was still so confused.

"What's stopping you?"

"I'm scared that I'm seeking something from him that he will never be able to give me," I admitted.

"But it sounds like it's something that you're leaning toward since you're still thinking about it."

"I am."

His arm looped around my neck. Then I felt his lips press against my forehead.

I held his elbow and, with a deep sigh, told him, "C'mon. Let's watch that movie."

WE HADN'T MADE it an hour into the movie before we were tearing at one another.

As he swam in and out of me, I clung to him with my arms tightly wrapped around his neck. I stared up at the ceiling, basking in the electricity between us. I wanted to be rational, to remember that I barely knew this man, that we had just met. But I couldn't deny that gut feeling that something special was happening. With each stroke, I could feel our connection deepening. I could feel his passion and his desire for me, and I knew that, despite the rash of our connection, I had found someone special.

"This pussy feels amazing." His words were like honey, soothing and sweet, against my ear as he rode me missionary.

With his body flush against mine, I felt safe and cherished, like I didn't have to hide any part of myself from him. He accepted me for who I was, with all of my flaws and imperfections. And I knew that I would do anything to keep this connection alive, to nurture it and let it grow into something beautiful.

He rested on his elbows and pulled my eyes to his. I could feel the heat rising in my cheeks as his gaze locked onto mine. The rest of the world, my past, and my problems withered away. I felt his warmth seeping into my skin.

"Cum."

I gasped as that soft roar sent explosive waves through me. He wouldn't take his eyes off of me, making me fight for the ability to breathe. I felt captive to him but simultaneously so free and alive in a way that I never had before. He made me feel beautiful and wanted, like my past didn't matter, and all that mattered was the connection between us.

CHAPTER 21

OCEAN GRAHAM

T inhaled deeply and then exhaled slowly. Yet, standing in front of the Eggshack, I was still quite panicky. The breathing exercise hadn't helped at all. My nerves were shot. The seventy-degree August morning air was slightly cool as it brushed by my face. However, I was still sweating.

I checked the time on my cell phone. It was fifteen minutes until noon, twenty minutes past the time Richard was supposed to have met me there. After a few days of toying with the idea of meeting with Richard, I finally decided to do so. Lyfe had been right. Either way, I would end up with regrets, so I put on my big girl panties and arranged this breakfast with him.

However, as the minutes ticked by and I stood alone in front of the diner, looking completely abandoned, a familiar feeling washed over me. I was reminded of so many promises he hadn't kept.

I fought to push back those disheartening memories, however. I clung to hope and the joy I had been feeling for the past few days. I forced myself to focus on the good memories I had been collecting in the past week. I had feared that having sex with Lyfe would ruin his dedication to courting me differently, but that hadn't been the case at all. The depth of our conversations had only grown. Our dates were even more romantic. And our sex... *God*! It felt like each time he penetrated me was better than the last. Lyfe had the perfect name because he had been indeed pouring new existence back into my world. And his intentions were so pure.

As a CTA bus approached the bus stop in front of the restaurant, I became hopeful. That hope made me ashamed of myself because there I was, at twenty-seven years old, still clinging to the hope that Richard would finally do right by me. Yet, as I watched passengers file off, my eyes landed on an older version of the father I remembered. I squinted, ensuring that it was truly him. As he smiled at a toddler waddling into his path, I noticed that most of his teeth were gone. However, he shockingly looked properly groomed despite that. It was the most kempt he had appeared since I could remember. His clothes were clean and fit. His shoes weren't worn. His posture was upright, and his stride was level and confident.

I discreetly exhaled while thinking, *Thank God*. For the first time in twenty-seven years, Richard hadn't let me down.

I watched as his stride slowed. He started looking around the exterior of the restaurant. Assuming he was looking for me, I called out to him, "Richard!"

His attention found my voice. As he took me in with confusion dancing in his aged eyes, I waved, so he would know it was me.

Richard's eyes bulged with shock. Then he smiled and shuffled toward me. "Oh my God!" he gushed as he entered my space. "Look at you! Hi."

My lips found my ears nervously. "Hi."

A cloud of awkward tension formed between us. I spoke over it, telling him, "Come on. Let's go inside."

He nodded and followed. He then reached past me and opened the door like a gentleman. As I crossed the threshold, I relaxed. The jittery nerves were evaporating.

"For two?" the hostess asked.

"Yes," I answered.

"Right this way."

We followed her to a booth in the small diner. As we sat, she gave us each a menu and then told us, "Your waitress will be right with you."

"Thank you," I told her before she walked away.

As I got comfortable, I felt Richard's eyes on me. I looked up and, shockingly, saw a twinkle in his orbs that appeared so admiring that I blushed.

"You grew up to be so beautiful," he said.

"Thank you."

"How are you?" he asked excitedly.

"I'm okay."

Showing his gummy smile, he insisted excitedly, "Tell me all about you."

"Um... Well... I don't have much going on. I don't have any kids. I'm not married." Since I had stopped wearing my ring, I didn't feel the need to explain that I was getting a divorce. Besides, his presence alone hadn't earned him my complete honesty after his many years of absence in my life.

"Are you in college? Working?" he asked.

"I got my GED some years ago. Now, I'm a rental broker and a rideshare driver."

His eyes brightened. "That's great."

"Thank you. That's about it, though."

"You look good... healthy."

I swallowed hard at the intention of his words. During my addiction, I had bumped into my father many times. I had never told him I was on drugs, but he knew a fellow junkie when he saw one, just as I did. I was also sure that his friends in the streets had shared my demise with him and my mom.

"Thank you," I replied sheepishly.

"How long have you been clean?"

"Five years." And then I reluctantly asked, "Are you?"

"Yeah," he answered with a nod. "For a month now."

"That's great. I—"

"I'm Rachel. I'll be your server for today," a woman announced, rudely interrupting us without even a warm greeting.

She reached between us, placing glasses of water, napkins, and utensils on the table. She then pulled a notepad and pen from her apron's pocket and asked, "You all ready to place your orders?"

I grimaced, but her attitude was familiar. The diner wasn't in the most upper echelon neighborhood of the south suburbs. This is how certain businesses in the city were; poorly managed and employed by workers who just showed up to work so they wouldn't get fired. A lot of times, they had to have these attitudes to create a thick skin against the chaos they came in contact with on a daily.

"Um, yes," I answered, quickly picking up the paper menu. I scanned it and then told her, "I'll take the two slices of French toast with sausage patties."

"It comes with eggs. How do you want them?" she asked dryly.

"Scrambled with cheddar cheese."

She didn't even make eye contact as she asked, "Anything to drink?"

"Apple juice is fine."

"And for you, sir?" she asked Richard.

"Coffee is fine with me."

"You're not hungry?" I asked him as I returned the menu to the table.

He shook his head from left to right. "No, I'm fine."

"You sure? It's on me," I insisted.

"I'm good with just the coffee."

Rachel walked away without a word, taking her foul attitude along with her.

Shaking my head, I said, "*Anyway*, how have you been otherwise? You okay?"

"I'm okay. My kidney is acting up on me, but what can I expect?" He chuckled.

"Where are you living?"

"Here and there, mostly a friend's couch, though." He then leaned over, grinning with all gums. "Enough about me. I want to know about *you*. How did you become a... Uh...What did you call it? A rental what?"

"*Broker.*"

For the next twenty minutes, I told him about getting my GED and real estate license. As he listened closely, Rachel returned and jolted his coffee in front of him, along with my order. He drank his coffee while quietly listening to me. As we conversed, I realized I was actually having a real conversation with my father. He was seriously listening as if he cared about the details. As he smiled at me, I realized this was what I had been waiting for from my parents. It was too late for them to correct my childhood, but validation in my adulthood would be enough. It was too late to get it from my mother, and I had given up any anticipation of my father ever changing, so I had stopped hoping. However, as I felt my heart ease, I relaxed in his presence for the first time.

"I'm really glad you agreed to meet with me," he said.

He had finished his coffee by now. I was too full to finish the shivering eggs on my plate.

"I know I don't have that good of a track record, but I'm hoping to change that."

I nodded slowly. Apprehension was still in the back of my mind, but this breakfast had convinced me to ignore that.

"We can do it again," I told him sincerely.

His cheeks swelled. "Good."

Rachel returned, dropping the bill on the table. She then hurried away.

Shaking my head, I reached into my purse for a twenty-dollar bill and placed it on top of it.

"Ready to get out of here?" my father asked.

"Yes. I can take you wherever you're going."

He smiled. "Oh, thank you."

"Just let me use the restroom really quick."

I jumped up from the table and followed the signs to the women's restroom. I then hurried inside, feeling excited anticipation for the rest of the day. Lyfe and I had a date planned. He hadn't told me what we were going to do. He only gave me a time to meet him, which made me even more excited.

After using the facilities and washing my hands, I used a paper towel to open the door and then hurried out of the restroom.

I looked across the small diner at the table where Richard and I had been sitting, waving as a signal that we could leave. Yet, my wave was met by no one. I inhaled sharply, shuffling toward the table, pushing my way through the tight spaces that the tables left a pathway for.

Approaching the table, I saw that the twenty I had left for the bill was gone. Gasping, I bent down, realizing that I had stupidly left my purse when rushing to the restroom. I was relieved to see that it was still there. Yet, it had been transferred to the side of the booth Richard had occupied, and it was open. I collapsed onto the booth's bench, reaching for the purse. Luckily, most of the contents were still inside. He had been decent enough to leave me with my wallet and phone, but all of my cash was gone.

At that moment, the fuel I had been using to keep going ran out. Shame and disgust for my own naïveté angered me and left me in rageful tears. Yet, I was more enraged with myself than Richard. He had only proven to be who he'd always been. *I* had been the desperate little girl who had only grown into an even more desperate woman who was still giving my heart to the wrong men.

LYFE MILLER

"No! No! No! No!" Landon chanted violently. "You can't go!"

I shook my head. Feeling overwhelmed, I leaned against the front door, holding my forehead. "Chill."

"No!" he yelled so aggressively that the veins in his neck popped out.

I looked at Esther as she stood at the island. She was as shocked as I was. Landon had been way clingier since I had been shot. But I hadn't known how much since I'd only been leaving the house with him or after he was already sleeping. But, today, I was spending time with Ocean, which required me to leave the house with him knowing.

"What's wrong, Landon?" I asked, trying to pry his feelings from him. "Are you scared I won't come back? I told you everything is okay now."

Ace had told me that Irv had put the word out that anyone's beef with me was over. I had no idea why he had suddenly tucked his tail and looked out for me, but his reputation was strong enough in the streets to end anyone's planned retaliation, so I appreciated it.

Perched on the edge of the couch, Landon grimaced, causing his nostrils to flare. "You don't know that! You said that before, but you got shot!"

"Land—"

"Just don't leave! Don't leave!" Landon's tight fists punched the couch.

"I'm not going anywhere that's not safe. I'm just going to meet Ocean," I explained to him as calmly as I could.

He groaned, revulsion filling his eyes. "Why are you going with *her*?"

"Because we're going on a date."

His frown deepened into pure disgust. "You're always with *her*."

I chuckled, and Esther shot me a warning stare.

"You don't need to go on dates!" he shouted, grabbing his hair tightly. "You need to stay here with me! I don't want you to leave me!"

I winced as he began rocking back and forth.

"I'm not, Landon. I promise," I assured him. I walked slowly toward the couch, sitting next to him.

I moved to lay a comforting hand on his shoulder. But before I could rest on it, he snatched away and jolted to his feet. "You can't promise me that!" he screamed as he stormed toward the stairs. "You can't! You can't! *You can't!*"

As he began to run up the steps, I jumped up from the couch.

"No, Lyfe, don't," Esther said as she walked toward me.

I sighed, looking up the stairs longingly. "I have to, Esther."

"You can't keep catering to him," she said softly.

Still, I moved to follow him up the stairs, but Esther stood in front of me, blocking my path. "Go on your date."

Defeated, my shoulders sank. "I can't. Not with him acting like this."

"He'll be okay. You have to have a life too. He has to learn how to cope with you not being around. He's about to be eighteen. He's almost grown. He has to learn how to cope so he can go to college, work, and live as an adult without depending on you."

As I continued to contemplate, Esther's lips pressed together. Looking behind me, she reached for the hook next to the front door. I heard my keys jingling. She then pressed them into my hand.

"Go," she urged firmly. "I'll tell his therapist about what happened today. She can talk to him."

Slightly groaning, I headed for the front door, cringing as I heard Landon's bedroom door slam shut.

Ocean emerged from her car with confusion painted over the makeup highlighting her beauty. I had parked beside her when I arrived on 31st and Lake Park moments after she'd arrived.

I bit the inside of my jaw, trying desperately to focus on what I was doing and not the lewd way her curves bounced as she slid on her flip-flops around the front of her car toward me.

"What are we doing here?" she asked as she looked around the lakefront. "We're going to the beach? You didn't tell me to bring a swimsuit."

A slick grin pierced through my beard as I leaned against my ride. "You don't need one. We're gonna have a picnic."

Her shoulders sank as she became completely overwhelmed with gratitude. Yet, except for a pleased smile, I saw tears pooling in her eyelids.

I laughed. "Are you crying?"

"Yes," she cried.

Confused, I inched toward her. "Because I'm taking you on a picnic?"

"No." She then began to sob.

I threw my arms around her, completely confused.

As she buried her face into my chest, I tried to make her laugh. "This is not the reaction I was hoping for."

"I'm sorry."

"What's wrong?" I continued to pry.

"I met with my father this morning."

I grimaced and mouthed, "Shit."

"It was awful." As she sobbed, she clung to me, digging her acrylic nails into my back. "He hasn't changed, and neither have I. I still let him manipulate me."

I softly pushed back, looking into her eyes. She closed them with shame. I let her go, using my thumbs to wipe away her tears. I then took her hand and bent down to pick up the basket sitting at my feet.

When she finally noticed it, she began to sob even more. "You even brought a basket."

A sympathetic chuckle erupted as I grabbed her hand. "Come on, girl."

"I'm sorry for crying."

"Stop apologizing, baby," I ordered softly as I squeezed her hand.

She took a deep breath, wiping her face. Since she was trying to calm herself down, I kept quiet as I led her to a grassy embankment near the sand. All the while, I was smothering the beast within that wanted to violently torture and then murder her father for breaking her heart again.

I sat the basket down and then took the thin, small blanket out of it. I then spread it out and motioned for her to sit. She kicked off her flip-flops and then gathered her cream, fitted dress that swept the ground and sat Indian style.

I sat next to her, emptying the basket. Her eyes softened as she watched me set the Rosé, champagne glasses, and a charcuterie board in front of her.

"This is so sweet," she nearly cried.

I shrugged a shoulder. "Just trying to do something different."

"I love it."

She giggled when I took the Bluetooth speaker out of the basket last. I had already synced it to my phone. So, as soon as I swiped to my iTunes app and started playing my playlist, Pop Smoke started playing through the speaker.

"*Awwww,*" she sang. "This is so sweet *and* ghetto. I love it."

We laughed as we leaned against one another. I put my arm around her before asking, "Do you want to tell me what he did?"

She looked out onto the lake, smiling at the kids playing in the water. The day had started off with cooler weather, but the afternoon was rising to a scorching eighty-five degrees.

She cringed, flushing with embarrassment. "We met at Eggshack. He looked sober. We had a great conversation..." Taking a deep breath, her head rocked from side to side. "Then, when we were about to leave, I excused myself to the bathroom." My eyes grew big with anticipation. "When I came back, he was gone and had taken all of my money from my purse."

I wrapped my arm around her and brought her into me.

"I'm okay," she insisted. "I can't blame him. I knew better. I haven't changed much from that stupid little girl with way too much hope in other people that have shown me who they really are time and time again."

"You have most definitely changed. You're not that broken little girl anymore, and your drama doesn't define you."

As our eyes locked, her gaze slowly formed immense admiration. "How do I continue to be a complete mess in front of you, and yet you *still* continue to look beyond it?"

"Because I don't see any of that when I look at you. I see you. Not a damsel in distress, not someone who needs to be fixed because you're perfect. I just see you."

Irv had probably called himself rehabilitating her, but he hadn't truly helped her. He had only fixed her up enough so she would be dependent upon him. He hadn't encouraged her to stand on her own. He hadn't forced his way through her boundaries to love her fully. But if I had to break through those barriers for her to truly be free, I was willing to do just that.

"W—what... what are you doing?" I stuttered with a deep chuckle as Ocean's hands slid into my jeans.

Her lustful, sneaky grin met my wonder. "I want to taste you."

Her head lowered into my lap as she pulled my dick out. Her eyes danced at the sight of the precum oozing from the tip of it. She then hungrily sucked my head, moaning in satisfaction at the taste.

Inch by inch, she swallowed every piece of me as she massaged by balls. I leaned back on my elbows, enjoying the warmth and wetness of her mouth as it covered my length.

By now, we had drunk the entire bottle of Rosé. The sun had set, but the beach was still alive. Most of the children had gone home. It was now the adults time to play. Most of the crowd was on the pier, in boats, or at the lakefront restaurant that served fast food and drinks.

Ocean was hidden by a bush alongside us. But the way that she was attacking my length told anyone that may have caught her that she didn't care at all. She sucked my dick like she was proud to be seen doing so.

Ocean breathed deeply through her nose as she guided my throbbing sex down her tight throat. Once she reached the base, she held it there for a moment, massaging my balls.

My head fell back as I moaned, "*Fuuuuck.*"

She swallowed me again and again and again.

"Come here," I ordered, tapping her shoulder.

I needed to feel her. I had become an addict myself, feigning the tight hug that her center gave me every time I entered her.

She looked at me, spit lubricating her mouth as she smirked devilishly. She then straddled me, hovering above my dick as it aimed for the door it wanted to enter over and over again.

She quivered as she slid down my length. Her saturated insides expanded to my size. She wrapped her arms around my neck, holding on tightly as my hands slid onto her ass cheeks and hid under her dress.

I loved the feel of her skin. When I touched her, it was as if our souls had been intimate in previous lives.

She began to rotate her hips in smooth, circular, slow motions.

"I love how you feel inside of me," she whimpered sensually.

Using my grip on her ass, I drove myself in deeper.

She inhaled sharply, her mouth falling agape as she gazed into my eyes. "What are you doing to me?"

"Making you feel good."

Her core pulsated, squeezing my steel. I softly bit down on her shoulder, fighting the urge to cum. "And what about my heart? What are you doing to my heart?"

I pushed back, looking into her eyes. "Mending it."

CHAPTER 22

OCEAN GRAHAM

"Bae, hold this while I play this game with Landon."

Tearing myself from my consuming thoughts, I looked over at Lyfe, who was handing me his drink. He, Landon, and I were at Dave and Buster's. Landon had reluctantly come along with us. I was happy that Lyfe had invited him to come because Landon had never hidden his disdain for my growing presence in he and Lyfe's tight circle. I was hoping that with each forced interaction, he would begin to accept me.

I took the drink from Lyfe and stood close by as he and Landon played Typhoon. As they sat side by side, my mind began to drift again.

I should have been proud of myself for maintaining my sobriety through all of the hell I had been through for the past month. Yet, I felt the total opposite. I was concerned that I was allowing this courtship with Lyfe to self-medicate my pain just as I had with opioids since every time I was around him, I was on a high.

Lyfe was a good man. In return, I wanted to be just as good, just as perfect. I didn't want to depend on his existence to be stable. I feared that was happening since, though I had tried very hard not to, I had replaced one love for another potential one so quickly.

Lyfe's presence in my life introduced a desire to get even more help. I was sober, but I was not completely healed. I was still struggling emotionally. Even knowing the truth of Irv's toxicity, the vision of Bridget's pregnant belly often played in my mind, riddling me with guilt and the hurt of the loss of my child. I didn't want to be a basket case whenever I was around Lyfe. I wanted to be as strong and confident as he was. Yet, only NA meetings could help me achieve that, and I hated those meetings. Being around people with pasts like mine, and hearing their stories, brought back memories that I was tired of living with daily.

"You want something else to drink?"

I blinked, bringing myself back to reality. I had been in my own thoughts most of the time since that horrible breakfast with my father.

"Sure," I told Lyfe, handing him my empty cup.

"I'll be right back. Landon is still playing the game."

I looked inside the Typhoon game and then nodded at Lyfe. "Okay."

I watched him walk off, admiring his soaring, broad stature. As he pierced his way through the crowd, many women, old and young, white and brown, admired his masculinity and swag as he floated toward the bar.

My phone rang, causing me to tear my eyes away from a man that had been impressing me more and more each day. I had assumed that his spontaneity could not get better than the day we had first met. Yet, each day, he proved me wrong. Every day I opened my eyes, he took me on a new adventure or showed me a different way he could care for me.

I answered the call through my air pods. "Hello?"

"Ocean?"

"Miss Graham?" I asked, recognizing her voice.

LYFE MILLER

As I walked toward the bar, my phone started to ring in my ear.

I answered, tapping my right air pod. "Hello?"

"What up, bro?" Ace returned. "What you on?"

"At Dave and Buster's with Landon and Ocean."

"Landon *and* Ocean? How did you get that to happen?"

"I *made* Landon come. Trust me, he didn't want to. He doesn't like how much time I've been spending with Ocean."

"You knew that was gonna happen, though."

"Yeah, I guess I was just kinda hoping that it wouldn't."

"He'll get used to sharing you."

I took long strides through the lively crowd. "He's gonna have to."

I had always catered to Landon. It had been only us growing up, especially after my mother passed. A woman had never been worth me forcing Landon to share our comfortable bubble. But Ocean was worth that and much more.

"Oh, he's gonna 'have to', huh?" Ace taunted me. "That's how you feel?"

I grinned, saying, "Hell yeah."

Just then, I caught the desperate eyes of a group of women that were surrounding the foosball table. Each one of them was beautiful, but they didn't hold a candle to Ocean. My obsession with her left no comparison to her beauty, inside and out.

Ace continued to poke fun at me. "Ocean got you that open?"

I chuckled. "Whatever, bro."

"It's okay if you're feeling her."

"I know it is," I said proudly.

Ace laughed. "When are you buying a ring?"

"Whoa, you goin' too far now. I'm feeling her, but *marriage*, bro?"

"Aye, she wifey material. I heard she's the one who bossed up on Irv about you."

"About *me?*"

"Yeah. She told him to put the word out that all retaliation against you was to cease."

Smiling, my brows raised high. "Straight up?" Suddenly, my dick started hardening in my jeans. This was one of the characteristics Ocean possessed that I admired. She had her shit together with a career and her own possessions, but she was still street enough that she could speak to them. I was grinning as I approached the bar.

"She doesn't play about you," Ace bragged.

I was happy to hear that because I played no games about Ocean Graham either.

OCEAN GRAHAM

"Yes, this is me, honey," Irv's mother replied. "How are you?"

I began to pace the small area between the Typhoon game and the one next to me with five teenagers surrounding it. I wondered why I'd gotten this random phone call. The last thing I needed was the pressure of Irv's mother's judgment and ridicule.

"I'm okay," I answered hesitantly.

"Are you?" she pressed.

"Yes, actually, I am," I answered wholeheartedly. By the grace of God, despite all of the drama, I was still smiling and still sober.

"Well, I spoke to Irvin, and he told me you all were getting a divorce."

I mentally prepared myself for her under-handed ridicule. Irv's mother hadn't been fond of me from the moment she'd met me. I couldn't have blamed her. I was thirteen years younger than her son, who was obviously much more well-off than I was. Patricia, Irv's mother, was from the southside of Chicago. Though she had matured into a prestigious Chicago Public School superintendent, she was still from the hood and remembered how an addict looked. She had sniffed out my addiction as soon as I was introduced to her.

For the next five years, I looked forward to finally having a mother figure in my life, especially since she was such an attentive and loving mother to Irv. However, she had always fed me with a long-handled spoon.

"Mmm humph," I uttered, waiting for more.

"I'm sorry."

Blinking owlishly, I asked in pure disbelief, "What are you sorry for?"

"He was honest about the child he has on the way."

"Oh, he was?"

That stung. I imagined that he had only been honest with his mother because his narcissism had used my inability to have his child as a reason why he was having one with someone else.

"He was," she said with discernment in her tone.

I bit back the sorrow that swam up to my heart every time I thought about Irv finally having the child I wanted to be the one to give him. I swallowed the pain of having to hold my deceased newborn while watching the disappointment in Irv's expression. Having to figure out a name for a child who would never live had been heart-wrenching. But I had managed to. I'd named my baby Lake Graham.

"I'm so sorry, honey. I know we never had a very close relationship, but I am still a woman. I don't condone what my son did. Not at all."

My eyes closed as I relished her apology. I had been waiting for that same sincere apology from Irv. I had never gotten it, though. I had only gotten space and coldness. Yet, for his mother to finally see me worthy of sympathy was good enough for me.

"Thank you."

"You're welcome, hun. Call me if you ever need me."

"I will."

"Have a good day."

"You too."

As I hung up, I knew I would never call her, though. She was Irv's mother. She had never stepped into that maternal role for me, so she was to be left in the same distant past where I had left her son.

I felt his shadow casting over me before he'd said a word.

"Here, bae."

I looked up from putting my phone into my purse and saw Lyfe standing over me, handing me another Sangria.

I forced a smile. "Thanks, baby."

His eyes narrowed. I knew he was about to question my mood, but he'd looked toward where Landon was sitting and then lost focus.

"Where is Landon?"

My brows curled, confused, as I looked toward the game. "He's right—"

He wasn't there.

Shit.

Lyfe instantly began to look around frantically. "Where did he go?!"

His eyes scanned the game room wildly. Watching his fear grow into a crippling state made my guilt rise.

I stuttered over a fearfully beating heart. "I-I... Um..."

His eyes narrowed as he glared at me. He grimaced, then pulled them away from me as he tossed our drinks down on the game in front of him.

"Landon?!" He began to call out for his brother as he took long, hurried strides through the game room.

Trembling with guilt, I followed him. I had been so wrapped up in my own thoughts that I hadn't watched Landon with the attention I should have. I had no idea when he had even left, which covered me in fear.

"Maybe he went to the restroom," I offered,

Lyfe did not act as if he had heard me. He didn't even acknowledge me.

"Lyfe?" I called as I fought to keep up with him.

"What?!" he spat.

I flinched. He had used a tone he had never used with me. The look of disgust and irritation he gave me when he barely gave me his eyes was unbearable.

Sheepishly, I replied, "I said that maybe he went to the restroom."

Without a word, he made an about-face, going toward the restrooms, causing me to chase after him.

LYFE MILLER

"Fuck!" I bellowed, making everyone jump in fear around me.

Gritting, I ended the call, fighting the urge to hurl my phone across the lobby. I couldn't count how many times I had called Landon's cell. Each call had gone unanswered.

I began to pace as I heard Susan, the manager of the Dave and Busters, say, "Sir, we've searched the entire facility at least three times. He's not here. We have someone reviewing the surveillance footage from our security cameras."

I cringed. Dread was rendering me nearly disabled. The sympathetic eyes the security guards and employees were giving me were only confirming that I was not having a nightmare, that this was real. In fact, as they all stood around me completely speechless, they were validating that I was standing in one of my greatest fears.

Landon was missing.

He had never run away.

Never.

I wondered where he could have gone and why. I feared that a corrupt person would see him, be intrigued by his disability, and take advantage of him. This world was evil. In the hood, we feared being shot. But there are even more dangers in the world filled with diabolical people who do horrific things to others, especially the weak. The possibilities were driving me into a rage that I couldn't smother.

Finally, the police entered Dave and Buster's. My eyes widened with hope. I had phoned them thirty minutes prior after Ocean, Dave and Buster's security, and I had searched the family entertainment facility for the third time. Ocean stood next to me, tearful. I couldn't even look at her. I knew she was consumed with guilt, but I couldn't console her. Not right now.

"Over here, officers," Susan called out.

The two officers stalked toward us.

"What's going on?" one of them asked. His badge read Kilpatrick.

The other's read Samuels.

"My brother is missing," I rushed to inform them. "He was playing one of the games when I walked away to go to the bar. When I came back, he was gone. He's seventeen." The officer's concern transferred to being aloof until I added, "And he's autistic."

For fifteen minutes, I gave the officers more details than they had asked for, providing them with many photos of Landon. Because of his disorder, I did not have to wait the usual seventy-two hours to file a missing person's report.

After noting all of the details, Samuels assured me, "We'll go drive around the neighborhood to see if he's just wandering around. We'll send another officer to assist in reviewing the security cameras."

"Thank you," I said with gratitude.

"Maybe we should do the same thing," Ocean suggested.

Without a word, I followed the officers toward the exit. I hated that I was so agitated that I couldn't say a word to Ocean. Landon wasn't her responsibility. He was *mine*. Therefore, I was so disappointed in myself that I couldn't speak unnecessary words. Landon was my obligation, the only and biggest one I'd had since my mother's death. I owed it to him and my mother to never put him in danger. That had been my only job, and I had failed.

I marched behind the officers, brows tightly furrowed. Concern and worry were laced in my eyes as the setting sun met me on the sidewalk in Oak Park. Seeing that the night was nearing, I became even more hysterical, fearing the worst.

"We'll call you, of course, when we find him or find out anything," Kilpatrick told me as he approached the passenger's door of his squad car. "We'll send this report over to the Special Victims Unit right away."

"Thank you," I dryly replied, stalking toward my own truck a few feet away.

I could feel Ocean still behind me, following me meekly. As I reached my truck, I caught a glimpse of the anguish absorbing her.

She felt guilty. I wanted to heal that for her, but imagining Landon out in the world alone and scared was brutal. I couldn't cure my own guilt, so there was no way I could cure hers. My own shame was giving me violent nausea that was becoming harder to control by the minute.

Without a word, I started my truck. As soon as she climbed in, I threw it into drive and peeled out of the parking lot, thoroughly checking every nook and cranny of Park Drive. I had never felt so lost and helpless. My stomach twisted into intolerable knots as my mother's words rang in my ear. *"You'll be all Landon has after I'm gone. Take care of your brother, Lyfe."*

THIRTEEN YEARS AGO

CHAPTER 23
LYFE MILLER

"So, when you gon' let me come over?"

Tiana sucked her teeth. "What you wanna come over here for, Lyfe?" Though she had tried to appear irritated by my question, I could hear giddiness in her tone a mile away.

"I just want to hang out with you," I lied.

Hanging out was far from what I wanted to do. As a senior in high school, getting the pussy was all that was on my mind. Tiana had a phat ass I was trying to see outside of her Apple Bottom jeans. Thinking about it, I felt my dick getting hard inside of my Sean Johns. As I lay back on my bed, I adjusted it so it had room to grow.

"Mmm humph," she teased with a giggle.

"Lyfe!"

My mother's heavy Jamaican accent pierced through our small two-bedroom apartment in Washington Park.

"Yeah, Ma?" I called out.

"*Yeah*?!" she snapped, mocking me.

I covered the receiver of my Blackberry so Tiana couldn't hear me submitting so fearfully to my mother. "Yes, ma'am?"

I was about to be eighteen years old, grown in my eyes. Yet, to my Jamaican-born mother, no age was old enough to disrespect your mother and get away with it.

"Come here. I need to talk to you," she called out in a commanding voice.

"Shit," I mumbled. Then I told Tiana, "Let me call you back."

"Okay."

"You better answer too, with your sexy ass," I flirted.

She giggled. "I will. I promise."

After hanging up, I got out of bed, adjusting my erection and pulling down my baggy white tee to hide it further.

I thought back quickly. I wondered what I had done this time. The possibilities were endless. I had managed to be passing my senior year at Marshall High School by the skin of my teeth. I discovered that I was a very talented artist in an art class freshman year. My art teachers had collaborated with my mother and gotten me enrolled in all sorts of after-school programs so I could perfect my skills. They were convinced that I could get a scholarship for college. I was following their lead out of the joy I had for art and pure fear of my mother's wrath if I didn't. However, the streets of Washington Park intrigued me. I hadn't fallen victim to gangs or selling drugs yet. But I had a lot of homies that had, so I had ditched school quite a few times with them. I also hit a growth spurt in my junior year. I'd shot up to well over six feet. The Caribbean cuisine I was constantly fed had me thick like an NFL player. So, in addition to hanging in the streets, I was becoming a lady's man. Both were driving my mother crazy.

Ambling out of my bedroom, I caught a glimpse of my little brother, Landon. He was sitting on the couch staring at the TV, fully indulged in Cartoon Network. Per usual, his fingers were kneading at the hem of his shirt as he rocked from side to side. To this day, he had yet to say a word. He would only make noises.

As my little brother developed, he slowly began to regress. My mother simply assumed that his development would take longer than other children and that he would be caught up by the time he finished kindergarten. But during my sophomore year of high school, I was able to identify that Landon was autistic. I learned the behaviors and physical signs of the disorder in a psychology class. When I told my mother, she took Landon to a doctor who had diagnosed him. He needed social and behavioral therapies that weren't covered by insurance. My mother couldn't afford it, so he couldn't get the treatment he needed. His symptoms worsened as he got older. There were free therapy services for children his age, but since my mother was working, she didn't qualify for them. I didn't understand that because we weren't rich. We just weren't so poor that we qualified for government assistance since my mother was too prideful to come all the way to this country and not work hard.

"Yes, ma'am?" I asked as I entered the kitchen.

I could smell the curry goat and rice and peas simmering on the stove a few feet away. My stomach began to growl with greed.

She sighed deeply. "Have a seat."

Grimacing, I was frustrated, unable to think of what I had done to cause the look of disdain on her face.

"I need to talk to you about something serious."

I sat down slowly. She placed the spoon she'd been stirring the contents of the pot with down on the stove and sat across from me.

My heart started beating feverishly with fear. But as she took my hand, my fright turned to wonder.

"I... I..." Her sudden sadness and fear devoured me. Her inability to find words was alarming.

"What's going on, Mama?" I pressed her.

"I... Uh..." She swallowed a lump in her throat as if it were the fear she needed to consume before she could say the words, "I'm dying."

My eyes narrowed as I snatched my hand back. "You're what?"

"I'm dying." She swallowed hard, holding herself. "I have colon cancer, and it's stage 4. I learned about it six months ago."

I blinked and shook my head as if I were hearing things. "Chemo won't help?"

Her eyes lowered sadly. "No, not with my tumor. It's inoperable. I've been getting chemother—"

"When?" I interjected, confusion escalating.

"While you've been at school. I didn't want to tell you because I didn't want you to be scared."

My eyes blinked uncontrollably as I attempted to wrap my head around what she was saying. "Okay, so get more chemo," I suggested frantically.

Her lips pressed together as she shook her head. "It's not working. The tumor is getting larger. It's growing into other organs." Tears blanketed her eyes. "I'm dying, sweetheart."

I jumped up, causing the chair to jolt back, making a screeching sound against the tile.

My mother saw the anger on my face as I began to pace.

"Sit down, Lyfe," she demanded gently.

"This isn't right!" I started to explode. "*No*, you can't die! What about me?! What about Landon?! Mama, no..." I felt the tears stinging my eyes. I couldn't imagine life without my mother. She was a stern disciplinarian, but she was also my best friend. She wasn't supposed to die. She was too strong of a woman to succumb to disease and leave us. I hadn't seen that coming.

"Lyfe, *sit*," she gritted.

Hearing her grave tone, I swallowed hard and retook my seat.

The look in her eyes let me know that telling me this was the worst thing she had ever had to do. Suddenly, I realized I had to be the man she had been grooming me to be. I couldn't fall apart. I had to be strong for her.

She took my hand again, wincing at the tear that had fallen from my eye. "I'm so sorry," she consoled, her voice trembling. "I didn't want to have to tell you this, but they told me I don't have much time left."

My jaws tightened as I clambered to hold on to the little strength I had. "How long?"

"A year at the most."

I cowered. The death sentence felt like tomorrow, and like it was my own. When her tears started to fall, I broke down. My mother was statuesque. She was the definition of a strong woman. She had come to this country along with her sister, became employed, and started a family. Unfortunately, my father had not stuck around, and neither had Landon's. I believe both men had left because they were intimidated by her strength and bite. She was a fierce woman, the type I wanted to eventually marry. And she was a great mother. Beyond that, she was a dynamic person. She had fed the neighborhood many times simply because she had food to spare. She had been transportation for neighbors in need simply because she was one of the few people in the neighborhood with a vehicle.

She didn't deserve this.

My head lowered onto my folded arms as they rested on the table. I began to sob uncontrollably. I heard my mother stand. I then felt her wrap an arm around me.

"I'm so sorry," she said in my ear. "I love you, and you can cry as much as you need to. Mourn my death along with me while I'm still alive. Because when I'm gone, you can't focus on that. You'll have to focus on yourself and your brother. Please take care of your brother."

FIVE YEARS LATER

LYFE MILLER

"Mommy! I want Mommy!" It wasn't until my mother's death that Landon finally found his voice. "Mommy!"

Sighing, I decided not to continue to wrestle with him. I groaned and told him, "Fine, if you don't want to eat, dude, then don't eat."

I walked away from the table, leaving him alone in the kitchen in front of two uneaten slices of pizza.

My mother had been deceased for three years at this point. She had held on for two additional years after receiving the prognosis that she only had a year to live. She had fought such a battle that I was convinced she would beat cancer. But cancer ultimately won.

I'd been a father for the last five years. Since my mother told me she was terminally ill, I stepped up and took on a bigger role in Landon's life, preparing myself to be his sole guardian.

It was hard to watch my mother die in hospice, but I managed because I had been unable to truly focus on her dying since Landon needed so much attention. Not even at her funeral had I been able to mourn her because Landon had had an outburst, and no one could contain him but me.

Now that my mother was gone, he depended on me as much as he had depended on her. Yet, he seemed to have taken ten steps back. Because of his autism, he couldn't communicate his feelings regarding my mother's death. I wondered if he even understood what had happened. He would only lash out and throw tantrums.

I had no idea how to raise a child. I especially didn't know how to raise one with autism. And I knew nothing about learning to do all of that while mourning the death of my wonderful mother. I was in over my head.

Ace gave me a sympathetic gaze as I moped into the living room. "You good, bro?" he asked in spite of the obvious.

I scoffed. "That lil' dude gonna run me crazy."

Ace only shook his head sadly before taking a swig of a Corona.

I plopped down on the couch, feeling the weight of the world on my broad shoulders. "That's why I gotta do this shit," I said, looking at half a kilo of cocaine on the coffee table.

He and I had managed to convince his connect to front me the weight so I could start making the money I needed to get Landon into therapy. I had tried to help him myself. I had studied autism profusely. But it wasn't working. He was almost ten years old now. Yet, he was still communicating like a three-year-old toddler.

To take care of us, I had been working as a sales consultant at Sprint while selling some of my art here and there. But therapy for Landon at his age would be more expensive than I could afford while trying to feed and clothe myself and a boy the size of a grown man.

The nine-to-five wasn't cutting it, and the art wasn't selling. I had quit Sprint the moment I'd gotten the word from the connect that he was willing to front me the work. I was planning to hustle until Landon was able to live a normal life, despite his disorder, so that when I died, he would be okay.

While eyeing the cocaine, I suddenly felt like that time for Landon would come sooner than later. Yet, the fear of falling victim to the streets couldn't stop me. I had made a promise to my mother to take care of Landon, and I couldn't let her down.

Doing so would be the end of me.

PRESENT DAY

CHAPTER 24
OCEAN GRAHAM

"Fuck, fuck, fuck, fuck, *fuck!*"

I cringed as Lyfe chanted angrily while pacing a groove in the carpet in his living room. Watching him panic was unbearable. The tightness in my chest intensified as self-loathing thoughts cluttered my mind.

It was now nearing midnight. We had just arrived at his home after searching every block in Oak Park for hours. I was so exhausted from the constant adrenaline of false hope. Every time we saw someone who resembled Landon, we were filled with such gratitude and relief, only to be let down when we realized it wasn't him.

The guilt in my heart was intolerable. I wanted to run away and hide from the sheer terror in Lyfe's eyes, but it would be so rude of me to leave him alone at a time like this, especially when it was my fault.

"I'm so sorry, Lyfe," I apologized in the midst of my tears.

I held my breath, waiting for him to say something to ease my guilt. His pacing froze. His head tilted toward the ceiling as his eyes squeezed shut.

"It's not your fault. I should have been watching him. It's my job to keep an eye on him. I can't expect anybody to take care of him like I do."

I cringed as those words stabbed into my heart. I threw my face into my hands to hide my tears. I felt terrible. Again, I was the fuck-up I'd always been. I should have watched him. Yet, instead, I had been too involved in my own drama. Again, my chaos was affecting Lyfe's life.

As I began to sob, I heard him suck his teeth. I peered between my fingers to see him glowering at nothing in particular. My lips parted to give him my deepest apologies, but then the doorbell rang. I gasped as Lyfe darted toward it. My eyes widened with hope as he tore it open. My heart then sank at the solemn expression on the faces of the officers standing on the other side. I held my breath, incapable of taking the news. The room started to spin. The earth began to quake under my feet. The room went deafly silent. Then the officers stepped apart as their lips began to move. That's when a stubborn-faced Landon appeared from behind them.

The relief was so powerful that I nearly felt faint as I finally began to breathe again. Happy tears poured from my eyes as their voices slowly became audible to me again. But then I noticed the bruises and cuts scattered about Landon's beautiful face.

"What happened to you?" Lyfe exclaimed with relief as he took Landon in his arms.

Of course, Landon wrestled his way out of Lyfe's grasp.

"He crossed paths with some troublemakers. I guess they could tell he was a little different. Assholes roughed him up." Lyfe began to seethe with rage as one of the officers continued to explain, "Luckily, some men driving by stopped them from beating him up and drove him to a police station."

"You all right?" Lyfe asked Landon.

Landon's expression was bawled up with frustration as he stared at the ground. "I'm fine," he mumbled like a stubborn toddler.

"He's okay," one of the officers assured Lyfe. "Just a few scrapes. He actually gave those assholes a run for their money."

"Why did you leave?" Lyfe asked Landon.

"Because you're always with *her*!" He jabbed a finger my way, his eyes still on the ground. I gasped. The pure repulsion in his expression for me was paralyzing. "It's supposed to be just you and me! *You and me*! But you keep leaving me for *her*. Then you left me with her, and she wasn't even watching me!"

I broke down, sobbing.

Landon took off toward the stairs, climbing them two at a time.

Lyfe moved to go after him but then hesitated, telling the officers, "I'll be right back. Give me a few minutes."

They nodded as Lyfe took off after Landon. The sympathy in the officers' eyes as they looked at me was too much to bear. I clambered for my purse and keys. I then stood and rushed toward the front door.

"Excuse me," I said tearfully as I pushed past them and through the doorway. I sprinted down the front-porch steps, sobbing uncontrollably.

Thankfully, I had driven to Lyfe's house that morning. I hurried to my car, popping the locks. I then hopped in, turning on the engine with trembling hands. As I drove off, I could see Lyfe standing in the doorway, watching me. Yet, he never tried to stop me.

LYFE MILLER

The next morning, I lay in bed, staring up at the ceiling. I hadn't slept at all during the night. Adrenaline was still soaring. Beyond that, I was still reeling with anger, wanting to find the motherfuckers that had jumped my brother. The officers had told me that they were some teenaged, white, privileged boys with nothing else to do but walk around Oak Park, causing havoc. I had a bullet for each of those motherfuckers, even though they had been arrested.

Reluctantly, I tore my eyes away from the ceiling and reached for my phone. I hoped Ocean had called but prayed that she hadn't. My feelings for her were fearfully strong. However, no feeling could match the love and devotion I had for my brother. I didn't blame her for what had happened the night before. Yet, I did blame her past, which often caused her to mentally check out often. I didn't want the woman I had chosen to cause me to let my mother down. So, when the officers told me that she had run out in tears, I didn't stop her. Confusion had left me wondering had that been the right thing to do.

So, since then, I had done nothing.

Yet, just a few hours without hearing from her already had me suffering with desperation to be in her presence. My phone rang as I stared at it. My eyes narrowed at the unfamiliar number as I answered. "Hello?"

"Hi," the professional male voice greeted. "Can I speak to Lyfe?"

"That's me."

"Good!" he exclaimed with relief. "My name is Brian. I got your number off of your website."

I scratched my forehead and wondered where the hell this call was going. I hadn't updated my website in years, nor had I gotten any sales or inquiries.

"My client came across your artwork on Instagram and would like to hire you to do a mural in his home."

My brows curled with perplexity. "Your client?"

"Yes. He's an R&B artist from Chicago who lives in LA now. You may have heard of him: Midwest Dallas."

I jolted straight up in bed, eyes stretching wide with amazement. "Word?" I pressed, blinking slowly.

Midwest Dallas had become the prince of R&B since his debut on the scene in 2019. His first album, *Mia*, had been in heavy rotation when seducing bedroom victims. Brian had spoken casually, as if he was asking me to do a mural for a peasant instead of a Grammy Award-winning recording artist.

"Yes," he assured me. "I'd like to fly you out to LA so you two can meet and go over ideas if that's possible."

Still flustered, I found it hard to answer him. "For real?"

Brian chuckled, clearly amused at my awe. "Yes. Absolutely I am."

OCEAN GRAHAM

Pulling up to my home after work, I felt jealous of Lyfe. I would rather have been shot in my back because being heartbroken at work was much worse. It *had* to be. My entire day had been torturous. I had barely made it through the showings on my schedule that day. I would have done some rideshare driving to occupy my mind, but I couldn't manage to force a smile anymore.

The heavy weight of missing Lyfe left me barely able to carry my own weight as I climbed out of the car. I moped up the sidewalk, regretting going into my empty house. It hadn't even been a full twenty-four hours since I'd last seen Lyfe. Yet, it felt like a lifetime.

I would have to get used to it, however. I had to be a big girl because there was no way that Lyfe and I could ever be together. His commitment to Landon surpassed the dramatics that I had caused in his life since we'd met.

My feet felt like dead weight as I climbed my porch steps. Even though Landon had been found, I was still filled with guilt. I drew in a heavy breath, causing my cheeks to inflate, and then exhaled as I gripped the railing.

It was a beautiful August afternoon. Feeling the sun on my skin even reminded me of Lyfe. On a day like this, we would have been enjoying the weather along with each other. Visions of him tasting my tongue in the sunshine made my heart ache. Memories of riding him on the lakefront as the sun set gave me tearful chills.

I could then hear my cell ringing in my purse. I reluctantly pulled it out because I didn't want it to be Lyfe. I needed to hear his voice like I needed my next breath, but I wasn't good for him.

It was Sharon, my divorce attorney, so I answered, "Hello?"

"Hi, Ocean. How are you?"

"I'm okay."

"Well, I just emailed you the divorce decree." She spoke hurriedly, as if this was one of many calls on her to-do list. "I need your signature. Irvin has already signed on his end."

I grimaced, unable to take any more blows. I looked up at the sky, wondering why I was being tested constantly.

"Okay," I simply answered.

"Once you sign, I will submit it to the judge for approval. It won't require a hearing. Print them out because I need your actual signature. Then fax them back to me."

"I got it." Once on the porch, I checked the mail.

"Thanks. Talk to you soon."

I ended the call before pushing my key into the lock.

"Ocean?"

Initially, hearing the sudden boom of a deep voice made me stiffen, nearly paralyzed with fear. Then I recognized that it was him, and chills ran down my spine. I didn't turn around, however. I couldn't look at him. I began to frantically unlock the front door as my voice trembled when I released the words, "No, Lyfe."

"We need to talk."

I began to shake, his voice coming closer and closer as he climbed the stairs.

"No!" I shouted. "Just go away. We can't do this anymore!"

Finally, the door opened, giving me the only relief I'd felt in days. I hurried inside, closing my eyes as I shut the door so I wouldn't get a glimpse of Lyfe. If I had seen him, I would have melted into his hands. I would interject myself back into his life selfishly, adding more drama than I already had. I locked the door and fell against it. Tears fell as I slid down the cold wood, squatting with my face in my hands.

"Ocean, open the door," Lyfe softly demanded from the other side.

"Go home, Lyfe!" I screamed through my tears. "*Please* go home!"

I struggled to my feet and ran into my room. If I were to do what was best for him, I couldn't hear his voice. I closed my bedroom door, salty tears seeping onto my quivering lips.

When Lyfe began to bang on the door, I fell onto the bed. I put my pillow over my head, muffling the sounds of his fists connecting with the timber. I lay there crying into my comforter, my makeup smearing against my soft, blush duvet cover. Then it was suddenly silent. The pounding had stopped. Then Lyfe's heavy footsteps descending the porch stairs pierced through my bedroom window.

I inhaled sharply, flinging myself out of the bed. I rushed to my bedroom window, which faced the porch. I discreetly peered out of the blinds. I was only able to see the back of his large, delicious frame. Yet, laying my eyes on any part of him was enough to end me.

Any control I had quickly vanished. Sadness and anger exploded. I lost it, leaving the window and looking around my bedroom, heaving. I was so tired. I was beyond done with ruining everything around me. I was sick of losing.

I rushed toward my dresser and swept everything off it forcefully with sweaty palms. Perfume bottles crashed against the walls. Toiletries tumbled over as others hit the floor, spilling their contents all over the carpet. I screamed at the top of my lungs as I tore the drawers open. One after the other, I opened them, throwing underwear, socks, and lingerie onto the floor. It felt good to release the anger on something, on *anything*.

As I flung a few items of clothing into the air, a small baggie fell out slowly. I watched it as curiosity halted my tears momentarily. As it hit the ground, I realized it was the bag of heroin I had stolen from Lyfe's stash some time ago.

I gasped and snatched it up from the floor. I then rushed out of the room toward the kitchen. I wasn't thinking. My body was moving on its own. I simply wanted the pain to go away.

It had been years since I had cooked heroin, but it was like riding a bike. It had all come back to me so easily. Soon, I was fishing out hardened pieces of crystal from the concoction I had mixed up and cooked perfectly.

In the past, I had been very resourceful whenever I had to figure out ways to smoke heroin. I had been a genius at making something out of nothing. Therefore, I found some aluminum foil and eagerly sat at the table. I began to make an aluminum pipe. It was perfect as far as I was concerned because it would do the trick in the place of glass. Putting the makeshift pipe to my lips was euphoric. The stench of the burning substance brought back memories of pure bliss.

My mouth began to water. My heart began to palpitate with anticipation of finally leaving the painful memories, even though it would only be for a short while.

TWELVE YEARS AGO

CHAPTER 25
OCEAN GRAHAM

By the time I turned fifteen, the streets had taken the place of my parents. Usually, I would cut school because I was tired of being bullied for my tattered, smelly clothes or my unkempt hair. My parents and I had been kicked out of our apartment because of their drug use. We were forced to move into a cheap rowhouse near 30th and King Drive. Because I attended high school in the area, many of my classmates had seen me with my parents. Many of their parents had either sold to mine, my parents had tried to panhandle from them or had stolen from them. The list of embarrassing circumstances went on and on.

I did have friends, however, who were in the streets as well.

"I can't believe nobody is serving. What the fuck? Drug dealers take breaks?" Netta fussed.

Netta was one of them. She had attended school, so I'd met her at the bus stop outside of Dunbar after dismissal. Since then, we had been waiting for the corner boys to appear so we could cop some weed and then go to the park and get high.

"There goes Smoke right there." Netta pointed excitedly toward the corner.

"Bet." I smiled as we hurried toward him.

"Aye, let me get a dub," I told him once we'd reached the corner.

Smoke frowned, looking down at my short frame. "You too young to be smoking weed, ain't you?"

I kissed my teeth. "Last time I checked, I didn't have a father, so give me the fucking weed," I snapped.

Scoffing, he reached into his pocket and then angrily pressed the bag of weed into my hand. He snatched the bill from my other one and dismissed me, "Get the fuck on."

I shrugged my shoulders, and Netta giggled while skipping away.

The only thing that had changed since I was twelve was that I had managed to keep a few dollars in my pocket. Since the first time I'd hit that joint in that gangway, I had formed a dependence on weed. I then understood why my parents were addicts. The way an addicted person chased a high was savage. Stealing was the norm for me. I had gotten really good at it. Anything I needed, I took. I had been threatened with arrest a few times but never charged because I was so young, and the officers often felt sorry for me. Unbeknownst to me, the streets were forcing me to become just like my parents. I was no longer stealing for survival. Since I was too young to get a job, stealing had become a hustle. I would steal from stores and sell the items to feed my weed habit and party with my friends.

"You got some blunts?" I asked Netta.

She cowered, shaking her head.

I then started walking toward the local gas station. Netta followed.

$\sim$

Two hours later, I was on my way home to feed a severe case of the munchies.

"Hey, Ocean!"

I looked up the street where her voice was coming from. Ivory jogged toward me with her bookbag bouncing on her back. Unlike most of the other girls in school, Ivory had taken a liking to me. I felt it was because the stories I would tell her during English class fascinated her.

"What's up, Ivory?" I greeted her.

"Hey," she replied with a smile.

I looked her over in envy as I always did. Ivory was so beautiful to me. Her parents kept her looking good in Baby Phat, Apple Bottoms, and even Sergio Valente. Her straight, silky hair was always professionally styled, and she smelled like flowers all the time.

"Why haven't you been to school in so long?" she asked.

It had been nearly a week. I would rather walk the streets alone than willingly enter that school just to be the bud of bougie bitches' jokes.

I frowned, telling her, "I'm sick of those bitches."

"Well, Mrs. Williams asked about you today. She said she was going to call your parents."

I laughed. "Good luck with that."

"Where are you on your way to?"

"Home to get something to eat."

"Okay, well, call me after you eat so I can tell you what's been happening in school since you've been gone."

"Okay," I assured her before she walked off.

Ten minutes later, I unlocked the door of my home. My stomach was in knots, so I rushed to pry the door open, eager to get to my stash.

I had become a professional at hiding things from my parents as well. I had created my own stash spot in the floorboards of my bedroom. Therefore, the money, stolen items, and food had been safe inside since we'd moved in.

Surprisingly, my father was sitting on the couch. A man was sitting next to him.

"Hey, Stink," he greeted me.

"Hey," I dryly replied.

My parents were actually under the impression that they loved me. When they were sober, they had the audacity to speak to me as if I mattered to them. It was as if their neglect was nonexistent to them.

I hurried inside my room, mouth watering in anticipation of the Ramen noodles, honey bun, and Doritos I had hidden away as I closed the door.

"Ocean." I heard my father's voice on the other side as the door-knob turned.

I paused in front of the folding chair in my room as he opened the door and invited himself inside.

"I've been waiting for you to get home from school all day." He closed the door as he asked, "Where you been?"

I eyed him suspiciously. He was more fidgety than usual, and his sudden attention was suspect.

"What you want, Dad?" I asked directly, too hungry for his games.

"My friend, Tommie, out there is going to come in here and talk to you for a minute."

My face dissolved into a confused snarl. "He what? *No.* I don't want to talk to him."

"Please, Ocean? He's been asking about you, and I told him he could meet you."

"Why do you want your grown friend to meet me?" I spewed.

He nervously looked from me to the door of my bedroom.

"Unt uh!" I snapped. "Can you get out of my room, please?"

An eerie feeling had come over me. The mania in his eyes was way too suspicious. Finally, desperation like I had never seen before appeared in his eyes.

"He's coming in here," he insisted in a tone that he never used with me. "And you better act right. Otherwise, you gotta go. I know you've been ditching school. You probably been with some boys anyway, so this won't be that hard."

My brows curled downward with curiosity. "What are you talking about?"

"Do what I say!" he snapped through gritted teeth. His sudden rage made me jump out of my skin. "Or get out!"

My heart started to beat out of control. My parents didn't do much at all for me, but I needed the little bit that they did do. I definitely needed the shelter. It was apparent that my father was so desperate that he would put me out if I didn't comply. So, I decided to obey as I plopped down in the folding chair.

"Thank you." He was so relieved that it was sickening. He shuffled toward the door in his raggedy shoes. Before leaving out, he looked back at me, saying, "I told him not to hurt you."

I was shivering with nerves as Ron entered the room. I looked up at him with innocent eyes, nervously wondering what he wanted. Yet, when he closed and locked the door, taking off his shirt, I knew.

Tears instantly came to my eyes. I was heartbroken. My parents had denied me everything a child deserved. And now, my own father was forcing me to give up my virginity too. My sadness transformed into rage toward Richard's audacity and sickness.

I stared up at the beer-bellied man. He was a nice-looking older guy. He was clean, and his hair was even freshly lined. If he was an addict, he was a functioning one. Yet, he was still old and filled with perversion as he eyed me lustfully.

"How much?" I blurted as I glared at him.

He looked at me, tilting his head to the side. "Huh?"

"How much are you giving him for me to do this?"

He scoffed at my wisdom. He held a wicked smile as he answered, "Fifty."

I was sick. Fifty dollars was all that my body was worth to my own father. My rage turned into fight. I knew I didn't have a choice. I really believed my father would put me out if I didn't do this. I also feared that this man would simply take what he wanted if I didn't comply. But I would be damned if I allowed Richard to take this from me too without me having a say so. He had already taken so much already.

"Make it a hundred," I sassed confidently.

Tommie scoffed. "What?"

"Make it a hundred, or I'll tell the whole neighborhood you're a pedophile. I'm only fifteen, and you're what? Forty?"

He sucked his teeth and reached inside his pocket. "Fine," he spit, taking his hand out. He peeled some bills off of a stack and handed them to me.

I took them, counted them, and then stuffed them into my sports bra.

Tommie then sat on the floor Indian style. He reached into his pocket again. He then revealed what I knew to be a pipe. As he prepared it, I looked at it in wonder. I'd heard what heroin did to people. I had heard it gave first-time users such a euphoric feeling that they chased it for the rest of their lives.

"Can I have some?" I needed something more than weed to get me through *this* type of betrayal.

Looking up at me, he raised an eyebrow high. "You sure?"

"Yeah." I shrugged. "I smoke weed all the time."

"This isn't weed, sweetheart," he spoke with so much passion that it sounded like he was reciting poetry. "This is a high you'll never come back from. You'll look for it in everything you do from this point on."

"Are you going to give it to me or not?" I spat.

He shrugged, shaking his head slowly as he handed it to me. "Here."

I put the pipe to my lips just as I had seen my parents do many times. He then lit it. As soon as I saw the smoke rising, I inhaled. Within seconds, pure euphoria overtook me, swallowing me whole. I was numb, much more so than the feeling weed gave me. I felt so good that it was frightening, but I was obsessed with it at the same time. I'd left my body and floated to the sky. Amongst the clouds, I was light and free.

My father had been the one to show me the value of my body, and he was the source of my addiction.

That night, after having sex with Tommie, I left home willingly, and I never went back. My father had hurt me to the core, and my mother was too much of an addict to care or defend me. But I, too, was hooked then.

I chased that initial high every damn day of my life after that. Many nights, I slept in hoe motels infested with roaches and bed bugs, but that was all I could afford, considering how much the cost of my habit increased. It had gotten so bad that I would rather sleep on the streets than spend the money I needed to feed my addiction. So, oftentimes, I could have been found sleeping under viaducts, bridges, and even at bus stops.

Over time, I slowly dissolved into the mess my parents had left behind. Yet, no one had cared to clean it up.

PRESENT DAY

OCEAN WATERS

"Welcome to the New Life Christian Center meeting of Narcotics Anonymous. My name is Sophia R., and I am an addict. Is this anyone's first NA meeting?"

Since I hadn't been to an NA meeting in a long time, I raised my hand, along with the two other people in the small room at the church. Seven others sat with us in a circle as we sat on metal folding chairs.

"I, as well as everyone in here, am proud of you for being here," Sophia told the first-timers with a smile. "We are excited for you to start working on the steps to recovery. This is a safe space. There is no judgment within these walls, and confidentiality is our foundation. That means whatever happens or whatever is said here must remain here. If you need a sponsor, please let me know after the meeting is over. Now, let's start this meeting off with the Serenity Prayer. Let's stand and join hands."

Breathing in deeply, I stood and bowed my head, taking the hand of the person on each side of me, and mouthed the prayer along with Sophia and the others.

"God, grant me the serenity to accept the things I cannot change, the courage to change the things I can, and the wisdom to know the difference. Living one day at a time, enjoying one moment at a time, accepting hardship as the pathway to peace. Taking, as He did, this sinful world as it is, not as I would have it. Trusting that He will make all things right if I surrender to His will. That I may be reasonably happy in this life, And supremely happy with Him forever in the next. Amen."

We released one another's hands and returned to our seats.

Sophia then said, "All of our meetings are closed meetings. These meetings are only for addicts or those who think they might have a drug problem. Are there any non-addicts here today?"

Sophia waited for anyone to answer. When no one did, she replied, "Now, let's go over the twelve steps of NA."

After reciting and explaining the twelve steps, Sophia went over what an addict was. She then opened the floor for introductions.

Nervously, I raised my hand. Others had as well, but when Sophia's eyes landed on me, she smiled softly. "You. You can go first."

I anxiously stood, forcing my shaky words to leave my throat. "Hi. My name is Ocean G-" I stopped myself, realizing that since I had signed those divorce papers two days prior, I was no longer a Graham. "Ocean W., and I am an addict."

"Hi, Ocean," the group greeted in unison.

I toyed with the hem of my shirt to calm my frazzled nerves as I continued, "I've actually been in recovery for five years. However, I almost relapsed a few days ago."

The moment I smelled that heroin burning, I became sick with the haunting memories of what that drug had done to me, to my family. I threw it down to the floor, disgusted with myself. But that wasn't enough. So, I scooped it up, ran to the bathroom, and flushed it down the toilet.

Many people in the group gave me gazes full of sympathy and support as I continued, "I have had lots of emotional turmoil going on in my life that have caused memories of past traumatic events to resurface. And I almost gave in. But, thank God, I didn't. But I now know that I need to start attending meetings again and maybe even seek therapy so I won't ever come that close to relapsing again and so I can be a healthier, sober person for myself and the people around me."

Sophia, along with other members of the group, smiled and clapped as I returned to my seat. As she called on the next person to introduce themselves, happy tears filled my eyes.

I sat in my chair, listening to the struggles of addiction of others that sounded oh-so-familiar to me. Sitting there, I realized what I had been missing and needed. Suddenly, I didn't feel alone in this trauma and fight anymore.

As I listened to the next introduction, I felt my phone vibrating in my pocket. I took it out and discreetly looked at it. Seeing Lyfe's name on the Caller ID, I cringed and declined the call. He had been calling randomly since the day I had sent him away from my home. Yet, I couldn't answer for many reasons.

It had taken me a few days since nearly relapsing to go to a meeting. I had been living daily with the finalization of my marriage and losing Lyfe. But I realized that, regardless, neither would have lasted, nor would I ever be able to be in another loving relationship again until I got some help.

I wasn't completely healed, but this was a huge step in the right direction.

~

"Urgh." As I drove home, I suddenly felt the donuts that I had scarfed down during the meeting threaten to resurface. I fought to keep control of my car as a violent wave of nausea swam through me. "Oh my God." The sensation became so intense that I quickly pulled over, causing horns to blare at me.

Once on the shoulder of the expressway, I threw the gear into park and hurriedly pushed open the driver's door. I only had time to lean over before I was regurgitating.

"Shit!" I panted once it was over. I flung myself back into my seat. I then searched my console for tissues. Luckily, my car was fully equipped with cleaning products to keep my car clean when I did rideshare.

I found some napkins in the console and wiped my mouth. Before pulling off, I ensured that the threat of sickness was gone.

Sure that it was, I pulled off, curious as to why I would throw up something that never bothered me before.

"Oh shit." My brows rose as I eased back into traffic. While keeping my eyes on the road, I took my phone out of the cup holder and scrolled to the app that I used to track my menstrual cycle.

After the first few times we'd had sex, Lyfe and I had abandoned using condoms. He insisted that I was his and there was no need. However, he had been pulling out because we weren't ready to have kids yet.

"Damn," I whined when I saw that my cycle was two weeks late.

The sex life in my marriage had been so scarce that I hadn't had a need to keep up with my cycle. I hadn't broken that habit in the short time that I had been sleeping with Lyfe.

I had spent months ignoring the guilt of losing my first child. Now, it was engulfing me. Stinging tears of guilt and fear came to my eyes, blinding me. I blinked, fighting to see the road as I approached my exit.

LYFE MILLER

"There they go right there." Ace sat up with excitement as the group of teenagers came into view from my ride.

My eyes narrowed as I seethed, remembering the bruises they'd left on Landon.

Because of their arrest, I had access to the names of the boys who'd attacked Landon. I had since been following one of thier posts and stories on Instagram since his profile was the only one that was public. Naive, he put his every move on social media. That afternoon, he posted several videos of him and some friends at the park. I had recognized the faces of his friends as the others that had attacked Landon.

I wanted to put a bullet through thier eyes. However, the murder of four white teenagers in Oakbrook would have been blasted all over social media until an arrest was made. I could not foolishly leave Landon alone because I was in jail for murder.

But they could get beat within an inch of their lives.

I turned toward the backseat where Ace's corner boys were

267

waiting eagerly. They were all under the age of eighteen and trained to go. Two more of their homies were behind us in Ace's ride.

"Do *not* kill them," I told them sternly. "But make them wish they were dead."

"Fa sho," Lil' D rushed as he threw the backdoor open. They then all filed out, heads covered with hoods. Many of them still wore masks, as if we were still in the height of the pandemic.

They bounced across the street excitedly. This type of action had them salivating. I hadn't needed to promise them anything in exchange for this. They were happy to have permission to cause trouble once me and Ace had given them the word.

I watched with anticipation as their homies behind us joined them in the middle of the street. They then ran toward the park, where I could see Landon's assailants sitting on benches, smoking weed. My chest rose repeatedly, anger causing my heart to pump wildly. Yet, admittedly, some of my frustrations had Ocean's name on them.

It was over between us. And even though I understood her reasons why, I was frustrated that those reasons even existed. I hated what had happened to her that made her unable to be a part of my life. I even hated my own past for putting me in the position of having to let her go so that I could put all of my attention on Landon.

Initially, I didn't care about any of that. My need for her was more prevalent, which had brought me to her house the day before. However, her rejection had made it so that I could no longer ignore the truth. I wanted her, but I couldn't chase her. I wanted to fix her, but my obligation was to fix Landon.

Ace began to laugh as the attack began. The group of white boys hadn't seen our lil' homies coming. They attacked them suddenly with wild, vicious blows that sent them flying off of the bench. As they kicked and punched the white boys, a cloud of sand formed around them, making it nearly impossible to see the mayhem unfolding.

"They gonna kill those white boys," Ace bellowed with laughter.

"I wish they could."

"Ooo shit!" Ace gasped as Lil' D kicked one of them in the face so hard that we could see blood fly from his mouth from the curb.

I began to blow the horn frantically, a signal for them to stop. Their hard-headed asses landed a few more blows, causing me to lay on the horn, before they took off toward my ride, laughing hysterically.

The white boys squirmed, rolling in the sand, finding it hard to stand. As the lil' homies jumped in, rejoicing and recalling what they had just done, I didn't feel vindicated. I drove off, feeling as if this wasn't enough. In exchange for my brother's suffering, they didn't deserve to even be breathing. But it was because of responsibility and maturity that this would have to be enough.

A FEW DAYS LATER...

LYFE MILLER

"Here we are, Mr. Miller."

My eyes brightened as the driver approached two large iron gates. They opened automatically. I leaned against the rear passenger's window of the Range Rover, looking up at the mansion with wide, eager eyes. I swallowed hard, masking my amazement so I wouldn't appear as naïve and awestruck as I felt in this new land.

I was in Los Angeles. Brian had been official. For days after his call, and each time he called after that to confirm details, I thought this was all a prank someone was pulling on me. Even after I received the first-class flight information and confirmed it with Delta, I still wasn't convinced.

Now, I was climbing out of the truck that had picked me up from the airport. I hadn't felt more important in my life than when I left baggage claim to see a man dressed in all black and a top hat, holding a sign with my name boldly printed on it. There had even been a bottle of Hennessy XO awaiting me in the back seat. Yet, as I walked up the steps of the luxurious property, I was still in disbelief.

I was waiting to be awakened from this dream by a taunting laugh from someone teasing me for having the audacity to believe that something so surreal could happen to a hood nigga like me. However, the fourteen-foot, blue-green glass doors of the magnificent estate on the prestigious street of Holmby Hills opened, and indeed the face of Midwest Dallas appeared.

"Lyfe! What up, bro?!" He was humbly just as excited to see me.

I forced my grin to appear confidently as I met him at the doorway. His extended hand took mine, and we shook up like we were just two street dudes from the same trenches of the Chi.

"Nice to meet you," he told me.

"Man, likewise, for sure."

His eyes bucked and then quickly narrowed. "Gawd damn, bro, your voice is deep as fuck." I chuckled as he stepped back, allowing me into the breathing foyer. "How was your trip?"

"It was *great*," I had to admit.

The first-class experience started in the Delta club at the airport. I had taken full advantage of the bar and full-service buffet.

I had nervously gulped down cognac during the flight to calm my nerves in complete disbelief at the exceptional hospitality in the skies. I was disappointedly tipsy as I left the plane, but seeing the driver and style he greeted me with in the 2023 Range Rover sobered me up quickly.

"This is a dope crib, man," I told Midwest Dallas.

In the foyer, I was standing in daylight that shined down from a forty-six-foot-high dome that was two stories overhead. Suspended from the center of the dome, a massive eighteenth-century baccarat crystal chandelier hung. Looking up and taking in the view, I remembered Midwest Dallas' story, which had appeared in blogs numerous times. He'd also recalled portions of his bio in multiple interviews. He was a hustler from the Chi whose wife had died giving birth to his son, Kenny. He had always been a talented singer, but he'd never taken it seriously until his best friend forced him to record some music once he was released from prison. After going viral on social media, his career catapulted. I wondered if my story could end in such a fairy tale as well. Unfortunately, if it did, it wouldn't be with my dream girl by my side since the woman of my dreams refused to speak to me.

"You want a tour?" Midwest Dallas offered.

My eyes brightened on their own, showing my excitement. Yet, I replied coolly, "Yeah, that would be dope."

Surrounding the foyer was the library, massive living room, formal dining room, and two marble powder rooms, which all had high ceilings and large French doors. The large master suite had three fireplaces, sitting room, wrap-around balcony, wet bar, and a marble spa. In addition, there were three guest suites with private baths, self-contained staff quarters, and an elevator servicing all three floors of the mansion.

As we approached a door, he told me, "I'm sorry my wife isn't here for you to meet her. She had a gig in Atlanta."

"Totally understandable."

"She still insists on working, even though I told her she doesn't have to. You know how independent Chicago chicks are."

Since he'd chuckled at that playful jab, so did I. "Oh, fa sho."

After he opened the door, I followed him down a flight of stairs.

"This is my studio where I want the mural to be painted."

I nodded slowly, looking around the enormous space. Brian had already told me the vision Midwest Dallas had, so as he motioned for me to have a seat on the leather couch, I reached into my bookbag. It was the same bookbag I hustled with. So, as I did, a surreal feeling came over me. Instead of reaching into it for cocaine, I was pulling out the sketches I had created for him on the four-hour plane ride.

275

As he took them in, his eyes danced. Yet, I still held my breath, waiting for his approval. He had requested a mural of his family to draw inspiration from while he wrote and recorded music in his studio. Brian had mentioned that Midwest Dallas spent so much time in the studio that he would look at pictures of his family to motivate himself to keep going. Therefore, he felt like decorating the black walls with images of his wife, Kenny, and their newborn baby girl would be ideal. I had taken pictures from his Instagram to come up with many concepts.

Looking down at the images, a pleased grin made an appearance through his beard.

"Man, these are *dope*." Then his eyes squinted as he frowned at the sketches, giving them the African-American confirmation that I had killed it.

Relieved, I grinned from ear-to-ear, showing every tooth in my mouth. "Cool. Good. I'm glad."

"You are so fucking talented, bro. Your images are very realistic. Have you ever thought about becoming a tattoo artist? Your tattoos would be dope as fuck."

I shook my head. "Tattooing was never my thing. I like a bigger canvas than skin."

Still scanning the sketches, he slowly bobbed his head. "I feel you."

I started to go over the colors he wanted me to use. Once my lingo became too artsy and technical for his vocabulary, he told me he trusted me to do my thing.

After choosing one of my concepts, he asked, "How long would something like this take you to do?"

"I'm assuming like a week."

He nodded slowly as he began to think. "Okay. Let's make the arrangements for you to come back and knock this out. If you aren't comfortable being away from your brother that long, he's welcome to come with you."

Caught off guard, I blinked a few times before asking, "You know about my brother?"

"I've seen him on your Instagram. It's dope as fuck that you're raising him."

It touched me that he would even research my story and look outside of his own needs to accommodate not only me but my brother as well. A bit speechless, I focused on the floor, anything to keep Midwest Dallas from seeing the emotions his compassion had brought out of me.

"And, after thinking about it, there is a large blank wall in Kenny's room that I couldn't figure out what to do with," he said. "If you could create a painting of his mom to cover it, that would be great. Hate to just throw that at you."

I looked at him, still in awe. "Nah, it's cool." My response was blasé, but I was unraveling with appreciation and disbelief within.

"Just add it to my bill. Whatever it costs."

I discreetly sighed deeply, releasing every anxiety I'd had about being able to take care of Landon and live long enough to do so. I suddenly saw hope where there hadn't been any before. I could finally envision Landon and I living happily and safely ever after with every resource he needed to prosper.

I just wished that I saw Ocean in that picture as well. Even while my life was changing dreamily, while I rode first class, while I met with a super star, I thought of her and wished that she was there. She belonged there, no matter how much she thought differently.

CHAPTER 26
OCEAN WATERS

"Thank you," I rushed as I took the bag from the Instacart driver.

She gave me a sympathetic gaze as she replied, "You're welcome," and left the porch.

I hurriedly closed the door, rushed into my bedroom, and then the master bath. My hands were shaking as I took the pregnancy test from the bag.

I had finally gotten the courage to take a test. But I still couldn't bring myself to buy one, so I ordered it through Instacart.

Still trembling, I took it from the box and followed the directions.

Once I was done, I placed it on the sink, set the timer on my cell for three minutes, and began to speak positive affirmations to myself.

I was so appreciative that I had started back going to NA. Those meetings helped me deal with the overwhelming notion of possibly being pregnant again. I had been sick every now and then. Suddenly, the smell of my own perfume nauseated me. So, I knew that I was with child. But I needed to confirm so that I could face the next rollercoaster in my dramatic theme park of a life.

I had avoided it long enough.

The timer sounded off, sending a piercing sound of doom into the air, which echoed in the quiet bathroom.

Cringing, I stood.

As I stared down at the word "POSITIVE", tears streamed down my face. After losing my baby, I had hoped and prayed for another chance to be a mother. But now, as I faced the reality of a pregnancy with a man I barely knew, I felt a sense of hopelessness and heartbreak. Our relationship was over. I couldn't bring myself to cause him and Landon anymore stress. And the thought of raising a child alone was chilling.

Every time I thought about the future, I felt a sense of despair and loneliness. I had been through so much, and now I was facing another challenge that seemed insurmountable. The thought of bringing a child into the world without the support of a partner filled me with dread. Because of how I was raised, I promised myself that the children I birthed would be in a two-parent, loving, and clean household where they would need for nothing. Yet, I was single and barely holding on to my sobriety. All I had was love to give.

As I looked back on me and Lyfe's brief time together, I couldn't help but feel a sense of loss and regret. We had shared something special, something that I had been searching for my entire life. But now, because of circumstances beyond our control, it was over. And as I clutched the pregnancy test in my hand, I knew that I had to find a way to be strong for myself and for my unborn child, no matter how difficult it seemed.

~

As I showed my company's most recent vacancy in a three-story building in Bronzeville a few hours later, I felt hopeful. If love was all that I had to give to this child, then that was a good start because I hadn't even had that. Using the teaching of NA, I was focusing on the positives of being pregnant. I had a chance to bring a life into this world that would love me unconditionally.

I was proud of myself for that. I wished that I had kept up with the NA meetings from the beginning, but it was never too late to correct my wrongs. Now, I planned to attend NA meetings weekly, along with therapy for the trauma I had experienced. My first therapy appointment was in a few days.

"So, what are you guys thinking?" I asked the interracial couple that I had been showing the unit to.

Sierra, a Hispanic woman, smiled brightly. She looked around the living room as she bounced their six-month-old daughter on her hip. Their child was so beautiful that I hadn't been able to stop gushing at her adorable fat cheeks and huge kinky coils, which mimicked the curls atop her father's fade.

"I love it," she told me, and she then looked over at her husband.

"If you like it, I love it, baby," he said sweetly.

I swooned, admiring his sensitivity toward his wife. It made me miss Lyfe, knowing he had always given me whatever my heart desired while being my security blanket. I missed him dearly, but I knew my absence from his life was best for him and Landon, so I pushed those wishful fantasies to the back of my mind.

"How do we go about filling out an application?" Sierra asked.

"As soon as I am done doing tours today, I will forward applications to everyone interested."

"Oh no," she pouted. "Are there a lot of people interested?"

"There were only two," I answered honestly. As her pout deepened, I told her, "But if you fill it out fast and get approved before the others, all you have to do is put your deposit down first to secure the unit."

"Okay, I'll be looking out for your email then," she said with a nervous grin.

"Great. I only have one more showing today. They should be arriving any minute, and then I'll get that application right out to you."

"Thanks," her husband, Kyle, said, taking his wife's hand.

He then began to guide her toward the front door of the unit. As he opened it, she gave the open concept one more once over. She then sighed deeply with a pleasing smile. I joined her in the grin because I knew exactly what she was feeling. If I'd had a family, I would have loved this place as well. It was over two thousand square feet with spacious rooms and a master bathroom to die for. The elevated Jacuzzi with a mirror as its backdrop was a selling point in itself.

Feeling her hesitation, Kyle looked back. He chuckled deeply while opening the door, saying, "Come on, baby."

"*Okayyy,*" she whined, following him out.

Giggling as well, I told them, "It was very nice to meet-"

My farewell lodged in my throat as Lyfe's large stature emerged up the staircase behind them.

"Looks like your last appointment is here," Kyle announced, eyeing his wife teasingly.

"You'll *hate* this place," Sierra told Lyfe. "I literally just saw a roach."

She'd made me laugh over my astonishment at seeing him there. His deep rumble filled up the hallway, causing Sierra's eyes to bulge. As her husband guided her down the steps, I caught her give Lyfe a once-over as well. She then looked back at me and winked before they disappeared down the stairs.

Finally, he was standing before me, his masculine scent suffocating me as his intimidating orbs took me in, hypnotizing me with his sweltering swag and masculinity.

"W-What... What are you doing here?" I stuttered.

He didn't ask for permission to enter the condo. He simply made his way inside, gently pushing by me, giving himself permission.

I felt butterflies fighting chaotically in my stomach. "I have an appointment in a few minutes."

"I *am* your appointment." He turned toward me, watching me as I closed the door. "I booked the appointment under a fake name since you won't talk to me."

I sheepishly hid from his gaze. I attempted to walk away, but he blocked my path, pinning me between his large frame and the door. He then reached behind me. To my surprise, I heard the door locks engage with a click. I swallowed hard, gathering my composure. I collected all the energy in my body so I could stand firm.

Though I was pregnant with his child, we couldn't be together. Landon wasn't ready. I was still healing. Lyfe couldn't take care of me *and* Landon.

"Lyfe, you can't—"

He grabbed my chin and swallowed my words with a deep kiss that took my air. Just the taste of him was enough for me to give up all resistance. I threw my arms around him and allowed the kiss to absorb me back into the intoxicating passion that was me and Lyfe. We began panting as his hand went from my chin to gently holding my throat as he pinned me against the door.

Suddenly, I was suspended in the air. I gasped as he tossed my legs around his waist and held me there as he pushed my knee-length dress up around my waist, all while our tongues continued to slow dance.

He was able to hold me up with one arm as he pulled his

manhood from his jeans. He then dove into my needy flesh with one thrust.

"Ah!" I exclaimed.

"I missed this pussy," he growled into our kiss.

I whimpered as I wrapped my arms around his neck, holding on tight. His grip was tight on my waist, with both hands bouncing me up and down on his erection as he pressed me against the door.

"I love you," swam from his throat into our breathy kiss.

I quivered in response, holding on to him tighter.

"You hear me?" he asked, swimming deep in my juices. "I love you."

I cried out with moans of immense bliss, pure natural bliss that gave me a high I finally wasn't ashamed of.

LYFE MILLER

I'd meant those three words. My trip to Los Angeles had only proven that. I had spent the day with a Grammy Award-winning artist. He had even taken me to get something to eat later that evening. We had bumped into some of his industry homies. Stunning women flocked around him as we ate. All along, thoughts of Ocean stalked me. I wanted her to experience this with me. I felt like finally, my life was changing for the better, and I needed her to be by my side.

I *needed* her.

She was broken. But I couldn't see my life without her pieces in it. She was wounded, but I was ready to kiss each tattered scar until it healed.

"You can never run again."

After she'd cum multiple times, I gave myself permission to cum as well. Now, we were lying on the fresh carpet in the empty condo, trying to catch our breaths from the intense lovemaking session that had lasted for over an hour and had traveled there from the front door.

Since my arm was under her, I used its strength to bring her toward me. She rolled over and landed on my chest. "You hear me?" I asked into her curly hair. I wasn't asking her to be mine. I was *demanding* it. "I'm not a square guy," I spoke into the silence. "I'm from the streets, but I know nothing about being with a person with your past. All I know is I don't give a fuck about it, besides the fact that I will consider it in how I love you."

She said nothing in response, but her heart was speaking for her as it beat thunderously against my sweaty chest.

"Okay," she finally replied in the sweetest whisper.

In response, I bent down and kissed the top of her head.

She then reached up; her coffin-shaped nails traveled into my beard and started to play with its coils. "I love you too."

I was happy she couldn't see the grin on my face, but I was sure she could feel my heart skipping beats.

"Then why were you running from me?"

"Because Landon hates me, and I know your devotion to him. I don't want you to ever have to choose."

"Then he'll have to learn."

"That isn't working, obviously. He ran away because of me and got hurt."

"So, you're going to run away from him forever?"

"*Yes.*"

Even though her tone was dead serious, she giggled.

Her laugh then faded off into a sigh. "I might not have to run forever, though. Who's to say we will last that long?"

"You don't want us to?" I asked.

She sighed, burying herself in my chest. "Of course I do. I'm not trying to be a Debbie Downer, but you just never know. You're so unreal to me. This feels like a dream that I am going to be brutally awakened from. Considering my past, I don't even feel like I deserve you. Life has taught me that you cannot assume what will happen in life. The moment you think you know something for certain, life will throw you the biggest fucking curve ball."

"I want us to last forever," I assured her, knowing she needed to hear that. "And I plan on ensuring that we do. Fuck those curve balls. I'll handle them like Kobe on the court, baby."

Suddenly, she burst into tears. She covered her face with trembling hands, causing my brows to meet with concern.

"Baby, what's wrong?"

She replied with uncontrollable sobs. I sat up, bringing her along with me.

"Talk to me," I begged.

She couldn't talk. She was crying too hysterically. She could hardly catch her breath.

"Ocean," I called softly.

"I'm pregnant," I sobbed.

I scoffed with a small smile as her shoulders sank. Finally, she pulled her hands away, revealing her tear-soaked orbs. "Are you laughing?!"

I was still smiling as I put a soothing hand on her thigh. "Yeah."

"What's funny about this?!"

"Because you're crying like this is a bad thing."

Her eyes narrowed. "You don't think it is?"

"I wasn't planning on it, obviously. I thought I was pulling out, but I guess my lil' niggas got some go."

"Stop playing, Lyfe!" she cried. "We've only been at this for a short time. You don't know me."

"But I know that I want you, and that means *all* of you. I just told you that I want us to last forever. Babies come with that. This one is just earlier than we thought it would be."

Tears continued to flow, though she was relieved.

"Come here." I wrapped my arms around her waist, and she laid her head on my shoulder. Wild curls danced in my face as I lost my fingertips in her roots. "Of course, I would want us to have waited until later. But I'm happy for you. This is your moment to get back something you lost. I'll never take that from you."

OCEAN WATERS

Lyfe had given me a few minutes to cry on his shoulder. However, they weren't tears of sadness; they were of relief and appreciation.

"You good now?" he finally asked as I lifted my head.

Nodding, I dried my face with the back of my hand.

"Good, because I have something to tell you."

I immediately got nervous. Of course, I did. My life was full of more downs than ups. Every time I got comfortable, something happened to catapult me into the dismal reality that I had been born into.

"What?" I asked reluctantly. I was submitting to him, but I honestly didn't want to know. I wanted to stay in this healthy bliss that those beautiful three words had poured over me.

"I got a call from Midwest Dallas' manager."

My eyes grew owlishly through the kinky curls that fell in my face. "The singer?!" I spit in disbelief.

"Yep."

My mouth fell agape cartoonishly. He softly pushed my curls

behind my ear. Happiness contorted his express into boyish bashfulness.

"What did he want?" I asked with as much anticipation as if I had gotten the call myself.

Lyfe looked to still be in disbelief himself. He looked up at the ceiling, shaking his head as he recalled the phone call, doubt still dancing in his eyes.

"He randomly called me and said that Midwest Dallas had come across my artwork on social media because he was looking for someone from his hometown to do a mural in his house. I didn't believe it, but it was legit. He flew me out to LA-"

"What?!" I exclaimed. I sat all the way up then. I crossed my legs Indian style next to him, grinning from ear to ear. "When did all of this happen?"

"He called me the morning after we'd gone to Dave and Buster's."

The reminder instantly caused guilt to return. Seeing it, he reached over and started to rub my thigh. I loved how he didn't ignore my feelings and always catered to them.

"So, when did you go to LA?"

"Yesterday."

"Oh! My! God!" I was beaming. "How was it?!"

"It was..." His smile met the ceiling. He shook his head, at a loss for words. "It was crazy, baby. I couldn't believe it. You should have seen his house. And he was cool as hell. Money didn't change him at all. He was still just a cool nigga from the crib."

"Wow," I whispered. I stared down at him, blinking owlishly. "So, you did the mural and came home that fast?"

"We only met to go over ideas. So, I came home this morning. The mural is going to take me about a week."

My eyes tripled in size. "You're going to go to LA for a week? Landon can't function being away from you that long."

"Midwest Dallas is paying for Esther and Landon to fly out too."

My mouth dropped. "Oh my God! That is *so* fucking dope."

This is when I knew I was smitten. I was so unconditionally happy for him, as if this blessing had been mine. I genuinely loved him because I was so happy for this opportunity that he well-deserved. His dedication to being a good man and brother had awarded him this fortunate blessing. Everyone with the kind of drive he had deserved this streak of luck. It was what every person in the hood, getting it out the mud, prayed for.

"You're coming with me."

Reluctance instantly replaced my excitement. "No, Lyfe. Landon isn't ready for me to be around like that. I won't run from you anymore, I promise. But I'm not going to throw my presence in Landon's face like that. I can't take the guilt. I already messed—"

"You didn't mess up," he insisted, his large hand softly stroking my face. "That wasn't your fault."

"It *was*. You asked me to watch him, but I was too busy dealing with my own shit."

"You know how many times I fucked up when I became his sole guardian?"

I scoffed. "You never lost him, though. I'm damn sure of that."

He squeezed my thigh. "Aye."

I reluctantly looked at him, pouting. "Yeah?"

"We have feelings for each other, but I know Landon is a lot. He comes with me. He always will. You ready for that?"

I wasn't even sure if I could handle my own issues, nor was I sure if it was the right time for me to dive into this passionate relationship with Lyfe. Therefore, being willing to take on Landon was a stretch that I knew I wasn't mentally ready for. However, as I looked into Lyfe's eyes, I wanted to try. I was determined to try and be the very best at it.

Giving him an admirable gaze, I promised him, "You're ready for this baby, so I'll do any and everything in my power to be more than ready for everything that comes with you, including Landon."

LYFE MILLER

Regardless of my assurance, Ocean was still shell-shocked from Landon's disappearance, so she hadn't come back home with me as I'd asked. I had let her get away with that because I hadn't seen him since leaving for the airport the morning prior.

I was so happy that Ocean had another chance to be a mother. I had never had the chance to envision myself as a father because I had so much on my plate with Landon. However, I was willing to figure out how I would shuffle being a father to two if that meant that Ocean got the baby she wanted and needed.

Esther had offered to be more hands-on with him because she loved us, and her heart went out to me as a single man raising an autistic teenager. So, she offered to spend the night while I went to LA. I was scheduled to return to the Golden State in a week. Midwest Dallas had offered to include the cost of bringing Esther and Landon with the deposit that he would make in a few days. I hoped Ocean would come with me regardless of her reservations about Landon. After meeting and seeing the pure love and devotion Midwest Dallas had for his family, I really wanted that for myself, Landon, and Ocean.

"So, this is really happening?" Esther's eyes were wide with excitement as she teetered on the edge of the couch next to me.

Landon was seated on the other side of me, focused on a scientific documentary on television.

"Yeah." I nodded, still in disbelief.

I had been on the phone with Esther nonstop while I was in LA, keeping her abreast of everything that was happening. She was so concerned about my safety and the authenticity of the meeting that I didn't feel like I had a choice. I liked it, though, because her concern reminded me of a mother's love.

She gushed, rocking with happiness. "This is so exciting!"

"It is." I smiled proudly. "Thanks for staying here while I went to see Ocean."

When I had landed in Chicago that morning, I was supposed to have gone straight home to relieve Esther, but I needed to see Ocean. I couldn't take it any longer. So, I asked her to give me a few more hours. I had then gone to Ocean's company's website and scheduled a viewing with any apartment that she was showing that day.

"I told you I got you," Esther said, slightly nudging me with her elbow. "Plus, I'm invested in you and Ocean as much as I am invested in you and Landon. I like her. I want you guys to work out. All three of you feel like family now. I love you guys. *And* I get to go to LA for a week. I've never even been on a plane before."

"You haven't?" I asked with surprise.

I had only been on a plane to nearby cities like Detroit and Minnesota, but considering how successful Esther was, I was sure she had flown quite a few times.

She shook her head with nervous yet excited anticipation. "Nope. When I go visit my family down south, I always drive."

I looked over at Landon, even though he was completely absorbed in the documentary called The Molecule of Life he'd found on YouTube.

"This'll be your first time flying, too," I told him. "You ready to get on a plane, Landon?"

"Yes, planes aren't dangerous at all," he said with a shrug, like my question was silly. "Riding in a car is more dangerous, so there's nothing to be scared of."

No matter how long I had been raising him, I would never get used to his melancholy and matter-of-fact tone that constantly made me feel like *I* was the one with the social disorder.

An hour later, Esther left. I was lying across my bed, staring up at the ceiling. Landon was still deeply indulged in his documentary, so I had gone into my bedroom to recoup from all that had happened over the last two days.

Life changed so fast that in an instant, so many life-altering, unexpected occurrences can happen. In those moments, we could either wind up suffering, grieving, or rejoicing. Either way, those were the memories that were created to last a lifetime. I'd had so many instances of my life suddenly changing for the worst that I was basking in the blissful feeling that, finally, it had suddenly changed for the better.

Midwest Dallas had assured me that he would document my work on his social media platforms and tag me. Since I was a fellow dude from the same streets as he was raised in, he had taken a personal interest in putting me on. Many had promised that to others, yet never came through. So, I was just appreciative of the bag I was about to make by working for him. It would be enough to assist in getting me out of the streets. I was simply grateful for that.

And I finally had my woman. I had to forcefully take her, but she was mine. As I recalled the memories of Ocean leaking on my dick earlier that afternoon, I felt a heavy weight accompany me on my bed. Opening my eyes, I saw Landon sitting at the foot of it, staring off into the abyss.

My lips parted to ask what he needed, but before I could, he asked, "Are you sad?"

My brows curled with confusion. "No. Why do you think I'm sad?"

"Since I ran away, you haven't been the same," he answered, stemming with his fingers. "You've been sad. I can tell. It's because you haven't been with Ocean."

There was no question in his tone. He knew what he was talking about. Despite his disability, he knew me. In fact, it was because of his disability that he knew exactly what he was talking about.

Still, I lied, "No, it's not."

I loved him so much that I never wanted him to think I had to choose between him and anyone else, even though I had been wracking my brain for solutions to the problem of Landon not wanting to share me with anyone else.

"You're not telling the truth."

"I'm okay, jerk," I tried to convince him with a bit of humor.

"You are *not*," he forced out at a high pitch.

Since he was getting frustrated, I got serious and honest. "You're right. That's true, dude. I've been missing Ocean."

He sighed, his body recoiling. "I can tell. You used to be happy. Like how you make me happy." He then blew another heavy breath, this time long and hard. Then he actually looked at me in my eyes, a rare moment that I took advantage of. "You can't just be with only me forever. I know that. I'm being... *selfish*. Ocean can come over. She can be your girlfriend. That way, we *all* can be happy."

Landon's words brought tears to my eyes that my masculinity didn't have the strength to hide. The tears weren't about him opening his heart to Ocean. I was tearful because my brother/son was growing up. This was a milestone. The therapy I had risked my life to afford was working.

A sense of relief, joy, and pride swelled my chest. This was a huge sign of progress in his development, and it gave me hope for their future. I felt like all the hard work and effort that I had put into supporting his development was finally paying off. Small progressions had happened over the years, but this was a huge one.

I sat up, throwing my arms around him. I expected him to fight his way out of my embrace, but he didn't. He actually put his arms around me as well and returned my affection, causing me to hold him tighter as tears fell into my beard.

"Thanks, bro," I managed to say through my emotions.

"You're welcome," he replied robotically, "Even though I still think her name doesn't make any sense *at all*."

CHAPTER 27
OCEAN WATERS

I had hidden from Landon for a week. A seventeen-year-old boy had me literally shook. Lyfe and I were fresh, but the uniqueness in our chemistry and connection was undeniable. It was so special that I didn't want it ruined by anything frivolous. Therefore, I had been taking my twelve steps and therapy seriously while not stepping on Landon's toes.

Yet, I was now being forced to face what felt like the only remaining obstacle preventing my relationship with Lyfe from fully flourishing. Taking a deep breath, I rang Lyfe's doorbell. My heart fluttered with reluctance to face how Landon would treat me. Lyfe had shared with me that Landon had actually told him he would accept me into their world. However, I wasn't sure how long that would truly last.

I was ready for the fight, though. No matter how nervous I was, I was ready to put forth the effort in handling Landon with love, in the very same way Lyfe was handling my mental obstacles that often interjected their way into our relationship.

Soon, the door opened, and an energetically excited Esther was on the other side. "Hey, Ocean!"

I giggled at the big floppy hat she was wearing, along with a floor-length maxi dress. I was used to seeing her in her scrubs. That day, she looked radiant, and she was glowing.

"Where is your luggage, girl?" she asked me as she left the doorway.

"Lyfe told me to leave it in the car until the driver arrived."

Esther squealed and did a little dance. "Can you believe this is happening?"

With an excited deep breath, I smiled as I closed the door. "No, I'm still in shock."

For the last week, this trip was really all Lyfe, and I had talked about, along with him going over specifics for the murals to get my opinion. He was driving himself crazy, ensuring that everything would be perfect. I totally understood because we both felt like this could open more doors for his artistic talents.

Esther grinned from ear to ear, clapping her hands together quietly. "I still can't believe it either. No one deserves this opportunity more than Lyfe."

"I totally agree," I replied, sitting on the couch.

Esther was about to say something else until heavy footsteps were heard above us. Soon, Landon appeared, lugging a suitcase with him as he carried a bookbag on his back. I tried to hide my nerves, but there was no use. I felt like my heart was beating so thunderously that it was causing the cotton of my cami to tremble. Esther looked over at me and smiled with sympathy.

"You got everything you need?" Esther asked Landon as he arrived at the landing.

"Yes," he said point blank, nodding slowly.

As he rolled his luggage near the front door, I admired how much he looked like Lyfe. His slim-fit jeans and black anime tee clung to his thick, elongated frame nicely. He had even begun to grow out a beard, which I was sure Lyfe had something to do with. The only differences between the two were a few inches in height and the hesitance in Landon's stance. As he looked at the floor and rocked from side to side, one could tell there was something different yet special about him.

As I smiled at his appearance, he sighed so deeply that it caught me and Esther's attention. She opened her mouth to speak to him, but when he suddenly started to amble toward me, she became speechless. I was as well, wondering what he was doing until he stood in front of me, bent down, and actually threw his arms around me.

"*Oh,*" I softly exclaimed with surprise.

He blurted, "Hi, Ocean."

Tears started to rise to the surface of my brown orbs. "Hi, Landon."

Still embracing me, he said, "I told Lyfe you could be his girlfriend."

"Oh, did you?" I asked as he released me.

He nodded hard, staring at the wall behind me. "Yes. I was being selfish. You make him happy like he makes me happy."

"Oh my God," I gushed, the tears falling regardless of how hard I tried to keep my composure. "Well, thank you, Landon. I really appreciate that."

He bent down and whispered, "My brother *really, really* likes you."

Esther and I fell out in uncontrollable giggles just as Lyfe emerged from his bedroom, looking like a whole meal, dragging a suitcase behind him.

"It's true," Landon whispered again, completely ignoring that Lyfe was now in the room. "He was *so* sad and—"

"Aye!" Lyfe snapped. "You in here telling my business?"

Landon giggled and hurried away toward Esther like a child who knew he was in trouble.

As I wiped my tears away, Lyfe's shadow cast over me. "What are you crying for, baby?"

"He hugged me," I whimpered tearfully.

Lyfe smiled at my tears and reached for my hand. "Come on, crybaby. The driver is outside."

Taking his hand, I stood and followed him toward the door. On our way, Esther excitedly flung the door open. She was not trying to hide her excitement at all.

Seeing the shiny, expensive truck waiting at the curb, she gasped. "*Oooh*! They sent us a Bentley truck, chile!"

"Esther, why are you screaming?" Landon asked as she took his hand.

"Because this is exciting, Landon!" she purposely squealed, causing Landon to press his free hand over his ear.

Lyfe and I chuckled with amusement as he let my hand go to grab Landon's suitcase as well.

"Mr. Miller, no!" a man exclaimed.

We all looked out of the doorway to see an older, White gentleman dressed in a black suit jogging toward the house past Landon and Esther.

"Please let me get that for you," he said, quickly climbing the stairs.

Esther turned around with an impressed expression as her eyebrow raised. She grinned so wide that it nearly pushed past her cheeks.

"I can't handle Esther *and* Landon. She is doing the most."

JESSICA N. WATKINS

I smiled. "She is just excited."

"I know. But I can't handle her excitement and mine."

Lyfe shook his head with a chuckle as the driver landed on the porch.

"I'm Ben." He extended his hand toward Lyfe. "Nice to meet you, Mr. Miller."

As they shook hands, Lyfe returned, "Nice to meet you as well."

Ben took the suitcases and hurried down the steps. I admired the boyish nervousness and disbelief in Lyfe's eyes. I took his hand, getting his attention. Standing on my tiptoes, I grabbed his chin with my other hand, my fingernails becoming lost in his thick beard. I then kissed him softly on the lips, mine being so appreciative of finally tasting him for the first time that day.

"You've got this," I assured him. "You're a talented artist, and you've been preparing for an opportunity like this your whole life. You deserve this."

I was so proud to finally be the strength he needed. He had always been my security and my comfort, but I was finally able to be his backbone.

I was honored.

He smiled into my eyes, and as he nodded, his chest rose, telling me his confidence was returning. "C'mon," he said, squeezing my hand. "Let's do this."

LYFE MILLER

Several hours later, Ocean strongly clung to my hand as we climbed the steps of Midwest Dallas' mansion.

"I *cannot* believe this," Ocean breathed.

She had been teetering between inspiring me and freaking out for the entire plane ride and drive. But I appreciated her pushing past her nerves to pour into me. Though she was excited, she continued to give me words of encouragement. If I had any doubt about how this would all work out, she had ensured that I felt like a fucking beast that was going to succeed like a boss.

This time when the doors opened, Midwest Dallas' wife, Harmony, had opened them with a baby on her hip so beautiful that it was seemingly making Ocean's womb cry. She gushed at the baby before even giving Harmony eye contact.

"Well, hello, Lyfe," Harmony greeted. "Nice to finally meet you. I'm sorry I didn't get a chance to meet you when you were here last time."

As she extended her arm out to embrace me, I assured her, "It's nice to meet you, and it's okay. I understand. You're a busy woman."

I had been following Harmony online for years, admittedly only because she was a beautiful woman with curves for days. She was a very successful makeup artist to the stars. She often flew all over the country for gigs with actors, musicians, and even politicians.

As many people did, Harmony instantly gushed. "Wow, your voice is beautiful."

I grinned slightly with appreciation. "Thank you. This is my girl-friend, Ocean."

As they greeted one another, I took a few seconds to realize what I had said. I had already staked my claim on Ocean, but I had never had to say the words out loud that she was mine. As I watched her embrace Harmony, I actually felt honored to be able to claim her. No matter what she had done in her past, the woman she was today was exceptional. Her strength to keep fighting her demons was so coura-geous, and that was more attractive than the exaggerated curves of her body.

Harmony softly nudged Ocean with her shoulder. "How do you handle him talking to you with that voice all the time?"

Ocean blushed. "Barely."

As we all laughed, her daughter did as well, stealing all of our attention with her adorable smile.

"And this is my sweet baby girl, Heaven," Harmony told us as she bounced her.

"*Awww*, hi, Heaven." Ocean smiled into the baby's face as she shook her little hand. "That's the perfect name for such an angelic face."

Sympathy accompanied my smile as I watched Ocean. I knew that the trauma of losing her child was something she fought with daily. Yet, hope accompanied the sympathy as I silently prayed that nine months from now, she would be holding our child.

"I'll show you guys to the studio. Dallas is already down there recording, as always," Harmony teased with a slight eye roll. As she closed the door, she added, "Oh, where are your brother and his caregiver? I thought they were traveling with you?"

I replied, "Esther felt like she and Landon would be in the way, so after checking into the hotel, they went to the mall."

"Oh, they wouldn't have been in the way at all," Harmony insisted.

"I know. I believe she knew that too. She just wanted to go to the mall."

Harmony giggled as she led us to the studio. Along the way, Ocean looked around the mansion with wide eyes, clinging to my hand as we headed toward the room where I would make my first major artistic mark.

OCEAN WATERS

It was so heartwarming to see Lyfe establishing himself as an artist. It showed his many layers. He was a diverse man with multiple dimensions that were slowly being revealed to me each day I spent with him.

As he created the mural, I was able to see him in a new light. His creative genius was mesmerizing. The images of Kenny, Heaven, and Harmony were so lifelike that I felt like they would start moving and talking to us.

"Wow, man, you are getting a lot done in one day," Dallas told him as he came back into the studio.

Looking behind him, it was so hard to contain my shock. Kane & Abel followed him.

My eyes bounced from them to Lyfe as I fought to keep my composure. But Lyfe's focus was on the drawing of Kenny he was completing, so he didn't notice the additional superstars in the room with us.

Kane and Abel were the most popular rappers at the time. They were my favorite trap artists. They had won multiple Grammys, as well as other music awards, and they had over a billion followers on Instagram. They were constantly in the blogs, flying on jets, buying million-dollar pieces of jewelry, and being linked to one Instagram model or female celebrity to another.

Finally, Lyfe looked up. "When I get in a zone, it's hard for me to stop." His eyes then expanded a bit when he noticed the popular rap duo behind Midwest Dallas.

"Kane, Abel, this is my boy, Lyfe," he introduced.

They actually walked around Midwest Dallas and shook my baby's hand.

"What up, bro?" Abel greeted.

"Nice to meet you," Kane told him. "Man, that mural is dope as fuck."

"Thank you," Lyfe grinned with pride. Then he noticed me excitedly teetering on the edge of the couch. "This is my girlfriend, Ocean."

They both turned and when they smiled at me, I could have died! Then they actually walked toward me, so I stood on wobbly legs trying to keep my cool. "Hi. It's really nice to meet you guys. I'm a *huge* fan."

As they hugged each side of me with one arm, I couldn't help but let out a little squeal.

I could hear Midwest Dallas and Lyfe chuckling as Abel said, "That's what's up. We love our fans, especially ones as beautiful as you. You want a pic?"

"Can I?" I swooned.

"Yeah, come on," Kane replied.

I rushed toward my phone, which was behind me on the couch. I then hurriedly handed it to Lyfe. We took the picture quickly as he said, "You gonna leave me for them, baby?"

"No." I blushed.

After taking the picture, I thanked them and eased back to my corner before I got in trouble.

"Kane & Abel are about to do a feature on one of my next singles," Midwest Dallas told us. "This some exclusive shit y'all about to hear. I don't have to make y'all sign any NDAs, do I?" he teased.

I shook my head, eyes still giddy with excitement.

Lyfe chuckled as he returned to his drawing. "You got it, bro. I doubt I'll even hear it. I'm focused over here."

I couldn't understand how Lyfe could contain himself in the presence of these stars. He was making me force myself to boss up. But that was how Chi-Town men were. No matter who was in the room, they kept their cool and their guard up so everyone around would know that no matter what, they weren't to be fucked with.

"You see this shit, bro?" Abel asked Kane as he stared at Lyfe's art. "This shit like 3D. It looks like Kenny is about to run up on me."

"Yeah, he talented as fuck," Kane added as he sat in front of the production console.

"This is the type of shit D-boy needs for his project," Abel told him.

Hearing D-boy's name, my eyes widened animatedly.

I need some sunglasses.

I was failing at acting nonchalantly.

He's never going to bring me back with him again.

D-boy was another famous rapper. He was more of a hip-hop icon, however, with countless platinum albums. He was also a super producer.

"You're right," Kane agreed with excitement.

"What project is that?" Midwest Dallas asked them.

Meanwhile, I was focused on Lyfe, wondering how he could just casually keep drawing while these celebrities were putting his name in the same sentence as a legend.

"He's been pitching this idea for an animated series to a few networks. Some Boondocks-type shit. He told me the other day he was looking for the right artist." Suddenly, he gave his attention to Lyfe. "Aye, you mind if I give him your number?"

Lyfe casually turned around, nodding. "That's what's up."

Abel handed him his phone, and my baby locked his phone number in it!

I was about to burst, but Lyfe was his usual cool, dominant self. He kept a stoic expression as he punched his number in.

"Thanks, man. I think you're exactly what he's looking for." Abel then shook up with Lyfe.

Still perched on the edge of the couch, I watched like a proud mama. Once giving him his phone back, Abel joined Kane and Midwest Dallas at the production console.

Lyfe turned back toward his mural, but along the way, his eyes met mine. It was then that he allowed himself to lose his cool. He grinned from ear to ear, causing me to quietly giggle until my face started hurting. He blew me a kiss before refocusing on his work.

I'm sucking the skin off his dick later.

We didn't get into our suite until five that morning. Lyfe had worked that entire time. He hadn't even stopped to eat. All night, I had pinched myself as I'd watched Midwest Dallas and Kane & Abel create a masterpiece of a record. While doing so, they admired my man for the masterpiece he was creating as well.

Harmony had come to hang out with me a few times since she felt like I was stuck down there with all men. We talked briefly about my pregnancy, and she gave me a lot of tips on managing a newborn while having a partner that would be as busy as her husband was. But most of the time, she was tending to her kids because she had been out of town for the last week on a movie set.

Once back in the room, I hurried to get into the shower. It had been a long day full of a lot of emotions, so I assumed Lyfe would be passed out once I was done. However, as I stepped into the shower and allowed the steaming water to wash over me, the bathroom door opened.

Wearing a sneaky smirk, he inched inside.

Blushing, I asked him, "Why are you creeping in here?"

"I'm coming to take a shower with my baby."

"I just knew you would be sleep."

"I'm too excited to sleep."

He began to reveal his perfection with each article of clothing he removed. I began to salivate at the thickness of his frame. Those thick thighs each had been able to hold up my two hundred-plus pounds on multiple occasions. They were anchors that refused to allow me to fall off his exhilarating ride.

However, Lyfe was filled with too much excitement from the day to even notice me admiring him.

"If D-Boy really calls me... Oh my God." He shook his head, the expression of disbelief still in his eyes that had been there for a week.

"He will, babe. Kane & Abel were so impressed with your work. You aren't anywhere near done with the mural, and they couldn't stop talking about it."

Lyfe inhaled nervously. I admired him, so happy for the opportunities that were coming his way.

He smiled boyishly as he inched toward the shower door. I stepped aside, giving his mass space to enter. He stood in front of me, and the water was no longer able to reach me. As the water hit his back, his lewd orbs engulfed me, giving me a threatening look that held a hint of a smile.

I flushed under his eyesight. "What?"

"You gonna leave me for one of those rapper niggas?"

I burst out laughing. "Hell no."

"You better. Them niggas got millions."

Tilting my head to the side, I allowed my smile to drop so my sincerity could not be overshadowed by it. "I'd rather have you."

His chest rose as he bit down on his soft bottom lip. "Is that right?"

"Yep. But then I'll be all alone because you're going to leave me for some Instagram model or celebrity when you get famous."

He shook his head confidently. "Never."

"How do you know that? Gorgeous women are going to be throwing themselves at you."

"Because while they may be gorgeous, you're fucking stunning and the only woman I want to be mine."

My center quivered at the deep rumble capturing me. As passion swam in his eyes, his bow-legged gape approached me, cornering me in the large shower. My back pushed into the tile as he pressed his chest against mine. He lowered his head, taking my mouth with his. As our breaths became one, I wondered why this man had chosen me. He'd had his pick of women with far less flaws, with more beauty, with undeniable perfection. Yet, he claimed me. He took me over and over again. I wanted to doubt his commitment to me, but the way he kissed me validated his need for me. He kissed me with hunger. He touched me with possession.

He grabbed my shoulder, spinning me around. He then grabbed my thigh, lifted my leg, and sat my foot on the small bench along the adjacent wall in the shower. He pressed my back down, giving it the arch he desired.

He then spread my ass cheeks wide with a firm grip. I braced myself for his penetration, planting my hands alongside me on the wall. Yet, instead of feeling his amazing tool plummet into me, my center was met with laps of his tongue in my juices.

"Uh!" I exclaimed, melting into the wall.

He slurped at my center, devouring me, causing my legs to shake weakly as an explosive orgasm tumbled down to my core.

"I'm cumming, baby," I warned with a whimper.

"Give it to me," he softly roared into my interior. "Drown me, baby."

OCEAN WATERS

A sharp pain ripped through my body, jolting me awake. Before I could react to the pain, I felt liquid gushing down my legs. I jumped out of bed, frightened that I was ruining the white sheets. The room was dark as I sprinted to the bathroom, cringing from the sudden cramps.

As I burst into the bathroom, I realized what was happening.

I was having a miscarriage.

With a trembling hand, I turned on the light. I then reluctantly looked between my bare legs. My heart sank as I saw the blood.

I was losing another child.

Tears streamed down my face as I clutched my stomach, the pain growing more intense by the second. I felt a sense of despair and hopelessness wash over me.

I wondered why this kept happening to me, if this was what I were to reap from all of the bad seeds my past had sown. Maybe my punishment was to never be a mother.

The weight of my loss was crushing, and I didn't know how to bear it.

I sat on the toilet, feeling my baby slip away. I knew that I would never forget this moment. The pain, the heartbreak, the sense of loss - it would stay with me forever, only doubled this time. I cried out in anguish. I knew that I had to find a way to pick up the pieces and keep moving forward, no matter how difficult it seemed, because I couldn't afford to take any steps back.

"Bae?"

I cringed when I heard his voice on the other side of the bathroom door.

It opened, and when his beautiful, concerned orbs met mine, I began to sob uncontrollably.

He rushed to me on bare feet. He then kneeled in front of me. I threw my arms around his neck and cried on his shoulder.

"What's wrong?"

"I lost it. I lost the baby."

I felt his heart sink. And that only made me weep even more. Initially, I knew that he had mostly been okay with me having a child so early in our relationship because he knew that I needed it. But to feel his loss was crippling.

"What do you need?" he asked as he soothingly rubbed my back.

"An NA meeting."

CHAPTER 28
LYFE MILLER

"What about this?"

Ocean hadn't even looked at the Gucci tracksuit for longer than a second before she shook her head. "Nope," she answered softly.

My mouth dropped a bit. "Why? This is dope."

She sucked her teeth. Then her plump, suckable lips formed into a pout. "Exactly. It's *too* dope."

"Huh?" I asked with a confused chuckle.

"That's going to look *too* nice on you."

"So, I *shouldn't* buy it?"

"No. I don't want you in LA looking that good for those hoes."

Still laughing, I asked, "What hoes, baby?"

She kissed her teeth. "The hoes that are going to be surrounding you and D-Boy as he drags you all over LA."

Kane & Abel had actually come through. A month after returning from LA, I was being flown back out by D-Boy himself on a private jet. Aside from the accolades Kane, Abel, and Midwest Dallas had given my artistry, the images and videos of the murals I had done in Midwest Dallas' home had gone viral on social media. It had only taken hours for the Shaderoom and BallerAlert to repost them. By the time I had gotten off of the plane in Chicago, my followers had increased by tens of thousands. I received a call from D-boy days later, insisting that I come back to LA to begin the process of creating the animated series he planned to shop to major networks and streaming services. I was scheduled to leave in two weeks.

Aside from that, I had been getting so many DM's about my services that I had had to get a busy line. I was getting requests for artwork in homes, businesses, and even murals for the city of Chicago.

"Baby, there aren't going to be any—"

"Unt uh!" she interrupted. "You don't lie to me, so don't start now. You know damn well D-boy is going to have a host of hoes around him. Every time he posts an image or video, there are at least two bad bitches with him."

"Bad bitches?" I tilted my head and smiled devilishly. "You like girls?"

"What?!" she screeched.

"You said they were bad like you were checking them out. Let me find out you were doing more in the streets than drugs."

Gasping, she lunged toward me and punched me playfully. "Fuck you!" She laughed. "You know damn well I don't like girls. I've done some strange things for some change, but never that."

Chuckling, I told her, "I know, baby. I was just trying to make you laugh."

I draped my massive arm around her and then brought her to me involuntarily. She disappeared under my arm as I brought her along.

Then I continued to slowly scan the aisles of the men's department in Nordstrom.

I had never been one of the kinds of hustlers that wore my money on my body. My obligations had required that I spend my bands on therapists and home health aides versus Gucci, Prada, and Chanel. However, since I was being launched into this new circle of industry people so suddenly, I felt like my wardrobe needed an upgrade if I wanted to look the part.

"Bae?" I called her gently.

"Humph?"

"You know you don't have anything to worry about, right?"

"You say that, but you don't know that. Hell, you weren't expecting to meet me when you got in that Uber a few months ago, were you?"

"No. And that's why you aren't driving Uber anymore."

Ocean's eyes rolled slightly. "Mm humph."

"You're right, though. I guess all I can do is promise you that you're the only woman on my mind. As I take this journey, I'm taking the people along with me who I plan to take care of with this new opportunity. That's Landon and you. You hear me?"

As she nodded, I stopped my stride only long enough to kiss the top of her head.

"I know you love me," she said as we began to stroll again. "I don't want you to be worried that I will be some insecure, needy woman, nagging you about other women whenever you come home, and I know I won't always be able to travel with you. It's just that relationships are something new for you, and we're so fresh. I'm secure in my position in your life, but I'm human."

"I feel you, bae."

"Good. Then put that Gucci fit back." As I laughed, she added,

"Don't think I didn't notice that you didn't put it..." Suddenly, she stopped speaking, and her steps halted.

I looked down at her, curious. When I saw her staring ahead, I followed her eyesight.

Seeing Irv and Bridget walking our way, I brought her even closer to me.

"Come on," I demanded gently.

I brought her along with me, forcing her to continue our journey because she had nothing to fear. But as I looked down to ensure that she was okay, I saw her glance a few times at Bridget's massive belly. I then focused on Irv, realizing he was walking directly toward Ocean and me. I felt her tensing up the closer he came.

"You know I got you, right?" I reminded her.

Her voice shook as she answered, "Yeah."

"Then what you scared of, bae?"

"Nothing. Seeing him is just bringing up bad memories."

"I'll send him the other way. Just say the word."

Just then, Irv finally approached us. Bridget was a few feet away, scanning a rack of jeans. Knowing Irv and Bridget, I was sure he had told her to stand there, and she had obeyed like a puppy.

"What up, Lyfe?" Irv spoke as he closed the space between him and us.

I simply gave him a nod of acknowledgment, keeping my eyes zeroed in on his hands. To my surprise, his stance was unthreatening and almost passive as he fought to keep his eyes from zeroing in on Ocean. Although he was showing me respect, I kept my guard all the way up.

"You mind if I holler at Ocean for a minute?" he asked.

I looked down at Ocean, asking, "You want to talk to him?"

Irv actually looked a bit shocked, but he took the hit to his ego without saying a word.

"It's fine," she answered.

"Ah'ight. I'll be right over here." Yet, as I walked just a few steps away, I gave Irv a stern, threatening expression that he knew meant not to play with mine.

OCEAN WATERS

Lyfe walked not even a foot away.

"What's up?" I asked. I then pursed my lips together, folding my arms impatiently.

"I just wanted to tell you that I'm sorry for how things went down."

"Things went down?" I chuckled. "You mean you're sorry for cheating on me, creating a child with your side chick, and then trying to make me feel like an unfaithful whore because you wanted to be with her instead of me since I was all fixed up and no good to you anymore?"

Irv groaned slightly as guilt blanketed his dark brown face. "Yeah, that's what I mean."

As I scoffed, he slightly blew his breath, shame causing the corners of his lips to turn down. "You look happy. You deserve to be happy. Lyfe is a good dude. He's good for you—"

"And I'm good for him. I'm *great* for him," I added without him asking.

Irv nodded once sharply. "I agree. I wish you the best."

"Sorry. Can't say the same for you."

Pressing his lips together, he nodded slowly and then walked off toward his still very pregnant girlfriend, who looked to be due any minute.

I shuffled over to Lyfe, eager to get the hell away from Bridget's delusional contentment. I wondered if she knew that the healthier she became, the worse he would treat her. Recalling the many nights I had spent alone, I realized that my abandonment had been punishment for becoming a better person.

I grabbed Lyfe's hand gently as I approached him from behind.

"You good?" he asked.

"I'm great," I promised.

I truly was. To help manage the emotions of losing another baby, I had been in therapy every week, in addition to NA meetings two times a week. The consistent help had been a tremendous assistance in my healing and moving on. I was evolving into a stronger person each day. This time around, I was not blaming myself for the loss, and I had been able to combat depression.

After returning from LA, I went to see my OB/GYN. Since I had been so early in the pregnancy, there was no need for a D&C. She had ordered tests and ultrasounds to assure me that the miscarriage was a coincidence and did not at all mean that I would have problems conceiving and carrying another child to term. However, I was so shell-shocked that I had no plans of trying in the near future.

"What he say?" The inner corners of his brows were merging together, anger dancing in his eyes.

"He didn't say anything bad. He said I look happy, that you're a good dude, and he wishes me the best. He apologized too."

The anger disappeared and was replaced with a bit of shock. "Word?"

"Yep."

"Umph," he grunted as we started browsing again. "And you worried about me getting hoes."

"What's that mean?"

"Seems like your old hoe is having some reservations about the decisions he's made."

"I doubt that. But even if he is, I'm happy *exactly* where I am."

I truly was. As Lyfe and I walked further away, I felt like I was leaving any old regrets or worries about my failed marriage in that aisle with Irv and his toxicity. No matter if Lyfe and I would be together forever as we both intended, I would forever be thankful for his presence in my life which showed me a new quality of love. I would always be thankful for meeting Irv because, without him, I would most likely still be in the streets. Irv had rehabilitated me out of poverty and homelessness. He had fed me, which gave him the power to starve me.

Though I would forever be grateful, I now longed for the type of love that Lyfe gave me because it *nourished* me, leaving me with the inability ever to starve again.

Lyfe had come into my life and been so naturally supportive and loving. I wanted desperately to pay him back in every way that I could. I hoped that I could take some of the burdens of caring for Landon off of his shoulders. Esther was a godsend, but she wasn't available twenty-four/seven. So, after leaving the mall, I decided to take Landon to the museum so that he and I could have some bonding time. I had done extensive research on the ride home to find somewhere to take Landon where he would be happy and engaged. I only had to punch in

DNA exhibits for the Museum of Science and Industry to populate.

"You sure about this?"

I laughed, shaking my head. "Why do you keep asking me this?"

"Because he's a lot to handle."

"And I have to get accustomed to handling him, baby." Then I balanced on my tiptoes and lay a loving kiss on the seat I took quite often.

Sighing deeply, he nodded and stepped aside. I continued to shake my head at his reluctance as I left out of his bedroom.

Landon was standing at the front door, swaying as he stared at his tablet.

"Are you ready, Landon?"

Keeping his eyes on the screen, he nodded. "Yes."

"Okay, let's go."

"Be good, Landon," I heard Lyfe say behind us.

"I will," he pressed with an irritated frown.

As I opened the door, I turned my head, and my eyes rested on Lyfe, who was approaching us.

I allowed Landon to leave first.

"We won't be long," I assured Lyfe as he took the handle into his hands.

"Call me if you need me to come."

"I'm sure we'll be fine." Landon had been so welcoming to me that I doubted he would run away again. And I had been so scared straight that I didn't plan on letting him out of my sight. If I had to, he would even go to the ladies' room with me.

I gently grabbed Lyfe's chin. "You worried about him or me?"

"He'll be okay. He's already decided to accept you, so the way that his mind works, he's good. I'm worried about you. I don't want him to overwhelm you."

"You want to be with me forever, right?"

His deep-set eyes lowered with confidence and longing. "Of course."

"Then I have to learn how to handle him on my own. Not with you always hovering. So, *bye*."

I left the doorway and hurried behind Landon before Lyfe changed his mind.

"Are you excited about going to the Museum of Science and Industry, Landon?"

His smile met his ears as I popped the locks to my car. "Yes."

"Guess what?"

As we climbed into the car, he returned, "What?"

"Today is one of their National DNA Days."

He actually looked at me, giving me rare eye contact, which made me gush. We both smiled wide like Cheshire Cats.

As I turned on the engine, I saw Lyfe teetering in the doorway.

"Have you heard of National DNA Days?" I asked Landon.

He shook his head, securing his seat belt. "No."

Pulling off, I was so excited to finally tell him something that he didn't already know.

"National DNA Days at the Museum celebrates the successful completion of the Human Genome Project in 2003. You know what that is, right."

"Of course," he said haughtily.

"Of course you do," I laughed. "And it celebrates the discovery of DNA's double helix in 1953. In honor of these scientific discoveries, the museum has a lot of special events and exhibits. You should look it up on our way so that you know exactly what you want to do when we get there."

Excitedly, he started to punch away at his tablet.

327

Once we entered the museum, Landon began to look around, taking in his surroundings with wild anticipation dancing in his eyes.

But there was an exceptional amount of people in line, particularly kids. They bounced around wildly and loudly, making Landon flinch with irritation. I could see the anxiety slowly swallowing him. He began to rock back and forth, and I could see that he was starting to stem. I remembered what I had researched about how to soothe someone with autism. I gently placed my hand on his back, rubbing it in circles.

"It's okay, Landon," I said softly. "We're only going to be in line for a few minutes. Then we're going to look at the exhibits. Okay?"

Landon continued to stem, so I got nervous, feeling as if I was going to fail so early in our outing. But I kept rubbing his back, saying, "You are going to love the exhibits. I read that there is one where you can talk to a scientist from the University of Chicago about the latest in DNA research."

Eventually, he started to calm down.

"Okay," Landon finally said, looking up at me with a grateful smile.

I smiled back at him, feeling elated that I was able to help him feel more comfortable. "You're okay?"

He nodded sharply. "Yes."

"Good. Come on."

After paying to enter, we started exploring the DNA exhibits. Landon talked non-stop. He was so knowledgeable about science, and I was impressed.

We continued our tour of the museum, and Landon was so excited to show me all the cool things he knew.

"There is DNA in strawberries?" I asked aloud as I read a sign near the All Things DNA exhibit.

"Of course, there is," Landon said if I should have known. "Strawberries have large genomes; they are octoploid, which means they have eight of each type of chromosome in each cell. Thus, strawberries are an exceptional fruit to use in DNA extraction labs, and strawberries yield more DNA than any other fruit, like banana and kiwi."

I nodded as if I'd understood a word of what he'd said. "Umph."

As we walked, we chatted about science and DNA, and I could see Landon becoming more and more comfortable around me. I felt like we were bonding, and I was happy to be getting to know him better.

As we left the museum, Landon actually turned to me and draped his long arms around my shoulders.

"Thank you for bringing me here, Ocean," he said. "I had so much fun."

"I had fun too, Landon," I replied, fighting happy tears. "You taught me so much. Can I bring you here again one day?"

Landon nodded feverishly, and I knew that we had made a connection. I was excited to continue to bond with him and honored that I could possibly help Lyfe in a portion of the way he had helped me.

LYFE MILLER

There was no way that she was going to go over and beyond to be a part of Landon's life and I not rock this pussy in gratitude.

No sooner than she and Landon returned, we had dinner. My dick danced aggressively under the table the entire time.

After dinner, Landon disappeared upstairs. So, I took her into my bedroom and showed her my appreciation for hours.

"Suh criss."

Her body shivered as soon as my accent floated into her ear.

"Mi nuh waah tuh liv ah second widout yu."

Her tiny hands pressed into my chest. "Stop it. You know that ends me."

I granted her mercy but continued to attempt to reach heights in her pussy that I had yet to climb if it were possible.

"Oh, God," she whimpered, still trembling.

Her lips were pressed against my neck as her fingertips found my scalp. My dick concreted painfully.

"Amazing, You're fucking amazing." I felt myself unfolding, succumbing to the wet softness of her center.

She wrapped her legs around me, anchoring me inside of her. "I love you, baby," she whimpered.

"You're my dream come true," I returned.

My pelvis collided with hers as I stared into her eyes and worked myself deep inside of her. Waves of pleasure crashed between us.

An incoherent moan of desire poured from her throat as I fucked her squelching interior. Her legs shook and trembled as the building pressure rose within her.

Feral, I grunted as I thrust fully into her.

"Mmph!" she yelped.

I suddenly pulled out of her. I started to lay soft kisses from the nape of her neck and over the curvature of her neckbone. I then went to her milky breasts and took each one into my mouth. She gasped each time I took a large nipple between my lips.

I lay kisses from her ribs to the stretch marks that were evidence of the child that didn't live. I then spread her thighs wide open and lost my face in her slippery canal.

"God!" she yelped as I sucked her throbbing clit. "Yes, Lyfe!"

I french-kissed the pussy lovingly and used my mouth to speak silent words of affirmation to it.

"Shit!" she squealed. "Yes, baby! Eat that pussy."

I ate her until she had cum twice and was spent. I then rode her until it was my turn to explode, which had only taken minutes.

With a grunt, I pulled out and spilled my seed onto her stomach.

I reached over to the nightstand for the wipes and cleaned her off. After tossing the wipe in the trash near the bed, I collapsed next to her. She was still panting heavily as she reached for her phone next to the wipes and I for the remote.

There was no question if she was spending the night. Over the last month, we had become inseparable. She spent every night here, unless I had a job out of town. Since I had become so successful with my art, Esther had stepped up even more. She had offered to spend the nights with Landon that I was working.

"Oh my God!" Gasping, Ocean sprang upright, staring at her phone.

"What happened?"

"What the fuck?" Astonished, she stared at the screen in terror.

I sat up slowly, concerned. "Baby..."

Saying nothing, she handed me the phone. My eyes squinted as they fought to focus on the bright screen. It was a news article that had been shared by someone on her newsfeed. The title read: *Ivory Stelle murdered as her boyfriend slept in the next room, officials say.*

Blinking slowly, I read the article as Ocean sat in a daze, eerily silent.

Ivory had been asleep in her bedroom while her boyfriend, Romell, and his friend, Johnny, were partying in her living room. Throughout the night, Romell had fallen asleep in the living room when Johnny entered Ivory's bedroom and sexually assaulted her. During the assault, Ivory was choked to death. Johnny awakened Romell once he realized that Ivory was dead. The two men fled the scene and were on the run for only a few hours when they were captured by authorities.

Romell gave a full confession.

"That could have been me."

Narrowed, curious eyes went to Ocean. She stared ahead with a blank expression as she blinked slowly.

"What do you mean?"

She swallowed hard as her eyes lowered. "Johnny tried to rape me."

"When?!"

333

She jumped as my deep roar soared around the room.

"A while ago. While you were still in the hospital. The night we reconnected."

"Why didn't you tell me?!" My chest dramatically rose and fell as rage pumped through my veins.

"Because we were just getting to know each other. I was tired of all of the drama that constantly came with me. And we were so new-"

"I don't give a damn if we were so new that we were still wrapped in plastic! You tell me something like that."

Cringing, she finally gave me sorrowful eyes. "I'm sorry."

Sympathizing with the guilt in her slanted spheres, I put my arm around her neck and brought her under me.

"I'm sorry," she said again. "But I handled it. I fought him off of me and got out of there. I haven't spoken to her since. I even filed charges, but the DA refused to take it to trial because of my past record..." Her words trailed away as her voice began to crack.

Rocking her, I insisted, "It's okay. I understand. You don't have to say anything else."

The job of finding a man to protect her was over. She had found the man that would forever fill that position. But, most importantly, she had found a man that she didn't have to protect herself from, and that was what she had needed the most.

CHAPTER 29

OCEAN WATERS

"Ocean Graham?"

My heavy eyes reluctantly raised to see men standing in the doorway of my office. By the way that they were dressed, I knew that they were detectives.

"Yes?"

"May we come in?"

"Sure."

I pushed back from the computer that I had been barely looking at. Since I'd learned of Ivory's death two days ago, I had been shell-shocked. Despite how our friendship ended, I mourned the good times we'd had over the years and was so saddened that her naivety had led to her death. Moreover, it gave me chills that I could have been the one murdered by the hands of the same man. I thanked God that, for whatever reason, I had made it out of that situation alive.

"I am Detective White," the taller, Caucasian one introduced as they sat down in the seats across from my desk. "This is Detective Jenkins."

I nodded. "Hi. I assume this is about Ivory. I thought Romell made a full confession."

As I grabbed the latte that I had been sipping on all morning, the detective's eyes narrowed.

"Ivory?" Detective Jenkins questioned as he looked at his partner. "No, this is about Irvin Graham. Who is Ivory?"

I inhaled deeply, sitting up. "Irv? What happened to Irv?"

"He was arrested a few days ago. He's being indicted on Narcotics Trafficking and Criminal Drug Conspiracy." As I blinked slowly, he asked again, "Who is Ivory?"

I waved dismissively, shaking my head. "She was a friend of mine that was killed in her home a few days ago."

They nodded as Detective White recalled, "I know which case you're referring to. I'm sorry for your loss."

My heart was beating feverishly as I mumbled, "Thank you."

My mind was unraveling in disbelief as he said, "We want to ask you some questions about Irvin's case. We understand that you all aren't married anymore, but if you had any information for us, that would be great."

Redemption immediately entered my mind. I would have loved nothing more than to throw Irv under the bus. Yet, that would only tie me and Lyfe into his case as well. Irv had already taken so much from me. He wouldn't take my freedom and Lyfe too.

"I don't know anything about any drugs. He was a truck driver."

Detective Jenkins nodded. "You had no knowledge of his drug business?"

"None whatsoever. You might want to ask his girlfriend, Bridget. She would know more than I did since she spent more time with him than me."

"Yes, she is in custody, and we have been talking to her as well."

My laugh was short and full of sarcasm.

Sighing, Detective Jenkins stood and reached into his pocket. He then pulled out a card and slipped it onto my desk. "Well, if you think of anything and would like to be of any assistance, please give us a call."

"Have a nice day, gentlemen."

"You too, ma'am," Detective White farewelled as the other nodded and followed.

I discreetly blew a heavy breath. I then clambered for my phone and sent Lyfe a text message.

Ocean: *I need you to meet me for lunch. It's important.*

"THAT'S CRAZY."

Lyfe stared wide-eyed out of the passenger window.

"This isn't going to involve you, is it?" An hour later, my heart was still beating frantically. I had no feelings toward Irv's arrest. I was too far removed from him emotionally to care. And I was too grateful for the blessing of Lyfe being in my life to feel any type of vindication behind it. My only feelings were fear that somehow Lyfe would be involved. The thought of losing him was sending me into an anxiety I hadn't felt since burying myself in therapy.

Lyfe lay a comforting hand on my thigh as he shook his head. "I doubt it. Usually, when this happens, the DA cuts a deal if the accused gives up bigger names in the game. They wouldn't give a fuck about me."

"Are you sure?"

Looking away from the window, he gave me assuring eyes. "I'm positive. Besides, there is no proof that he served me. I was over-careful."

Relieved, I released a breath that I hadn't realized I had been holding.

"I wonder how long he's known he was being investigated."

Gasping, my eyes grew. "Do you think that's why he was so nice to me at the mall the other day? Because he knew he was about to be arrested and didn't want me to snitch?"

As it dawned on him, Lyfe slowly shook his head, disgust dancing in his eyes.

"That manipulating motherfucker," I spewed.

"He probably thought you were so mad at him that you would say something."

"But I knew nothing. My only proof is you, and I would never give you up."

His eyes were admirable as they locked on me. He then grabbed the back of my neck and brought me into a deep kiss.

"You got some clients this afternoon?" he asked against my lips.

"No." I was purring, center quivering.

"Cool. I need to take you somewhere."

"Where are we going?"

"None of your business, baby girl. Just go take your car home. I'll meet you there."

LYFE MILLER

"Why are we here?" Ocean's eyes slowly looked over at the graves that I passed as I drove through the cemetery.

I couldn't find the words to say.

"Lyfe?" Ocean questioned my silence curiously as I pulled over and parked.

"Hmm?"

"Why are we at a cemetery?"

I gently told her, "Get out, baby."

I climbed out of the truck. I then rounded the front end and met her at the passenger's side door as she opened it. I took her hand, helping her out of it. I then held my arm out so she could brace herself on it to keep her heels from sinking into the grass.

"Babe?" she called, her curiosity piqued.

I scoffed nervously. Concerned, she leaned into me to get my undivided attention back on her. "What's wrong? What's going on?"

"I didn't think this would make me so anxious. I feel silly for being nervous. She isn't even alive."

Ocean's face washed with confusion. "Huh?"

I squeezed her hand, smiling bashfully as if I were a fifteen-year-old boy all over again. "I want to introduce you to my mother, baby."

Her eyes filled with warmth and admiration. Her beautiful orbs danced with delight in the sun as she peered up at me.

I had stunned myself by even doing this, so I couldn't answer the questions in her eyes. I simply guided her toward my mother's resting place. Upon arriving at it, I let go of Ocean's hand and knelt in the grass next to her gravestone.

"Hey, Ma," I greeted her, touching the headshot of her encased in her gravestone. I then leaned over and kissed it.

Usually, when I visited her, I would just sit and talk to her as if she were alive. I would tell her things that were happening in my life and update her on Landon's progress. I was always so proud whenever I was able to tell her the accomplishments that Landon had been making and how he was growing. As soon as I had been able to, I had come to tell her how Landon had called himself giving me permission to have a girlfriend, and that he had actually hugged me.

"Ma, this is Ocean, my girlfriend." I looked back, reaching for Ocean's hand. She timidly inched closer with an anxious smile gracing her sweet face. "She's the one, Ma. You once told me I'll know when I've found the one when I fall in love without even knowing when or how. I'm there. I'm in love with her. I chase her, even though I already have her."

Taking Ocean to my mother's grave had been as significant as introducing her to my mother as if she were alive. It had given me the reassurance I needed that a force more powerful than any on this earth had put me in that Uber that day with Ocean. Therefore, there was no running from this mysterious grip this wayward woman had on my heart.

"I love you," Ocean purred in my ear as I drove my dick deep inside of her.

I nibbled on her neck, promising her, "I love you too, baby."

There was no place else I could go. My dick had traveled the furthest it could reach, but I wanted more. I wanted deeper. She moaned as I filled her up. I reached down between us, playing with her clit as I began to knock on the door of her cervix harder and harder until she was crying a symphony of praise in my ear.

"Yes," she growled. "Fuck!"

My balls collided with her ass hole, turning me on even more and causing my dick to pulsate against her walls.

Her hard nipples stabbed me in my chest as I rode her missionary style on her furry duvet cover.

I cringed at the way her tight walls hugged my dick, grabbing it and bringing it deeper inside of her warmth. I laced my fingers into her curls. I then softly pulled so that I could roam her neck. I lost myself in the crevices that tasted sweet, but I began to miss her tongue. So, I kissed the trail that led to those plump lips and took them with mine.

As I kissed her, I tasted wet salt. I pushed back, seeing that a lone tear had slid down her face.

"What's wrong?" I breathed, still feeling her walls clutch me.

"I feel so... so..."

I stopped my strokes, asking, "What?"

"No, don't stop," she begged. Then she used her hands on the small of my back to push me in deeper.

"Tell me what's wrong, baby."

She gasped as I began to stroke her again. She spread her legs wider, giving me full access to what was mine. She then giggled bashfully. "I just... I feel so... at peace, so safe, so free."

"That's how it feels to be where you were meant to be." Satisfied that her tears were happy ones, I dove deeper inside of her, racing my tongue to the deepest corner of her neck, causing her to shiver against my sweaty skin as I told her, "Welcome home, baby."

EPILOGUE

A year later, D-Boy's animated series was picked up by Netflix and approved for a second season before the first season had even debuted. Therefore, it was required that Lyfe relocate to Los Angeles since he would be working full-time on its production.

Since D-boy had worked collectively with Lyfe on the imagery, graphic design, and story concepts of the animation, he had acquired a leadership role in the creation of the series, making him not only one of the lead writers but also one of the executive producers. Using some of the finances he'd received from the contract with D-boy and Netflix, he'd purchased a five-bedroom home in Lancaster, California.

"*Ooooh*, this is nice!" Esther squealed as the tour of their new home came to a stop at her bedroom.

Esther had been happy to move with the brothers to California so that Lyfe could pursue his newfound career. However, Lyfe felt like she was much more than a caregiver. She had become the matriarch he and Landon still very much needed even though they were adults. Esther was more than a caregiver to Landon. She was also a support system to Lyfe and a matriarch that he depended on for wisdom.

"Take a look at the bathroom," the realtor, Ebony, encouraged her. Lyfe shook his head as Esther followed Ebony into the large bathroom of her suite, basically skipping.

"I got me a Jacuzzi?!" she could instantly be heard shrieking.

"Why is she screaming?" Landon groaned behind Lyfe.

"She's excited about her new room and this beautiful house," Lyfe told him.

"Aren't *you* excited?" Landon asked Ocean.

"Yes," she swooned, wearing an appreciative and adoring smile, which she'd had since they pulled up to the home on Dolomite Avenue.

"Well, *you* aren't screaming." Landon shrugged.

Ocean agreed with a nod. "Well, sometimes people are so excited that they don't know what to say."

"That's called being tongue-tied," Landon offered.

"It is," Ocean confirmed.

Landon bent down, whispering into Ocean's ear, "I wish Esther was tongue-tied."

Ocean and Lyfe fell out laughing as Ocean playfully hit his arm.

"Besides, she's going to wake the baby."

Beaming, Ocean looked down at the full head of curly hair that was propped against her chest in the baby carrier that was strapped to her chest. Bless Ing Miller was only a month old.

When Ocean learned that she was pregnant again so soon after her miscarriage, she was scared of the inevitable yet hopeful. As each month ticked by, Lyfe and Landon fell in love, but her angst grew.

She did not enjoy her pregnancy because she had spent it obsessing over doing whatever she could to bring the baby to term healthy.

Even during the delivery, she was on pins and needles until she heard her baby girl cry. *That* was the moment that she fell in love.

"C'mon, Landon," Ocean said, taking his hand. "Let's go figure out how to place the furniture in your room."

Since Ocean and Lyfe had only had virtual tours of the house before purchasing it, they hadn't been able to fully grasp the concept of the layout. Now that they were on their first physical tour after receiving the keys, Ocean was overwhelmed with ideas of how to decorate the place.

Landon groaned as Ocean dragged him out of the room. "This is unnecessary. I don't need a room here. I'll be staying on campus."

"But you'll need a room of your own for your breaks and when you want to come home."

Landon had been accepted into the University of Southern California. Lyfe had also acquired Landon and Esther a condo on campus so that Landon would be nearby as he studied forensic chemistry. During the semester, Esther planned to live with Landon to ensure that he maintained his therapy since Lyfe would be too busy with work to be as hands-on with Landon as he used to be.

"Why don't we go figure out how to decorate the baby's room instead?" Landon suggested.

Shaking her head, Ocean told him, "You're so stubborn, Landon. Fine."

Ocean followed Landon down the long hallway. Lyfe slowly followed, wearing a satisfied and adoring grin as he admired every inch of the home he had provided for his growing family.

"You shouldn't be walking around this much," Landon told her. "You are still healing from childbirth."

Ocean chuckled. At this point, she was used to his overbearing attitude. Landon obsessed over her pregnancy and the baby nearly as much as Lyfe, if not more.

As they stepped into the room, Ocean smiled, excited to finally see the details that she had been mulling over on the Trulia website for over a month.

"The crib should go here so that she gets lots of sunlight," Landon said as he stood in front of the picture window. "On average, there are two hundred and eighty-four sunny days per year in Los Angeles and only thirty-four days per year of precipitation. So..." Looking out of the window, Landon smiled slowly. "She will get a lot of sunlight, much more than she ever would have in Chicago."

"Landon, stop boring my fiancée with all your facts." Lyfe's booming voice suddenly entered the room behind them.

Landon laughed at Lyfe's teasing as Lyfe kissed Bless before wrapping his arms around Ocean from behind. They all then stared peacefully out of the picture window at the scenic view of California. The sun shined so brightly through it that it ricocheted off of Ocean's diamond engagement ring, which caused a cast of a multicolored rainbow amongst the walls in the bedroom.

"*Awww*, you guys are so cute," Ebony swooned as she entered the room.

Ocean blushed, and Lyfe smiled, but he never let her go. He never planned to, either. Lyfe felt bonded to Ocean for life. She was the equivalent of her name, deep as an ocean, and the further Lyfe went with her, the further he drowned in his love and commitment to her.

"I can't believe you guys have only been together for a little over a year," Ebony added. "You act as if you've been together forever. Where did you guys meet?"

Ocean looked behind her and up into Lyfe's eyes as they fell into insane giggles.

Ebony looked between the two of them, lost as to what the humor was. "What? What's so funny about that? I only asked how you guys met."

Still laughing, Lyfe told her, "We don't mean to laugh. It's just that the answer to that question is a very ... *interesting* story."

THE END

Don't miss a release by Jessica N. Watkins! To receive a text message announcing a new release, using your phone, text the keyword "Jessica" to 872-282-0790.

OTHER BOOKS BY JESSICA N. WATKINS

PROPERTY OF A SAVAGE (STANDALONE)

WHEN MY SOUL MET A THUG (STANDALONE)

SAY MY FUCKING NAME (STANDALONE)

A RICH MAN'S WIFE (COMPLETE SERIES)

A Rich Man's Wife

A Rich Man's Wife 2

EVERY LOVE STORY IS BEAUTIFUL, BUT OURS IS HOOD SERIES (COMPLETE SERIES)

Every Love Story Is Beautiful, But Ours Is Hood

Every Love Story Is Beautiful, But Ours Is Hood 2

Every Love Story Is Beautiful, But Ours Is Hood 3

WHEN THE SIDE NIGGA CATCH FEELINGS SERIES (COMPLETE SERIES)

When The Side Nigga Catch Feelings

When the Side Nigga Catch Feelings 2

IN TRUE THUG FASHION (COMPLETE SERIES)

In True Thug Fashion 1

In True Thug Fashion 2

In True Thug Fashion 3

SECRETS OF A SIDE BITCH SERIES (COMPLETE SERIES)

Secrets of a Side Bitch

Secrets of a Side Bitch 2

Secrets of a Side Bitch 3

Secrets of a Side Bitch – The Simone Story

Secrets of a Side Bitch 4

A SOUTHSIDE LOVE STORY (COMPLETED SERIES)

A South Side Love Story 2

A South Side Love Story 3

A South Side Love Story 4

CAPONE AND CAPRI SERIES (COMPLETE SERIES)

Capone and Capri

Capone and Capri 2

A THUG'S LOVE SERIES (COMPLETE SERIES)

A Thug's Love

A Thug's Love 2

A Thug's Love 3

A Thug's Love 4

A Thug's Love 5

NIGGAS AIN'T SHIT (COMPLETE SERIES)

CHICAGO URBAN BOOK EXPO WEEKEND

The biggest adult book fair featuring African-American authors in Chicago is coming August 20, 2023!

The Chicago Urban Book Expo was started by national bestselling author, Jessica N. Watkins, in 2015. Since, this book festival has grown into the largest in the Chicago-land area featuring African-American authors. Readers attend from across the country to meet some of their favorite authors of African-American literature! Free to all readers, the atmosphere is fun, with a soundtrack by the hottest Djs in Chicago, and lively, fueled by tasty libations.

Registration for the 8th Annual Chicago Urban Book Expo is open! There are a limited amount of author tables available. So, authors, please register ASAP! Readers, attendance is free, but please RSVP so that you can receive email updates about the event.

Reader registration: https://www.chicagourbanbookexpo.com/rsvp
FB Evite: https://fb.me/e/38rhfJu3X
FB Group: https://www.facebook.com/groups/1601970186766981

BLACK READING IS SEXY

Black Reading Is Sexy offers a variety of merchandise for the lovers of books written by **Black** authors about **Black** characters. Now, readers can enjoy so much more than just books.

The Buy Now, Pay Later option, Klarna, is available. You can start enjoying what you've ordered right away while using Klarna's pay later option. Simply choose KLARNA in the PAYMENT section of the CHECKOUT screen.

Made in the USA
Middletown, DE
05 July 2023

34598433R00205